"An author wi... ..."
—*New Yo...*
Janet Chapman

HIGHLANDER'S CURSE

"An enthralling and captivating romance replete with historical events, great emotional turmoil between the hero and heroine combined with a delicate touch of time travel and fae magic. A page-turner if there ever was one!" —*RT Book Reviews* (4½ stars)

"Time after time, Mayhue brings her readers tantalizingly close to emotional satisfaction."

Publishers Weekly

HEALING THE HIGHLANDER

"Amazing! The highly emotional, quick-paced plot makes this a page-turner. Deeply moving characters, fraught with emotional turmoil, the subtle entwining of Faerie magic and a highly charged, ever-expanding romance turn this into a keeper."

—*RT Book Reviews* (4½ stars)

A HIGHLANDER'S HOMECOMING

"Enthralling. . . . The combination of plot, deeply emotional characters, and ever-growing love is breathtaking." —*RT Book Reviews* (4½ stars)

A HIGHLANDER'S DESTINY

"Wondrous. . . . The characters are well written, the action is nonstop, and there's plenty of sizzling passion."   —*RT Book Reviews* (4 stars)

"This is one of those series that I tell everyone to read."   —Night Owl Reviews (5 stars)

A HIGHLANDER OF HER OWN

"A wonderful medieval time-travel romance. . . . Melissa Mayhue captures the complications and delights of both the modern woman and the fascination with the medieval world."

—*Denver Post*

"Fun and enjoyable."   —*RT Book Reviews*

SOUL OF A HIGHLANDER

Winner of the Golden Quill Award for Best Paranormal of 2009
Winner of the Winter Rose Award for Best Paranormal of 2009

"Mayhue's world is magical and great fun!"
—*RT Book Reviews* (4 stars)

"Absolutely riveting from start to finish."
—A Romance Review

HIGHLAND GUARDIAN

Winner of the HOLT Medallion for Best Paranormal of 2008
Winner of the Winter Rose Award for Best Paranormal of 2008

"Mayhue not only develops compelling protagonists, but her secondary characters are also rich and intriguing. An author with major potential!"

—*RT Book Reviews* (4 stars)

"An awesome story. . . . A lovely getaway to fantasy land." —Fallen Angels Reviews (5 Angels)

"A delightful world of the faerie. . . . The story flows with snappy dialogue and passionate temptations. It's sure to put a smile on your face." —Fresh Fiction

THIRTY NIGHTS WITH
A HIGHLAND HUSBAND

Winner of the Book Buyers Best Award for
Best Paranormal of 2008

"An enchanting time travel. . . . Infused with humor, engaging characters, and a twist or two."

—*RT Book Reviews* (4 stars)

"A wonderful time-travel romance."

—Fresh Fiction

"What a smasharoo debut! Newcomer Melissa Mayhue rocks the Scottish Highlands."

—A Romance Review

These titles are also available as eBooks

MELISSA MAYHUE

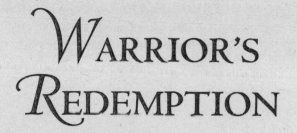

WARRIOR'S REDEMPTION

Pocket **STAR** Books

New York   London   Toronto   Sydney   New Delhi

The sale of this book without its cover is unauthorized. If you purchased this book without a cover, you should be aware that it was reported to the publisher as "unsold and destroyed." Neither the author nor the publisher has received payment for the sale of this "stripped book."

Pocket Star Books
A Division of Simon & Schuster, Inc.
1230 Avenue of the Americas
New York, NY 10020

This book is a work of fiction. Names, characters, places, and incidents either are products of the author's imagination or are used fictitiously. Any resemblance to actual events or locales or persons, living or dead, is entirely coincidental.

Copyright © 2011 by Melissa Mayhue

All rights reserved, including the right to reproduce this book or portions thereof in any form whatsoever. For information address Pocket Books Subsidiary Rights Department, 1230 Avenue of the Americas, New York, NY 10020

First Pocket Star Books paperback edition January 2012

POCKET STAR BOOKS and colophon are registered trademarks of Simon & Schuster, Inc.

For information about special discounts for bulk purchases, please contact Simon & Schuster Special Sales at 1-866-506-1949 or business@simonandschuster.com.

The Simon & Schuster Speakers Bureau can bring authors to your live event. For more information or to book an event contact the Simon & Schuster Speakers Bureau at 1-866-248-3049 or visit our website at www.simonspeakers.com.

Designed by Jacquelynne Hudson
Cover illustration by Kris Keller

Manufactured in the United States of America

10   9   8   7   6   5   4   3   2   1

ISBN 978-1-4516-4087-8
ISBN 978-1-4516-4090-8 (ebook)

This one is for the readers—all of you who, like me, love your characters complete with their own happy ever after!

ACKNOWLEDGMENTS

There are many people who play a part in the final form of each and every book I write. Without them, the stories wouldn't be the same.

For this book, I owe special thanks to these people:

Martin Mayhue—for the time and effort it took to actually brew up a batch of the Viking Bog Myrtle Beer so that I would know what I was talking about when I tried to describe it.

Nicholas Wade-Mayhue—whose artistic ability brought my vision to life in the form of the tattoo Odin's descendants wear.

Megan Mayhue of TrinketsNTidbits.com—whose talent with beaded jewelry yielded beautiful designs to represent the series.

Teresa Redmond-Ott—whose love for all animals is infectious and who graciously taught me more about chickens than I'd ever thought to ask.

Elaine Spencer—whose advice and guidance I value.

And

Megan McKeever—without whom my books just wouldn't be the same.

WARRIOR'S
REDEMPTION

Prologue

FAIRIES ABSOLUTELY WERE real. Dani didn't care what Aunt Jean claimed.

After Mrs. Palmer down at the new library had loaned her those wonderful books this past summer, she'd known it wasn't just her imagination. Lots of people believed in them. She'd spent the entire vacation between fourth and fifth grades reading all about Faeries.

"Dani?" Aunt Jean's voice carried all the way down to the chicken coops. "Dani! You better hurry up with those eggs, little girl, if you expect to get breakfast in you before the school bus gets here."

Dani grabbed the one egg that had been laid already, dodging the grumpy old brown hen's beak, and hurried back toward the farmhouse. She'd have to gather again when she got home from school, but at least Emma Hen had come through early, as usual.

A furtive glance toward the empty corner next to

the steps as she approached the house warned her of what was to come.

"Get your hands washed and sit yourself down."

Aunt Jean's no-nonsense expression was firmly in place, and Dani quickly did as she was told, slipping into her spot at the old kitchen table as her aunt slid a warm plate in front of her.

"What did I tell you about setting a saucer of milk out by the steps?" Aunt Jean waited, arms folded in front of her.

"Not to," Dani mumbled around her first bite of thick toast. "Draws snakes."

"So it's not that you forgot. You've just decided you're not going to mind me, is that it? You're just trying to be bad?"

"No, ma'am, I'm not trying to be bad. I promise." The Faeries liked milk and bread. It encouraged them to stay." My book said—"

"Nuh-uh." Aunt Jean turned back to the stove, scrambling Dani's egg, her gray curls swaying with the stubborn shaking of her head. "I don't want another word of that fairy nonsense, you hear me? There's no such thing as a fairy, but rattlers are real enough. Those damn snakes will smell that milk a mile off and next thing you know, you or me will be getting ourselves snakebit. And then what?"

"The Faeries would keep us safe, if you'd let me feed them," Dani muttered, tearing a corner off her toast and dropping it into her lap. If her aunt would just believe, the Faeries would hear all their wishes and make them come true. "I read that in one of my books."

"Danielle Faye Dearmon!" Aunt Jean turned around from the stove and leaned across the table. "I've had just about enough of this nonsense from you. Not everything in books is true just because somebody wrote it down. I'm serious as a heart attack about this, little girl. I want your promise right now that you won't put any more milk out by the steps for these damned imaginary fairies of yours or else I'm going to have to paddle your butt, you understand me? I want your promise on it, Dani. I want it now."

"Yes, ma'am." Dani didn't hesitate with her response. She had no choice. Her aunt was really serious this time. She almost never pulled out the "paddle your butt" threat. "I promise."

She meant to keep the promise, too. No more milk by the porch steps. But that didn't mean she wouldn't hunt down a new spot to feed the Faeries when she got home from school this afternoon. A better spot. One that Aunt Jean wouldn't find.

Because no matter that Aunt Jean was the best substitute mama on the face of the planet, in this one thing, she was completely wrong.

Faeries were absolutely real, and Dani meant to make sure she stayed on their good side.

One

HOWLS ECHOED THROUGH the forest of Wyddecol, so protracted and pain-ridden they tortured Elesyria's eardrums. Like those of some animal in its death throes, the screams pitched from fury to terror and back again.

She ran faster through the trees, seeking in vain to escape the torment of those sounds. Knowing she could never outrun that which came from her own throat.

It was her agony, her torment that tore the screams from her lungs as if the pain were a living creature eating at her innards.

Her daughter, her only child, her beautiful Isabella had disappeared from the World of Man.

On she ran, unseeing, dodging by instinct the low-hanging branches and fallen limbs. On, deeper into the forest, until at last she broke through into a clearing. Ahead lay the Temple of Danu, golden in its perpetual shaft of sunlight, encircled by its ring of massive stones.

Elesyria pushed herself harder, maintaining her pace up the long marble staircase. Not even at the doorway did she slow. No stopping to shed her sandals, no washing her feet, no bending low to show reverence at the doorway to the inner sanctum. Not this time. This time, for the first time ever, she simply didn't care.

Her precious Isabella was gone from the World of Man.

"Show yourself, I demand it! How could you allow this to happen?" she accused, ignoring the hysterical echo of her own words in the cavernous, rounded room. "You promised. She was to be cared for if I would but leave her with the Mortals and return to your service. You promised!"

She screamed the final words, her voice cracking as she sank to her knees. The tears, until now strangely absent, at last found their release, rolling down her cheeks to splatter on the white stone floor at her knees. "You promised," she accused one final time, her words no more than a whisper against the canvas of her grief.

"You would demand my presence in your world, Daughter of Danu?"

The words echoed off the arc of the room's high ceiling, bouncing, tumbling in a harmonious melody of sound.

"I would," Elesyria answered without hesitation. She had no care for the ancient protocols. No time to travel to the trance world. No desire to honor the bitch Goddess who had betrayed her.

In front of her a pale green mist coalesced, writhing and bubbling, shifting from one form to another until at last a tall, beautiful woman emerged. The Goddess, the Earth Mother, had arrived.

"Then I can only assume these are the direst of times. What troubles you, my child?"

"The loss of *my* child." Elesyria rose to her feet, well aware she breached all acceptable behavior in doing so. Eye contact with the Goddess was too painful, so she fixed her gaze on the other woman's chin. "Isabella is dead. You've broken your promise to me."

The Goddess lifted her hand as if to catch a handful of air in the room before rubbing her thumb against her fingers, much in the way a merchant might sample the feel of a fine silk.

"Isabella lives."

"Impossible!" Elesyria had been to the curtain between the worlds that very morning. She'd stood there as so often she did, stretching out her magic to caress the essence of the daughter she'd left behind. Only this time, there had been nothing. "She's not in the World of Man. I felt for her myself. That which had been her is gone."

"Nevertheless, Isabella's soul has not returned to the Fountain. She lives."

"How can that be?" Elesyria's legs buckled, too weak to hold her weight, and she dropped to her knees. "The place where I felt for her is as empty as my heart."

The Goddess lifted both arms and the mist returned, swirling in a sphere between her hands. It moved as if alive, frantic with a billion life-forms, its color shifting from the palest green to a brilliant emerald and back again. Then the Goddess clapped her hands together and the mist disappeared as quickly as it had formed.

"Not only does she live, she has joined with her SoulMate. Though, as you say, she is not in the time and place where you left her."

"What does that mean?"

The Goddess shrugged, palms held upward. "I cannot yet say. I know only what I feel when I search the Myst."

Elesyria's mind reeled in confusion. Isabella's space on the Mortal Plain was empty. She'd felt that for herself. And yet, the Goddess claimed her daughter lived. Lived and had found the one happiness every Fae sought: her own SoulMate!

"I need answers," she whispered, as much to herself as to the Goddess standing nearby.

"Indeed you do. Go with my blessings."

Her *blessings*? Not enough. Not by half.

Elesyria raised her head, coming as close to meeting the Earth Mother's eyes as she dared. "After all the years I've dedicated to your service, Goddess, I want more than your blessings. I want to travel through the curtain with the power to punish any who harmed my child."

"Crossing over with your Magic intact is forbidden by your High Council."

If the Goddess thought to dissuade her with something so trivial, she was seriously mistaken.

"I've no more care for the politics of Fae than I have for those of Man. I care only for the child grown to woman whom I left behind when I returned to my service in your temple. I must know the truth of her fate. I want to travel through the curtain. With my Magic."

"And if you find your daughter has not been harmed? If you find it is as I have indicated?"

If, pray the Goddess, Isabella lived happily joined to her SoulMate, as the Goddess insisted? "Then I want the power to reward those who aided her."

The visage in front of her shimmered from green to gold and back again.

"In offering reward as freely as you threaten punishment, Elesyria, you demonstrate your wisdom. So be it. You may retain your powers to use for this purpose and this purpose only. Your years of faithful service watching over my followers have earned at least this much from me. As you go forth, I will set in motion what I can to assist. Travel to the place where your daughter should be. Seek out the Tinklers when you arrive. They are my eyes and ears in the World of Man. If any can guide you to the truth, surely it will be they."

"Thank you, Earth Mother."

Elesyria bowed her head, honoring the Goddess before her. When she lifted her eyes once again, she was alone.

Rising to her feet, she squared her shoulders and hurried from the chamber, already seeing the spot where she would cross over in her mind's eye.

She would find the Tinklers the Goddess had spoken of and she would know the truth. She prayed the result would require her to use her Magic for the benefit of one who had helped her daughter, but if not?

Woe be unto any who had lifted a hand to bring harm down upon Isabella. They would feel her wrath even if it should shake the very foundations of the Mortals' world.

Two

Had it been only this morning he'd dared to complain aloud that his life couldn't possibly get any more complicated?

Malcolm MacDowylt, beleaguered laird of the MacGahan clan, pinched the skin on the bridge of his nose and wished to the gods he'd never stepped foot out of his bedchamber this day. The bird that had flown into his open window at sunrise should have been warning enough of the gods' intent at mischief. Foolishly, he'd ignored the sign and carried on.

Walk softly and have a care for your tongue, lad, lest you stir the anger of the old gods.

His father's voice echoed in his mind, naught but a memory now.

Aye, the old gods were busy this day. Neither his heavy burden of guilt nor the cursed drought that had plagued the land for months, threatening a winter of starvation for his people, had satisfied the denizens of Asgard. Not even his younger brother's arrival this very morning with the distressing news of his father's passing and his sister's resulting peril had satisfied their perverse pastime of plaguing him.

No, their judgment of his failures made clear their anger was in full bloom. Now, as if to drive home the spear of their discontent, they'd sent this *woman* to torment him.

"Am I to be kept waiting in attendance upon your daydreaming for the entire night, or will you send a servant to prepare my chamber?"

Of all the penance he might have expected the old gods to demand of him, he'd never imagined they would send Isabella's mother to torment him.

So much for his ability to imagine the worst. The truth of the matter stood before him in all her arrogant glory. Elesyria Aí Byrn clearly expected his meek compliance with her demands.

What choice had been left him? None. At least none that was honorable, and he would consider no others.

"As those who brought you here have seemingly left without you"—if they'd ever been there to begin with!—"I can hardly turn you out into the mercy of the night, now can I?"

"Tinklers," she murmured with smile and a sigh, her hand fluttering through the air like a midsummer butterfly. "Everyone knows how unreliable they are."

Tinklers unreliable? Not in his experience. They were, however, rumored to be agents of the Fae. Just as Isabella was rumored to have been born of a Fae mother. The very woman, it would appear, now standing in front of him, her foot tapping impatiently on the stone floor.

"Well? It's hardly proper to keep your own dear mother-in-law standing about on these old legs." The woman lifted a hand to her back and stretched as if she'd reached the limits of her endurance.

His own dear mother-in-law, indeed.

More like his own personal bundle of guilt.

"Janet!" he called, startled to find the old maid already at his side, her disapproving glare fastened on him. "Please show my—show Isabella's mother to a guest chamber and see that she's made comfortable."

"And high time it is, too," Janet muttered, a disapproving glare cast his direction. "It's more respect for yer elders you should be showing, if you dinna mind my saying so."

Not that it ever mattered what he minded when it came to the chief maid in his castle. Janet always freely spoke her mind. He had, after all, encouraged her to do so.

The women turned to leave the solar but his guest stopped, sending a warning smile in his direction. "I'll be about settling my things in my chamber for now, but come first light, I'll be back down. I'm wanting a chat with you, my son. There's much I'll be wanting to hear from your own lips. Much I have need to hear about what's happened to my Isabella."

Malcolm dipped his head in a respectful nod and, after the women departed, once again pinched the spot between his eyes as if by pressure alone he could force the worry from his brow.

There was one discussion he'd no desire to hurry into.

His marriage to Isabella had been nothing more than a means to an end. He'd barely known the woman, but the act had allowed him to become the MacGahan laird without a battle, without any loss of life. He'd even done everything in his power to see Isabella off on the road to her own happiness, but as it turned out, that wasn't meant to be. The guilt over her death had hung heavily on his shoulders since the moment his riders had returned with the fateful news.

"She has the look of her daughter about her, does she no?" Patrick, his brother and trusted second-in-command, approached from the corner of the room. "Though there's something about that woman . . ."

Patrick's words hung in the air between them, sending a prickle of discomfort down Malcolm's spine.

"Something? You think she lies about who she claims to be?"

Patrick shook his head slowly back and forth, his gaze fixed on the doorway. "No. I feel no sense of deceit about her. It's more of a . . ." His eyes tracked at last to meet Malcolm's. "I canna say what it is, Colm. Only that I've an unsettled feeling in her presence. She's trouble, that one."

Silence filled the room, pressing against Malcolm's eardrums as he considered the possibilities.

"Could there be any truth in the old stories, do you think?"

They'd both heard the rumors before they'd come

here last year to claim what was owed them by the old laird of the MacGahan. Rumors of the old laird's granddaughter, Isabella, having been born of a Faerie mother who'd long since disappeared from this world.

In spite of those rumors, Malcolm had journeyed here to demand that which he was owed, the holdings of the MacGahan in payment for the laird's debt to his own clan. After the old laird's mysterious death, Malcolm had married Isabella to peacefully secure his place as the new laird. That the marriage to him had not been Isabella's choice was only one complication.

Patrick shrugged and dropped into the nearest chair. "There's no one left from those days to speak on the truth of it, brother. And, whether or no, you've more pressing worries on this day than an aggrieved Elf in yer guest room."

Malcolm couldn't agree more.

"Have you decided what to do about Torquil's demand?"

Torquil.

Malcolm claimed the chair facing his brother, closing his eyes as he sat.

With their father's death, their elder half brother had become the new laird of the MacDowylt. And with his new title, Torquil now demanded homage and fealty from Malcolm. No matter that their father had given to Malcolm for his own all that he was able to collect from the MacGahan. No matter that he'd become the MacGahan laird with his father's blessing. As far as Torquil was concerned, all of it belonged to the MacDowylt clan and to him as the new Mac-

Dowylt laird. He saw Malcolm as little more than a caretaker and Castle MacGahan as nothing more than a source of silver for his coffers.

"Castle MacGahan can ill afford to pay homage to Torquil. We'll be lucky to feed our people through this winter as it is. And it should come as little surprise that I'll no be pledging my loyalty or my men to our brother's service."

His relationship with his elder brother had always been stormy. Unfortunately, it appeared his father's death had done nothing to calm those waters.

"And Christiana? Would you leave her fate to such as Torquil?" Patrick spoke calmly, only his eyes betraying his emotion. "He's neither the patience nor the understanding she requires. Her gifts confound him, and we both ken that forcing her into a marriage or sending her off to a convent will be naught but a disaster for all."

His younger sister's abilities to read the runes didn't confound Torquil. They made him drool with envy. Patrick knew that as well as he did. As well as they both understood what might happen if Torquil couldn't force Christiana to use her gifts for his benefit.

"We'll bring her here, where we can protect her."

Across from him, Patrick snorted his disbelief.

"Have you gone daft? You ken as well as I do he'll no let her come to us. No willingly. No here, where she might decide to use her gift for your benefit. She'd no be under his control and he'll be having none of that. I can scarce believe he allowed Dermid to journey here."

Their youngest brother's arrival had surprised Malcolm as well. Granted, someone had to deliver news of their father's demise and present Torquil's demands. But it seemed entirely out of character for Torquil to have sent Dermid.

"Aye," Malcolm agreed, frustrated at his own inability to interpret his elder brother's intent. "It's no like him to give up any pieces on his chessboard."

Whatever the new laird of the MacDowylt schemed, it made little difference. Malcolm's course was all too clear. He could no more leave his sister in Torquil's clutches than he could have turned Elesyria out into the cold this night.

"No matter the cost. We bring Christiana here."

Patrick nodded, rising slowly to his feet. "In that case, it's best I pay a visit to the MacKilyn. We've no enough men on our own to confront Tordenet Castle."

"Wait."

They would need help, no doubt. And Patrick was correct in wanting to ensure that the only remaining ally to Clan MacGahan supported them still. As much as it galled Malcolm, there was no option but to court the favor of Angus MacKilyn, as fickle an old man as ever walked the land.

But not by sending Patrick. He needed his brother here to keep watch over Elesyria until they could determine why she had come and what she wanted.

"Send Eric with a small party of men. I prefer your attention directed toward our houseguest, at least for the time being."

Just in case.

Again Patrick nodded, a small quirk of his eyebrow the closest he came to questioning Malcolm's decision. "As you wish, my laird. 'Tis a task well within the abilities of the captain of yer guard. I will see it done."

Malcolm leaned back in his chair, the sound of Patrick's retreating steps in his ears. Lifting a hand to his face, he massaged one finger across the bridge of his nose, giving thanks for his brother. If only everything else in his life could be as predictable and steady as Patrick.

Immediately, he sat forward, his eyes opened wide.

"I dinna mean it!" he offered to the empty room.

Best not give the old gods of Asgard any more targets this day.

Three

COMFORT, WYOMING
PRESENT DAY

WHERE THE HELL is she anyway? Hiding? She knows damn well I meant pumpkin, not pecan!"

"Now, Charlie, think of your blood pressure, darlin'. She'll be right back."

Dani Dearmon pulled the collar of her old sweater up against the wind and made her way through the early shower of snow crystals out to the ancient cottonwood tree, ignoring the upraised voices coming through the back door of the truck stop where she worked. She squinted against the biting sting of ice hitting her face and poured a capful of milk into the little bowl she'd fitted into the crook of the lowest branch.

"I certainly hope you appreciate this, Faeries," she muttered, turning from the tree and making her way back toward the sprawling building and the argument she knew awaited her.

Not an argument, really, she corrected herself.

More of a mini confrontation. But she was used to those now. Though they were old Charlie's stock and trade, she'd learned long ago that he must have been the original inspiration for the saying about someone's bark being worse than his bite.

"What's this I hear 'bout you having an oven full of pecan pies?" The old man stood in the center of her kitchen, his short stature and scraggly beard making him appear more like an out-of-place gnome than the owner of the biggest truck stop on this side of the state. "You lost what little sense you had? Halloween means pumpkin! Pumpkin is what you have for holidays, gal."

Dani turned from hanging her sweater on a peg by the door and smiled at the old man, taking time to pat his shoulder as she passed by him on her way to wash her hands.

"Not holidays at my house."

"He's talkin' regular Christian holidays. The ones decent folks celebrate," Verna, the oldest of the morning shift waitresses, added with a huff, her graying topknot shivering like a bowl of Jell-O as she spoke. "Not them evil Pagan things of yours. Don't think we don't see you sticking food out in that tree for your false gods."

Dani breathed in the calming smells of her kitchen and smiled, doing her best to ignore her fellow worker. "My Aunt Jean made pecan pies for every holiday. And you know for yourself, Charlie, my pecan pies will draw in every cowboy and trucker for a hundred miles."

As for Verna's comment, she planned to ignore the woman. No point in arguing with her. How could she expect her coworker to understand something her own family never had? She knew from experience that she should just let it go. Still, she couldn't stop herself. "And they're not gods of any sort. They're Faeries. Big difference."

"Get yourself back out front to your customers, Verna, and leave Dani be. She can believe in whatever she wants to." Charlie turned his scowl from one to the other of them. "No matter how crazy it is."

The woman pursed her lips in irritation and snatched up one of the fresh pans of cinnamon rolls Dani had finished icing before she'd gone outside. With a *harrumph* obviously meant to include everyone, Verna disappeared through the swinging door into the front of the diner.

"Guess we don't have any choice but to make do with what you got baking since you already did it," Charlie grumbled, scrunching his face into a scowl. "Don't know why I put up with your sass lip."

"Because she's the best baker in three counties and for some reason she likes us enough to stay on here and put up with you," Charlie's daughter answered. Evelyn, past fifty herself, grinned at Dani as she prodded her father's back, urging him forward. "Come on, Daddy. Get out of Dani's kitchen and let her do her thing."

"I'll do pumpkin next batch," Dani offered as a consolation to the old man's retreating back. "I promise."

"Damn straight you will," he asserted, snagging one of the fresh cinnamon rolls as he passed and stuffing it in his mouth. Dani shook her head, measuring out the ingredients for another batch of rolls, determined not to let any of this ruin her mood. This was the part of her day she liked best, early in the morning, when the kitchen was mostly all hers. Surrounded by the aroma of those things she'd made with her own two hands, she felt the closest she ever had to being where she belonged.

For a time she'd dreamed of going off to some fancy cooking school to become a real chef, but Aunt Jean's death five years ago had put an end to that. Probably just as well. Being a real chef would likely have meant working in a huge restaurant in a big city, and she knew for a fact she wouldn't have been happy in that environment. It simply wasn't where she was supposed to be.

"Damn Faeries," she muttered to herself, squishing the sticky mixture in the bowl between her fingers. Some days she honestly wished she'd never read that first book about them.

But she had, and from that moment on, she'd known in her heart they were real. More important, she'd known they had a purpose for her. A purpose and a place.

She just wished they'd hurry up and get around to letting her know about that purpose and place. She was tired beyond measure of always feeling as if she were in the wrong place at the wrong time.

Of all the places she'd worked in the past few

years, this had to be the best. The hours were long and the pay was pitiful, but they provided her with a place to live as well as meals.

They also treated her more like family than anyone had since she'd lost Aunt Jean. She could well imagine Charlie as a crusty old Scottish laird, straight out of one of her favorite books. He might raise hell with everyone around him but he protected his people from anyone else who might choose to do the same.

No, she knew this wasn't where she belonged, but it was as good a spot as any to be until the time came when the Faeries would finally send her where she did belong.

"Don't forget, you promised you'd go into Cheyenne with me this afternoon to pick up those new menus we ordered." Evelyn grinned at her from the doorway. "And I hear that new metaphysical shop has finally opened up next door to the printers. We can stop in and have a look around while we're there. Maybe find something pretty for them Faeries of yours."

"I'll be ready."

More than ready. A trip into the big city was usually a chore, but this time Dani was looking forward to it. Oh, there'd still be all the noise and the traffic that grated on her nerves, but she'd been waiting for months to visit the store Evelyn mentioned. Ever since she'd read about the mystical powers in crystals, she'd been itching to give them a try, and on their last visit into Cheyenne, she'd seen in the window that the new store would be stocking crystals.

With Halloween just a week away, maybe she'd finally found a way to contact the elusive Faeries she'd spent the last fifteen years believing in. Contact them and at long last set foot on the path to where she really belonged.

"I'm going to be ready for you this year, Faeries," she whispered, punching her fist into the ball of dough for emphasis.

She'd read through a stack of books and knew that on Halloween, or what used to be called Samhain, the curtain between the world of Man and Fae was at its weakest. If she was ever going to communicate with the Fae, this would be her time.

This was it. She felt it in her soul as if someone were whispering over her shoulder that after years of waiting, the Fae were about to disclose to her the purpose and the place they intended for her.

A purpose and a place where she belonged, because she knew for a fact she didn't belong here.

Four

ELESYRIA AL BYRN stopped outside the large wooden door, patting one hand over her hair in an effort to compose herself.

As she'd promised her Goddess before embarking on her quest, she was doing everything in her power to determine the facts of her daughter's disappearance before taking any action. But sorting through the events surrounding Isabella was proving a most difficult task.

Not to mention the toll it was taking on her emotions.

She'd spoken to the Tinklers. They had told her all about her daughter's escape from this castle along with a child and a man the Tinklers claimed was Isa's SoulMate. With their help, she had trekked to the place where they had left Isabella and felt for herself the waves of Faerie Magic flowing from walls of MacQuarrie Keep.

That wasn't all she'd felt.

In the dead of night, she'd visited the graves at

MacQuarrie Keep, one with a stone that bore the chiseled name ISABELLA MACGAHAN MACDOWYLT.

That visit had only deepened the mystery. Isabella did not lie in her grave. No one did. Just as no bodies occupied the graves of the man the Tinklers had claimed her daughter loved nor the boy who traveled with them.

Wherever Isabella and her Robert had gone, it was not into those dank, dark holes in the ground.

What was clear was that they had left this castle together. And from everything the Tinklers had told her, it appeared they could only have done that with the assistance of the man sitting behind the door she now faced.

The laird of the MacGahan, her daughter's widowed husband.

There was much she still needed to learn before her work here was done. Chief among that missing knowledge was whether Malcolm MacDowylt had acted to help or to harm her Isa. And the only way to assess that accurately was to determine the true inherent worth of the man himself.

Good or evil?

Worthy of her gift or deserving of her punishment?

Only time would tell. Time, and whatever test she could devise to provide the answers she sought.

With a long, slow, deliberate breath, she exhaled the turmoil of emotions assaulting her heart and cracked open the door. Only one question filled her mind now:

Who is Malcolm MacDowylt?

"Eric left at first light, taking three men along with him. They should reach MacKilyn Keep in two days' hard ride to present yer petition for aid. Within a sennight you should have yer answer." The voice of the man who'd kept to the shadows last night. "Unless the MacKilyn decides to drag his feet."

"Aye. He's an obstinate old bastard, that one. He kens he has us by the short hairs and I've no a doubt he'll use that advantage to exact some sort of—"

Malcolm's response came to an abrupt halt as she pushed the door fully open and entered to greet two sets of hardened eyes turned in her direction.

The owners of which were sadly mistaken if they thought to intimidate her with their stares. She could easily enough incinerate them both with a wave of her hand should she so choose.

And choose she might if the brazen young laird failed her test.

"Morning fare is served in the great hall, my lady, at the end of the corridor. Yer welcome to join those in attendance to break yer fast." Malcolm looked from her to the door as he spoke.

Luckily for him, she'd spent lifetimes honing her tolerance for fools.

"It's not my stomach that requires filling this morning, lad. It's my ears. I'm ready for that chat we discussed last night."

Did he pale at her words? His lips certainly tightened into a thin, straight line, and a look passed between him and the other man.

"Perhaps your guest would grant us time to discuss my daughter's final days in privacy." She waited, determined not to launch into the discussion in front of his man.

Again a look passed between the two men, this one alive in tension.

"I have no secrets from my brother, Patrick. He is as my right hand."

His brother, was it? Had she paid more attention, she might have guessed as much from the similarities in their appearance. They were of a size, the two of them, both tall and well-muscled. Battle-hardened men, she'd guess, from the identical expressions they wore to mask the depth of emotions roiling behind their intense blue eyes.

Schooling her own expression to a matching blandness, she crossed the room and seated herself, taking extra care to assume an air of calm and control as she once again met their gazes.

"As you wish. But know this, young laird of the MacGahan, I expect your complete honesty, no matter who is in the room with us."

His eyes flashed with what appeared to be an unguarded moment of anger before he caught himself and once again hid his emotion.

"I can assure you, my lady, that I am well past being a scholar at the master's knee and I am always truthful."

Malcolm's clipped tones conveyed more of his emotion than she suspected he would have liked.

"To a fault," his brother added.

"I'll be the judge of that." Elesyria glanced down to her hands clasped in her lap, marshaling her emotions for what she was about to ask. "I traveled to Castle MacQuarrie. I saw my daughter's gravestone." She paused, raising her gaze to meet his. "Are you responsible for her death?"

Pain leaked through the cracks in his mask. Pain and guilt, igniting her anger even as she caught scent of his emotions.

Let him try to deny it now.

The beast of retribution seethed in her heart, its deadly claws unsheathing, prodding her to her feet.

"Yes." He spoke the word quietly.

"You are not!" Patrick was at his side, a hand to his shoulder. "I canna allow you to claim as much to her own mother. Yer no to blame for what happened, Colm. You did everything in yer power to see her away and on the path to her own happiness."

Elesyria held her tongue as clouds of emotion rolled off the brothers, buffeting her senses. Patrick's story matched what she had heard from the Tinklers. But if it were truth, why did she sense so much guilt from the man who'd married her daughter?

"No." Malcolm shook his head slowly from side to side in denial of his brother's defense. "Had I forced her to stay here, she would yet live. All of them would. Isabella, the man who held her heart, even the poor, wee deformed lad. I sent them to meet their deaths."

Patrick turned from his brother, pounding a fist on the table next to him. "You allowed them to follow their own path. Who do you think you are? No even you could change what Skuld had woven for them."

"Skuld?" Elesyria had held silent for as long as she could. "I thought you were Scotsmen. Highlanders."

"We are sons of Scotland." Malcolm's chin lifted, his shoulders straightening. "Born and bred. But our father came to this land as Viking."

"Then you are Northmen."

"As you are Elven?" Patrick spoke, his back still to her.

It boded well that they knew of her kind. Elesyria crossed the floor, stopping less than a foot from the men.

"I haven't been called such for longer than I care to admit." Not since she'd last interacted with a Northman. How many centuries ago *had* that been? "My branch of the family prefers to think of ourselves as Faeric."

A sort of harrumphing noise escaped Malcolm's lips and he crossed his arms in front of him. "Ridiculous," he claimed, though he didn't sound as sure of that as he tried to appear.

Good. And now she would have the truth of that guilt surrounding him like a cloud.

She reached toward Malcolm, lifting her arm to touch her fingers to his temple, his cheek. He stood still, as if his body had turned to stone, his eyes boring into her, his pride preventing any movement.

There it was. Ripples of thick, oily guilt—not for

what he'd done himself, but guilt for what he felt he should have done. For what he felt he should have been able to prevent.

"Who are you, Malcolm MacDowylt?" She voiced the question, more to herself than to those present, as her fingers moved to his shoulder and then, ever so lightly, danced over his heart.

Pain lanced into her fingertips, like nettles of fire stinging her skin. She jerked her hand away, her gaze tracking to the reddened skin of her hand and back again to his eyes.

He seemed as surprised as she by what had just happened, grasping her shoulders with both his hands. "Are you well, my lady?"

A Faerie could not be harmed in the Mortal world. Most especially not a Faerie in full possession of her powers. Not unless . . .

Again she lifted her hand, careful to hover over his heart this time, not to actually touch that spot.

"Ah," she whispered. Had she been more intent on the search and less so on what she expected to find, she would have felt it before.

It was not a question of *who* this man was, but rather *what* he was.

More than Scotsman. More than Northman. More. Other. Strong Magic, old Magic surrounded him, raging in his blood.

At least she had some of her answers now. This man before her was no vessel of evil. He had done what he thought best for her Isabella, and he carried on his shoulders the weight of that decision.

It was reward rather than retribution she owed him.

But how in the name of Danu did one go about rewarding a descendent of the old gods themselves?

"I am satisfied with what I've found."

The barest tip of his head acknowledged her comment. "Then you will be leaving us soon to return to . . ." Malcolm paused, his eyes flickering to his brother and back again as he let the word linger a moment, as if in question. "To your own home."

"Not yet." She patted his hand and gifted him with her most pleasant smile. "I believe I'd like to get to know you a little better first. After all, my son, by virtue of your marriage to my daughter, we are family, are we not?"

More important, her work here was not yet finished. Not until she could find that which would make Malcolm MacDowylt a happy man.

Five

WHERE COULD THE annoying woman have gotten herself off to this time?

Patrick strode through the darkened castle corridors, taking little care to hide his irritation. For the last week it had seemed as though he couldn't turn a corner without bumping into Elesyria waiting there, but now that he actually sought her?

Nowhere to be found.

"Damn," he growled aloud as he made his way through the kitchens to pause at the door to the gardens.

Surely she wouldn't be out there. Not this late at night. Not in this cold.

And yet . . .

He'd checked everywhere within the castle proper to no avail. And hadn't she prattled on at the noonday meal about some sort of preparations for observing Samhain?

Watch her, Malcolm had asked of him, and watching her was exactly what he intended to do. He had given his word.

As he slipped out into the night, he sent a silent thanks to Freya for the full moon lighting his way even as he paused, listening for any telltale sounds.

Within moments he sensed her presence. Following his unexplainable instinct through the cook's garden and beyond the small orchard, he spotted her at last.

Noiselessly, he concealed himself behind a large tree, where he could watch without being seen.

What was the woman up to now?

Elesyria kneeled on the ground, at the very center of a circle of strewn stones, her arms lifted beseechingly toward the skies. For an instant, as if his eyes played tricks on him, he could have sworn another figure floated above her.

"Damned Elf," he muttered under his breath.

No doubt she practiced her own form of religion and, like as not, whatever she was up to now would do naught but bode ill for all of them. As if Malcolm needed one more burden placed upon his shoulders.

If that was her plan, she'd best be about thinking again, because he was having none of it.

Intending to stop whatever Elesyria attempted, Patrick stepped away from the tree but halted his movement as the woman he watched rose to her feet.

Moonlight glinted off her form, sparkling playfully over the unbound hair that cascaded down her back like a river of fire. She twirled in dance, arms lifted, her face shining with unbridled joy as her laughter tinkled like the music of water over stones.

Patrick ducked back behind the tree and rubbed a hand over his eyes.

Whether by trick of moonlight or magic, the woman before him was no gray-haired matron but a maiden. A lass at the peak of womanhood.

By Freya, she was beautiful!

In his chest, his heart pounded even as he fought to control his erratic breathing before he once again moved from behind the tree to catch another glimpse of her. Carelessly, his step snapped a dry branch, and across the field her head swiveled toward the spot where he stood. When their eyes met, the air shimmered as if a thick curtain had been pulled between them.

For the second time he wiped a hand over his eyes to clear his vision. When he looked again, the Elesyria he recognized approached him, her face much older than he'd imagined only moments before, but her eyes still shining with her joy.

"Good evening, Northman," she greeted sweetly. "Did you satisfy your curiosity with your spying on me?"

"Good evening, Elf."

He tipped his head respectfully, careful to hide the smile their shared greeting brought to his lips. A week ago he would have scoffed aloud at the suggestion that he would fall into such a comfortable routine with this woman.

In the face of his self-imposed control, her smile broadened, her eyes twinkling.

"Ah, Patrick, you are such a joy." She linked her

arm through his, patting his hand as she did. "Walk with me. I've had the most wonderful Samhain."

She was infectious in her happiness and, at last, he allowed himself the weakness of returning her smile.

"So tell me, my lady, what has made this evening so special for you?"

"My Goddess has brought me wonderful news. My Isabella lives, though far from this time. She's happier than I could ever have hoped, and I have your brother to thank for that."

"You spoke to . . . your Goddess." In light of her happiness, Patrick meant to remove any traces of doubt and sarcasm from his words. To his ears, though, he'd been less than successful. "She was here, was she?"

Who was he to question what comfort the woman took from her religion? If their positions were reversed, he couldn't say how he might react to the loss of a child. Even a child grown to full womanhood.

Again she grazed him with the glow of her smile and again, for just an instant, he could have sworn her visage shimmered between maiden and crone.

Likely he needed sleep. He should be flat upon his back lost in dreams rather than chasing after this woman into the early morn. But a promise was a promise.

"Yes. When the curtain between your world and mine thinned as is its custom on Samhain, my Goddess came to me, bringing her most welcome news. And that's not all."

She squeezed the arm that linked through hers

and tipped her head toward him, just as he'd often seen women do when they were about sharing secrets.

"There's more?"

"Yes," she breathed close to him, her words barely more than a whisper. "My Goddess, so wise and knowing, gave me the perfect solution to my dilemma of what to do about your brother."

Patrick wasn't at all sure he liked the sound of that.

"Then you'll be leaving us soon, my lady?"

"Oh my dear . . ." She pulled back from him, her laughter hitting the stones under their feet and bounding away like notes of music. "I can hardly leave now. *Now* is when our dear Malcolm will need me most. Look there!" She lifted a hand toward the sky. "Did you see? A shot of silver streaking through the sky. Proof the actions promised by my Goddess have been set in motion."

A hint of unease traveled across Patrick's shoulders. "Explain yerself," he demanded, perhaps a bit more forcefully than he'd intended. He was, after all, quite tired.

She shook her head, her eyes still shining with happiness. "No, dear Patrick. There is no explaining some mysteries. You'll simply have to wait to see for yourself."

No more words passed between them, Patrick's thoughts consumed with what the blasted Elf had in store for them and how in the world he would explain all this to Malcolm.

Six

"WORD IS, I make a mighty good bed warmer, darlin', and it's terrible cold out here tonight."

Like Dani couldn't have predicted this happening from the moment her date had arrived to pick her up this evening, a leer on his face and a bottle of Jack tucked into the back of his waistband.

She stepped backward into her doorway, turning her head from the scent of alcohol and too much aftershave wafting off her evening's companion.

"Whatcha say, Dani-girl? You gonna save me a long drive home tonight?" The corner of Lover Boy's mouth lifted in a half smile that had likely melted a whole slew of hearts in this part of the state. "I ain't had me no complaints yet."

Did he honestly expect that she'd be impressed by references from other women?

"There's always a first time for everything, you know."

His expression hardened and she immediately regretted her stab at humor. Aunt Jean always had said that sharp tongue of hers was going to get her into trouble.

"You turnin' me down?" No trace of humor in his response. "Or you gonna do the right thing and let me stay the night here after that fancy dinner I treated you to."

The vision of opening her purse and tossing cash at him flittered through her mind, quickly discarded. She'd put up with his wandering hands and his innuendo-filled conversation all night. That more than made up for the lousy fifteen dollars he'd dropped on her meal.

"I don't think that's such a good idea, Clay." Think? Hell, she knew. She was simply trying her best to be nice. "I have to be in the diner bright and early in the morning. Those cinnamon rolls don't bake themselves."

"Won't bother me none if you crawl out early." He leaned toward her, his oily half smile back in place, one hand reaching out to trail her cheek as if his physical touch might push her to decide in his favor.

Not happening. Another step back and she was inside, able to use the door as a barrier.

"Sorry, Clay. I had a nice evening, but I'm beat. See you later, okay?"

She didn't wait for his reply before shutting the door and sliding the bolt home, setting the glass chimes next to her door tinkling.

This was exactly the reason she didn't like to date customers who frequented the truck stop where she worked. More often than not, they assumed that just because she lived in a room at the attached motel she'd be quick to hop into bed with them at the end of the evening.

"As if," she whispered, tossing her purse on the table before crossing the room to perch on the edge of her one easy chair.

Just because she'd agreed to let this guy drive her all the way into Cheyenne for a decent meal she didn't have to cook herself was no call for him to go expecting more than a kiss on the cheek.

But he had expected more. They always expected more.

Too bad the few men she had dated since she'd been here weren't more honest with each other when they discussed the evening they'd spent with her. A little honesty might have saved good ol' Clay a long, disappointing drive home. Alone.

"Screw him," she growled, kicking off the uncomfortable heels she'd worn for her evening out.

The words had hardly passed her lips before she started to chuckle. "Or more precisely, *not*."

Besides, she had bigger plans for her evening than Clay Carter could possibly imagine.

She leaned forward and flipped on the television, waiting for the grainy picture to come into focus. As long as it was taking, the wind must be wreaking havoc with the satellite dish again. Not that it really mattered. She only turned it on for background noise while she got everything ready for what she'd planned tonight.

Within minutes, she was out of her dress and into

a comfy, oversize T-shirt. One more task and then she could get down to business. She pulled on a pair of jeans, slid her feet into some well-worn boots, and stuck her arms into the heavy sweater hanging by the door before opening her tiny refrigerator to remove a small carton of milk.

Opening the door, she stepped out into the cold and tugged the collar of her old sweater tight around her neck in an attempt to block the wind now tinged with the first light touch of sleet. She hurried across the parking lot and out to the back side of the little motel, away from the lights of the truck stop next door, to an ancient cottonwood tree. Squinting against the biting sting of tiny ice pellets hitting her face, she poured milk into the little bowl she'd fitted into the crook of the lowest branch.

"Here you go, Faeries. Hope you're all in a listening mood tonight."

She hadn't missed a day in fifteen years and she wasn't going to miss tonight, not even if it meant freezing her butt off out here. But she had to admit, one little sign of appreciation for a change would be a nice thing.

Ice clung to her hair by the time she stepped back inside her warm little room, melting almost immediately into little drops of cold water.

Great. Either she took time to dry it now, or she'd be a mass of out-of-control curls in the morning. A glance at the clock confirmed it was already after eleven. No time for primping her hair.

Curls it would be.

A quick towel-dry and she reached to turn off the television, stopping as an ad for some party shop in Denver caught her attention. The actors cavorted like amateurs in front of the camera, dressed up as witches and ghosts, inviting all the grown-up goblins in for a visit.

"Damn," she muttered as she hit the switch, sending the screen to black.

She'd better hurry or it would be too late. Tonight was Halloween, Samhain to the ancient peoples and to the Faeries. The one night of the year when the separation between the world of man and the world of Faeries was most penetrable. She'd waited for over three months for this very night, and there was no way she was going to miss this chance! Less than an hour left before it was over and she'd have to wait for another whole year for this opportunity to return again.

She had time. It was why she'd insisted on coming home when she had.

The little bag of stones lay at the bottom of her dresser drawer along with a thin, white candle, wrapped in the soft green velvet scarf she'd bought especially for them. They'd cost her more than a week's pay, but they were worth every penny. Or they would be, if they worked.

She shoved aside her small table and chair, clearing as much floor space as possible.

What she needed was a circle. Faeries loved circles.

One by one, she laid out her stones, reading from the strips of paper where she'd written their names and why she'd chosen them.

"Fairy quartz for heightened energy even while it calms. Apophyllite, the fairy stone, to help in working with Faeries. Staurolite, to channel information from the ancients."

She only hoped the ancient Fae were paying attention tonight.

"Amazonite for success and psychic abilities. Turquoise, for guidance through the unknown. Psilomelane, for scrying and out-of-body travel. Mica, to improve visions and mystical clarity. Jade, for dreams and realization of potential. Iolite, the shaman stone, to help with visions and spiritual growth. Chalcedony, the sacred Native American miracle stone. Clear quartz, a power stone to intensify the energy of my circle."

She set the last one in place and stood back to admire her work. It wasn't perfect by any means, but it would have to do. The quartz she'd truly wanted, one the shop owner had called a Time Link crystal, had reached for the sky with four beautifully shaped points that were said to give insight into the future as well as aid in finding meaning in the past. It had been very large and so far out of her price range, she'd had to settle for this one, with a point on only one side. A link to the past, the salesclerk had claimed. Close enough.

Eleven stones.

The twelfth was in the ring she wore on her right hand, her birthstone, a garnet. Her most valued possession, it had been a gift from her aunt on her sixteenth birthday.

"For romantic love, for passion, for sensuality and intimacy," she quoted, holding her hand out in front of her.

After an evening like she'd just suffered through, heaven knew she could use a dash of all those in her life.

Eleven stones for the Fae, one for her. Even the Fae should see that ratio as more than fair.

She pushed her hair back over her shoulder, realizing as she did so that she was still wearing her ratty, oversize T-shirt.

That would never do for meeting the Faerie Queen. If she showed up.

"*When* she shows up," she corrected herself. This was no time for doubting. "Not if. When. I meant to say when."

Another glance at the clock. Fifteen minutes left.

What did she have that was pretty? Not that she could hope to be as beautiful as a Faerie, but still, she should dress for the occasion. There was that long, gauzy sundress she'd bought at a garage sale a few years back. The one with little flowers embroidered over the bodice. Part of the appeal of the dress was that it always reminded her of something that would have been worn in a different century.

It would be perfect.

She pulled the tee off even as she headed for her drawers. In minutes she'd found what she wanted, dropping the cream-colored cloud of material down over her head before lighting the candle she'd left on the foot of her bed. It felt right.

Ten minutes.

Taking a deep breath, she stepped into the center of the circle and held her candle aloft. Its flame glinted off the facets cut into the stone of her ring. She closed her eyes to eliminate the distraction and forced all errant thoughts from her mind even as she expelled the air from her lungs.

Concentrate. The time had come.

"Your Highness?" She stumbled over the words, wondering at the last minute how she could possibly catch the Faerie Queen's attention. "Fifteen years, Your Highness. I've given you fifteen years. Milk for the Faeries every single day, even when I ate nothing for my own dinner." That sounded an awful lot like dramatic whining, not at all what she was going for. But she had been so patient for so long. Lord, but she was tired of waiting for them to notice her. Tired of just existing while she waited for whatever it was her life was intended to be to begin.

A deep breath to settle her nerves and she tried again.

"Fifteen years. I know that's probably not even a blink of an eye for you, but it's three-quarters of my life. Devoted to you. Believing in you no matter what anyone thought of me for it. Believing that you have some higher purpose for me. Knowing that I don't belong here and waiting for you to show me exactly where it is that I do belong. But now . . ."

Again she faltered. Now, what? What did she want, truly want, from the Fae?

"I'm ready. For whatever that purpose is. I'm tired

of waiting. Tired of watching the world pass me by. I'm tired of always being on the outside looking in. Please. I wish you would help me find the path to where I'm supposed to be. I just want to be where I belong. With people I can belong to."

Dani waited, the sound of blood pounding in her ears louder even than the semis pulling off the road outside.

Hair tickled at her face as if stirred by an errant breeze, followed by a light tinkling of the delicate chimes hanging by the door.

Her eyes snapped open in time to see the flame on her candle flicker and go out, leaving her bathed in a soft green glow of light.

That wasn't right. The lights had been on in the room. Regular, normal lights, not a single green bulb among them.

The errant breeze had morphed into an insistent wind, whipping the ends of her hair against her skin like little lashes.

She found herself unable to move, frozen to the spot while a million multicolored lights streamed across the room toward her. Over her, around her, through her, they filled her vision, lifting her up like a rag doll. She fought for her next breath as if the weight of the world sucked the air from her lungs. Her eyes fluttered shut as the sensation of her body hurtling through space overwhelmed her senses. And over it all, as impossible as it seemed, she could swear the last thing she heard was a woman's voice.

You had but to ask, daughter. So you wish it, so it will be.

Seven

HAVING A LUMP the size of a horse roiling around in his stomach was no way to begin the morning. Or perhaps it was the pressure on his chest that bothered him more. Like the whole of the world pressed in on him, cloaking him in a vague sense of foreboding, as if his honor and indeed his entire future rested on the most urgent action he must take.

If only he knew what that action might be.

Malcolm pinched the skin between his brows, applying pressure to the bone beneath, seeking physical relief from the worries that plagued him. Likely it was no more than the fitful night he'd spent, tossing and turning, tormented by dreams no man should be forced to endure. Dreams of others suffering because he hadn't taken action to save them. Dreams of failure.

"Shadows and nothing more," he growled, jerking his hand from his face and straightening his shoulders. "Meaningless."

If only his denial could lift the heavy mood he wore this day. With forced determination, he strode into the great hall, ignoring the voice in the back of his head urging him to make for his destrier and ride.

"Good morning, my laird." Patrick sat at the small table he favored away from the dais, his back to the wall near one of the great fireplaces. "Rest well, did you?"

Malcolm snorted his response, noting the dark circles under his brother's eyes. "No better than you, from the looks of it."

Patrick shrugged, lifting a hand to signal for a serving girl. "At least I had a good reason to have missed my sleep. Join me?"

With a nod, Malcolm slid onto the bench next to his brother, also facing out to look over the room. Too many years as a warrior to feel comfort in exposing his back, even in his own castle. Perhaps especially in his own castle.

"What ails you this morning, Colm? You've the look of a hunted animal about you."

Malcolm held his tongue as a young maid arrived at their table to deposit two large servings of porridge, waiting until she was well away from them.

"Naught but bad dreams," he muttered around a mouthful of the thick porridge. Hardly heroic for a grown man, a clan laird at that, to admit to being troubled by dreams as if he were but a wee bairn. "Though 'hunted animal' is a fair description of how I feel. It's as if I've a need to run. A need to set off for the forest to find . . ."

He let his words die in the air, filling his mouth with another bite to prevent himself from talking. He sounded like a man gone daft.

"To find what?" Patrick stared at him, his own food untouched.

This time it was his turn to shrug. "I canna say." That was part of the nameless anxiety that gnawed at his gut. "I dreamed of a ring of standing stones, but I've no memory of where. Of a woman's voice, but no her words. Of an urgent need to act, to be somewhere in particular, somewhere other than here, but I canna tell why or what it is I'm to do."

He opened his fingers, allowing the bread he'd used to scoop his porridge to fall to the table. The food had no taste this morning, dropping as it did onto the huge bubble of unease gurgling about in the pit of his stomach.

"Do you think it possible—"

Whatever Patrick might have thought to suggest was cut short by the arrival in the great hall of Elesyria.

"What are you doing here?" she demanded.

Malcolm found himself fighting the urge to beat a hasty retreat as the woman stormed toward the spot where he sat, stopping at last in front of him. Hands on her hips, she repeated the question she'd hurled at him from across the room.

"What are you doing here?"

Beside him, Patrick lapsed into a comfortable slouch, his back tipped against the wall behind them. "It is his hall, Elf. Who has a better right to be here than he does?"

Her eyes narrowed, the glitter of her irritation turned fully on Patrick. "I'm not questioning his rights, Northman. Only his good sense."

The glare moved from his brother to him, and once again Malcolm fought down the urge to make good his escape.

"Well? Was the Goddess herself not clear enough in her instructions?"

Instructions from a Goddess? Malcolm shook his head. Elf, Faerie, whatever this woman chose to call herself, she was clearly brainsick.

As if she could read his thoughts in his expression, she threw her hands into the air, casting her eyes upward "You see? You see what I'm forced to deal with?" On an exaggerated huff of breath, she dropped onto the bench across from him, pinning him with a look.

"Do you mean to tell me there's nothing more important you feel you should be doing this fine morning than sitting here shoving that sticky mess into your mouth?" She wiggled her finger toward the food in front of him, her gaze never leaving his face. "Nowhere else you feel you need to be?"

Malcolm schooled his expression, careful to avoid any hint of what he had shared with his brother only moments earlier. He'd rather roll in a muck heap than admit to this woman that he did indeed feel exactly as if he should be someplace else. It was without question none of her business. Not in the least. She'd be the last person walking the earth to whom he would—

"Suppose for a moment that's exactly how he feels

after a night of tormented dreams. What would you make of that, my lady?"

Unbelievably, from beside him, his brother gave voice to the very words he would have kept secret.

"Dreams, you say? You really don't understand, do you?" Elesyria sighed, shaking her head as if in disbelief. "Very well. I'll give you the benefit of the doubt. Perhaps communication from the Goddess was impeded by the same forces that prevented my touching you."

Again with the Goddess. This farce had gone on long enough.

Malcolm shoved against the bench with the backs of his legs as he pushed himself to stand. "I've a long day ahead of me and no time for any more of yer nonsense. Either of you."

With as much dignity as he could muster, he nodded to each of them in turn and headed for the door.

He almost made it.

"She'll die if you don't find her, you know. Out in this weather. Unprotected. She's but an innocent, sent here because of you. It's your conscience that will have to bear the burden of her death."

Elesyria's prediction froze his feet to the floor as surely as if the stones beneath him had turned to ice.

"What say you? Who's this woman of whom you speak?" He forced the words past a tongue gone thick and dry, turning slowly as he spoke to stare at the witch who claimed to be his mother-in-law. "I have no knowledge of any woman. And certainly no responsibility for her."

She shrugged her shoulders, a perfectly fabricated look of innocence spreading over her features. "I know not who she is, only that the Goddess was to send her here because of you. Perhaps as a test? Though I suppose it matters not, since she has little chance of survival out there." She fluttered her hand vaguely in the direction of the wall. "I do wonder, though, how long she might hang on. Suffering. In the cold. Lost. With no food or water. No protection. No—"

"Enough!" Malcolm roared, unable to listen to any more of her guilt-baiting.

What if the things she said were possible? There had been a woman central to his troubled dreams. He remembered that much. Could it be that this Faerie had conjured someone? Someone she'd stranded in the wilderness to meet some horrible fate? But why would she . . .

Revenge! The word lanced through his heart on a shaft of guilt. Revenge for the part he played in her daughter's fate. Revenge for his having failed to keep Isabella safe.

"Where do I find her?" He all but choked on the question.

Her lips thinned, all veneer of innocence gone. "I have no idea. It was you the Goddess chose to share that information with. Not me. Only you know the answer to that question."

His stomach lurched even as his breath caught in his chest, the morning's helpless distress rolling back over him full force. He could not stand by and allow another innocent woman's death. And yet, his dreams had been a jumble of unintelligible scenes and sounds. He had no way of knowing where she might be . . . if she even existed.

"You spoke of a ring of stones. I have seen such a place on my rides. A half day's journey north of here."

Malcolm jerked his gaze up, his attention riveted by his brother's claim. "You could find this spot again?" Patrick wandered on occasion, exploring the land for days at a time.

"Aye. I believe I can. If you think it's possible . . ."

Patrick's words hung in the silence between them, a siren call he had but to answer.

"It is possible," Elesyria broke the silence. "A stone circle has power to us. I would deem it more than possible, in fact. I would deem it probable."

It was settled then.

"We ride."

Without a word, Patrick was at his side, keeping pace as they ran from the keep to ready their mounts.

His only concern now was whether or not he could reach this mystery woman in time.

Eight

HOURS ON HORSEBACK had brought them well into the mountains and still Malcolm had found no sign of any ring of stones similar to what he'd seen in his dreams. His patience wore thin, his spirits as damp as the fine cold mist that stung his skin.

He wiped the moisture from his face, refusing to allow himself to brood over how much they could have used this weather a few months past. Instead he focused on their current quest.

"Are you sure we—"

"Yes," Patrick cut in, "just over this ridge, in the valley below.

Malcolm nodded, instinctively tightening his thighs against his mount's sides. The big horse's steps quickened over the rough terrain, moving faster as if keeping pace with the growing sense of urgency bearing pressure in his chest.

At the top of the ridge he pulled up the reins. Below him, the valley lay shrouded in a gray blanket of fine rain, all but obscuring a copse of trees off to his right.

"The stone circle lies at the very heart of the grove. If

we're to believe the Elf, we should find her there." Patrick pulled his horse to a stop soundlessly beside him.

If they were to believe. And how could he not? How could he ignore the nameless worry clawing at the back of his throat like a living creature?

A slight pressure with his heels and his horse sprang forward, taking the downward slope as quickly as possible.

It seemed an eternity cutting down the distance between them and their destination, but at last they made their way through the close-growing trees, to the opening at the very heart of the copse.

There, in the center of a stone ring, on a strangely green clump of vegetation, lay a crumpled body.

"By Freya," Malcolm hissed, sliding down from his mount and hitting the ground at a run. He remembered this place from his dream now, reality sharpening the hazy dream vision into clear focus.

She lay curled on the ground, wet hair the color of an autumn field splayed across her face.

It was only as he reached her side and knelt next to her that the enormity of her being here struck him. He'd dreamed it. He'd ridden all this way to find her. And yet, somehow, he'd half expected to find the ring of stones empty.

Expected or hoped?

With a shaking hand, he gently swept the hair from her face and ran one finger down her cheek.

By the Gods, she was lovely!

"She lives?" Patrick stood beside him, his eyes scanning the forest.

Aware of his brother's attention, Malcolm willed his hands to steady as he slipped his fingers to the side of her throat.

The beat beneath his touch was strong and regular. "She does."

"Then best we keep her that way by getting her out of here and back to Castle MacGahan. She's trouble enough without our adding more to it."

Acknowledging the wisdom of Patrick's words with only a nod of his head, he bent again over the woman. He thrust his arms under her shoulders and knees and rose to his feet, lifting her, cradling her close to his chest.

Her eyelids twitched and one corner of her softly pink lips lifted as if in amusement.

By the gods!

He would admit that his brother's worry for their safety was all too real. Someone had to be responsible for this woman being here. Someone who could yet lurk under cover of the forest. But Patrick was wrong about the woman herself. The beauty in his arms was anything but trouble. She couldn't be.

He breathed in the scent of her, light and fragrant, like a warm day in spring. Her skin, soft and flawless, brought to mind the petals of a newly unfurled flower.

That was her exactly. A delicate flower.

He turned his head to say as much as Patrick tracked round the circle, when a flash of movement caught his eye. The "delicate flower's" fist smashed into his jaw before he could draw his next breath.

"What the hell?" she demanded, her eyes sparkling with her emotion even as her fists flailed at his head and shoulders. "Get your hands off me. Right now! Put me down!"

While he would not harm her, he harbored no illusions as to her intent. The woman packed the punch of a blacksmith.

"Calm yerself, my lady," he cautioned as he allowed her feet to touch the ground without releasing his hold around her shoulders.

"Calm myself, my ass! Let. Me. Go." She shoved her weight against him, swinging her fist again as she tried to turn.

Prepared this time, her blow was easily deflected.

"As you will it, my lady." He lifted his hands into the air to signal his capitulation to her demands even as he stepped back.

Silence reigned in the circle as they waited, her gaze swinging wildly from him to Patrick and back again, her arms held in front of her as if in preparation for attack. Bright red splotches bloomed on her cheeks just before she blinked her eyes several times in an exaggerated manner, lifting her eyebrows as if it were the only way to force her eyelids to open.

"Whoa," she muttered, bringing one hand to her forehead. "Where am I? Who are . . . ?"

Her words trailed off as her head lolled over and her knees buckled beneath her, her body crumpling down.

"Bollocks!" Malcolm dove forward to catch her before she hit the ground, lifting her once again into his arms.

Behind him, Patrick snorted. "I said it before, did I no? Plain and simple. This one's trouble."

Settling onto his mount, his new charge in his arms, Malcolm shook his head in denial.

Not about the trouble part. Though Patrick always claimed that of any woman in his path, he could very well be right about trouble this time. But there was nothing either plain or simple about this woman. And even if she weren't the trouble his brother claimed, neither was she the delicate flower he'd earlier imagined. In fact, if he were to compare her to any flower at the moment, it would have to be one with thorns.

He rubbed a hand absently over the throb in his jaw.

Sharp, prickly thorns, with a temper to match.

Nine

DANI AWOKE FROM the nightmare, acutely aware of the chill in her room.

Damn.

The mind was certainly a powerful thing. That bizarre dream had felt so real, her hand actually hurt as if she had really slammed her fist into someone's face.

Not that she couldn't figure out why her subconscious would conjure up a scenario like men on horseback taking her captive. After all, she'd spent her evening fending off that octopus-handed, wannabe cowboy, Clay Carter. So much for the horses and captive part.

She pulled the heavy coverlet up and snuggled down in the big bed, thankful her alarm hadn't screamed at her yet. Just a few more minutes to savor bits and pieces of the dream. No matter how foolish it might be, a part of her wished some of that dream had been real.

Or maybe it was only the man she'd dreamed up whom she wished had been real.

It took no effort at all to re-create him in her mind's eye. Ol' Steely Jaw had been something to look at, all right, though if she was going to start regularly making up Scottish warriors to dream about, maybe it was time to give up reading so many of those Highland romances.

Or time to go buy some more.

She smiled to herself, thinking once more of the man. How her imagination had managed to create something as wonderful as him when she'd gone to bed thinking about that poop Clay was beyond her.

Wait.

The night before flickered through her mind like a grainy movie. She hadn't been thinking of Clay when she'd gone to bed. In fact, she couldn't actually remember going to bed. The last thing she remembered was standing in that Faerie Circle she'd built.

Dani tossed the covers off as she pushed up to sit. The light in the room came not from the streetlamps out in the parking lot but from the glow of burning wood in a fireplace across the room from where she huddled.

A fireplace that hadn't been there when she'd gone to sleep.

She held her breath, listening for any sound of the big rigs that came and went all through the night. Nothing. No sound at all but the crackling of the wood fire in a fireplace she didn't have.

This can't be real.

She denied her surroundings even as she crawled to the side of the bed and pushed away what appeared to be heavy curtains to peer down at the distance to the floor. Swinging her legs over the side, she dropped, a move she instantly regretted when her feet hit the cold stones.

Who in their right mind had cold freakin' floors like this, anyway? Even when she was a kid back on the farm they'd had scatter rugs on their old wood floors.

She hugged her arms tight around her middle, realizing as she did that what she was wearing was nothing she'd ever owned. It was a thick, long-sleeved, shapeless shift that just hung from her shoulders, so long it trailed on the floor.

Not that she was going to complain about it right now. It was a good bit warmer than the gauzy summer dress she remembered having on. At least, the last time she remembered anything at all.

This can't be real.

The room was big. Big enough, anyway, that the corners were swathed in dark. The kind of dark that could easily hide any number of unpleasant surprises for someone with an overactive imagination.

A ledge to the side of the fireplace held an unlit candle, which seemed a prudent item to get her hands on at the moment. A little more light would be welcome. Not that her imagination was overacting or anything.

Keeping her eyes fixed on her destination, she willed herself to take that first step. And the next. One foot in front of the other until—

"Shit!"

Her toe smacked into the unyielding stone of a raised hearth, and the second or so it took for the pain to race from her abused digit to her brain gave that imagination of hers more than enough diversion.

She balanced her weight on one leg, her good foot pressing down onto her injured toe as if force alone could stop the pain.

The initial wave passed, leaving only irritation in its wake.

Stupid girl.

If she'd paid more attention to her surroundings rather than letting the panic of them consume her, she could have avoided that little mishap.

Lesson learned.

Shifting her weight back to both feet, she stepped up onto the hearth and stretched to retrieve the candle. Bending down, she held it close to the glowing embers until its wick sizzled and caught fire.

Not even the additional light helped her make sense of her surroundings.

She could see now that there were rugs scattered around, furry things that she'd swear were animal skins. The room itself, or at least what she could clearly see, seemed entirely made of stone. Except for the two doors, which appeared to be wood.

Thick, heavy-looking wood. Like something out of a history lesson.

And absolutely, positively like nothing she'd seen anywhere in Comfort, Wyoming.

"I've got a feeling we're not in Kansas anymore," she whispered on a shaky breath as she stepped off the hearth toward the middle of the room.

Two doors.

If she wanted to find out where she was, her obvious choice seemed to be to go through one of them. But which one?

"And behind door number one," she muttered, deciding as she spoke aloud that she would try the door closest to the fireplace.

It opened easily enough. That had to be a good sign. At least whoever had put her here hadn't locked her in. She hesitated only a moment, gathering her courage, before stepping through into another, equally poorly lit, room.

The fireplace in here had burned down to a low ember, giving off even less light than in the first room, but she lifted her arm to hold the candle aloft and examined her surroundings.

This room was even larger than the one in which she had awoken. To her left, a small table with two chairs stood between her and another doorway, but it wasn't that direction that held her attention.

By far the largest single item in the room was a massive bed, with enormous wooden posters and a top rail from which hung dark folds of heavy-looking draperies.

Ominously, the draperies were drawn shut, obscuring whatever might be in the bed.

Whoever. Not whatever. *Whoever* might be in that bed.

Dani stilled, holding her breath, not even daring to blink, listening for any sound that might be coming from behind those draperies.

It took a bit to separate the pounding of blood in

her ears from the silence in the room, but she concentrated, willing herself to hear, and at last found what she sought.

A shudder ran up her arms and down her spine as her ears picked up the slow, steady *whoosh* of someone breathing.

The internal debate was short but intense, with fear encouraging her to run toward the other door while curiosity pushed her to look behind the draperies.

Aunt Jean's oft-used saying about what curiosity did to the cat rang through her thoughts even as she found herself tiptoeing toward the bed.

Mere inches from the bed, she stopped, one hand already on the curtains, fear and curiosity still locked in a vicious battle. Granted, whoever was behind those curtains should have the answers she needed. But what if they didn't feel particularly like sharing?

Her candle didn't make much of a weapon. Sure, she could set the bed on fire, but that wasn't likely to stop anyone who might be less than happy to see her here. At least, it wouldn't stop them in time to do her much good.

Holding the candle aloft, she examined the room again, this time with a purpose.

Two small bowls and a large vase sat on the table. That would have to do. Turning her back to the bed, she hurried over and set her candle on the table to pick up the vase. One sniff told her this was more decanter than flower holder. Scotch, she'd guess from the smell.

No matter. It was made of some sort of pottery and heavy enough that it should serve just fine as her new weapon.

She reached out to retrieve her candle and her hand froze as an impression of movement caught her eye. There, on the wall directly ahead of her, a misshapen blob flickered and danced. Fascinated, she stared for an instant, before her brain registered the form of shadow, a figure caught between her and the glow of the fireplace.

Arm raised, she stepped backward from the table and directly into a wall of hard flesh.

A wall with arms of steel that banded around her, one hand at her throat and the other covering her mouth before her first squeak had a chance to meet the night.

Panic speared through her chest and she swung the decanter up and over her head, wildly hoping to make contact with something. Faster than she could have imagined possible, the hand left her throat. The decanter flew from her fingers and shattered on the stone floor as her attacker deflected the blow by grabbing her wrist and twisting her arm up behind her.

"Stop it right now," a male voice ordered. "Behave yerself."

"Me, behave?" She sputtered from behind his hand even as he pulled his fingers away from her mouth. "I'm not the one who's attacking some innocent woman."

"Innocent women do not skulk about strange men's bedchambers. Which, by the way, would be better accomplished under cover of darkness, no by announcing yer presence with yer candle held high."

He had let go of her arm as he'd spoken and she whirled to face him, her fear quickly taking a backseat to a building anger.

"I wasn't . . ."

Though he no longer touched her, he hadn't backed away. A rather disconcerting fact she hadn't considered until she faced a wide expanse of naked chest.

"Um . . . skulking." She fumbled for what it was she'd intended to say. Probably best her mouth had gone dry before she could get herself really wound up for a tongue-lashing. A guy built like that could easily do some real damage if that was what he intended. "I wasn't skulking."

Since he didn't seem inclined to move away, she took a single backward step, forcing her eyes up to meet his as she did so. Recognition hit her hard, tightening her chest and sending an unpleasant flutter to her stomach. She stared into the face from her dreams, the face of the man who'd held her in his arms.

"In that case, my lady, I can only assume you had another reason for entering my bedchamber. It's only fair to warn you that had I wanted you in my bed, I would have placed you there myself rather than depositing you in yer own chamber."

"Had you wanted me in . . ." Any lingering shock fled in the face of his egotistical implication and once again she found herself reduced to a sputter. What a total arrogant prick! "Whatever you're thinking I'm doing in here, you better just think again. I was simply trying to find out where the hell I am and how I got here."

"You are at Castle MacGahan. As to how you got here, we found you in the woods and brought you here."

"In the woods. Of course you did." That made absolutely no sense. "There are no woods anywhere around Comfort." There weren't any castles either.

Though there had certainly been woods in the dream.

An unwelcome doubt crept under her bravado, rapidly replacing her anger. That was bad. Very bad. Anger kept the fear at bay. Doubt invited it in like an honored guest.

Putting distance between herself and this man suddenly seemed an excellent idea. She turned her back on him, taking a step toward the table, slowly, hoping she radiated an air of casual confidence. She kept going, one foot after the other, her eyes fixed on the opposite side of the table, wondering at what instant he might reach out to stop her.

"Perhaps you should consider returning to your own chamber now, my lady."

Perhaps not. Perhaps now she'd get the answers she wanted. With a good six feet and a strong table separating them, she turned to face him again, instantly wishing she hadn't.

It wasn't just a naked chest facing her this time. It was the whole of him.

She jerked her head down, fastening her gaze on the tabletop. "You should probably be putting some clothes on."

Whoever he was, he definitely didn't have any modesty issues. Not that he had anything to be modest about. *Damn.*

"What I should be, my lady, is in bed. Asleep. No standing about in the middle of the night, haggling with some mystery woman who has no name."

The uncomfortable heat that had started in her cheeks spread over her entire face and radiated down her neck.

"I have a name. It's Dani." She kept her eyes focused on the table, memorizing the pattern of the grain in the wood. "Danielle Dearmon. Not that you've exactly been all anxious to tell me who you are, either."

She was all too aware of movement across the room but refused to look. If he was headed her direction, she'd know well enough, all too soon.

"Malcolm MacDowylt. Laird and chieftain of Clan MacGahan. At your service, Lady Danielle."

He pronounced her name with a roll of the vowels that made her want to hear it again.

After a moment of internal debate, she risked a peek, relieved beyond measure to find he'd wrapped a length of cloth around himself like some medieval Highlander.

"Now that formal introductions have been made, I'd ask again that you be so kind as to make yer way back to yer own chamber so I can get a least a wee bit of sleep before sunrise."

Wrapped in a plaid, with his arms crossed over his chest in a way that made the tattoo covering his heart appear to pop out at her, he really did remind her of the cover of one of her favorite books. All he needed to complete the picture was a sword.

"Lady Danielle? Are you no listening to me, lass?"

No doubt but that was a Scottish accent she was hearing. Lord, could the night get any stranger?

Accent or not, she reminded herself, he could well be some psycho kidnapper for all she knew, since there was little other explanation for how she got here.

"Please just let me leave. All I want is to go home. I don't care who you are and I swear not to say anything to anyone." Pleading with these people never worked in books or movies, but she still had to try.

"Yer free to go anytime you like, though I canna say how far you'll get in the dark. It's what I want, as well. For you to go back to wherever it is you belong. But at this moment, I'll settle for having you on the other side of that door." He motioned his head toward the door she'd come through earlier. "And come first light, we'll get Elesyria in here and figure out exactly how to get you home. Will that do?"

Apparently, it would have to.

With an emphatic nod of his head, he moved back to his bed and climbed inside, pulling the curtain shut behind him in what Dani could only describe as a rather forceful gesture. No doubt about it, she'd been dismissed.

Free to go, was she? Testing his offer, she hurried

to the big door behind her and pulled it open to stare
into the darkest space she'd ever seen. It could be a
closet or the longest hallway in the world—she simply couldn't tell.

"You'll take yer candle with you, aye? There's no a
good reason to leave it burning and waste good wax."
The muffled words floated from behind the curtains
as if MacDowylt had already snuggled into his covers
for the night. "And shut the door behind you. I've no
fancy for that cold draft whipping through here on
this night."

So he knew the door was open. And he didn't care.

Her options suddenly felt more limited than when
she'd thought herself prisoner. She was free to wander around in a strange place in the pitch dark, but
there was no guarantee that would be any better than
the room next door.

Shivering from the cold, she picked up her candle and made her way back through the door where
she'd first entered, refusing to give that man the satisfaction of a response.

Back inside her own "chamber," as Malcolm had
called it, Dani looked around. There was still the second, untried, door.

As soon as she opened it, she realized it was more
likely hallway than closet. Facing the same direction
as the big door in the next room, it opened into the
same dark, cold space. She held her candle out in
front of her and confirmed her assessment in its wavering light.

Stepping back inside, she shut the door, pulling

the wooden bar down across it as a final measure. A glance to the door separating her room from Malcolm's confirmed there was no bar to secure that entrance, so she settled for dragging one of the heavy wooden chairs up against it.

There. That should serve her purpose.

She pulled one of the covers from her bed and wrapped it around her like a cocoon before dropping down on the hearth next to the fireplace. Though the stones weren't particularly comfortable, it would at least be a warmer place to wait for morning than sitting at the table.

Wait, not sleep. There was no way she could ever close her eyes and relax in this place.

WITH THE CLOSING of the second door, Malcolm sighed, feeling the first modicum of relief he'd known in the past twelve hours.

Danielle. Dani.

Her name was as uniquely lovely as the woman herself.

Not that he cared. He didn't. He had less use for the woman than he would have had for a horse with three legs. She was nothing to him but another burden on his already overloaded back.

He punched his pillow hard, wadding it into a ball under his head even as he jerked at his covers in a vain attempt to find his own rest.

She wanted to go home, did she? Wherever home was. At least that much was a relief. From the way Elesyria had fluttered around her when they'd arrived here hours ago, he'd feared that might not be the case. That damned Elven mother-in-law of his had all but declared the newcomer was here to stay and his responsibility to boot.

He rolled to his back, staring wide-eyed into the inky dark above him, his thoughts captured by the woman called Dani.

Likely she was some pampered elder daughter from a well-to-do family. She certainly didn't have the look of either a Tinkler or a starving peasant. For a fact, she seemed adequately filled out from having enjoyed a bountiful table wherever she'd come from. Filled out in all the right places, at that.

It was also fact that she had not the least bit of good sense about her, else she'd not have wandered into the stone circle so far from anywhere.

Though she had spirit. He'd give her that. He touched a finger to the sore spot on his jaw and smiled. She packed a fine wallop, too. And she was fair enough to look at, with her fine long hair the color of a winter sun and her curves that called out to a man.

It was those curves backlit as they'd been by the glow of the fireplace that had sent him scurrying like a frightened squirrel for his plaid, lest she spot evidence of just how fair his eyes found her.

Trouble, Patrick had named her and in truth his brother had the right of it. All women were trouble of the sort with which he had neither the time nor the patience to be bothered. Lucky for him this one seemed as anxious to be back where she belonged as he was to have her returned there. A very fortunate thing indeed, since he had more than enough trouble of his own. His people faced a long, hungry winter while his sister faced death or worse at the hands of their own brother. Compounding his problems, he had no idea whether or not his only ally would send men to his aid when the time came to go to battle against that brother.

And now he had this snippet of a female thrust into his care, requiring his time to see to her well-being, distracting him from the tasks that required his attention and planning.

Indeed, it was one very happy man he'd be as soon as he handed her over to those who rightfully bore the responsibility for her safety. He didn't need the burden of seeing to any woman's protection. His own history had already proven him to be a failure on that count.

On the morrow, they would straighten out their mystery and by sunset, he would have one less worry on his mind, because this Dani would go home.

Ten

"I DON'T BELIEVE IT'S possible for her to return to her home at this time, regardless of what either of you wants." The petite redhead who'd spoken smiled sweetly before popping a bite into her mouth.

It was partly the promise of food that had enticed Dani out of her room this morning, but now that it sat in front of her, she feared she'd gag if she tried to eat even a single bite.

"What?" At the far end of the table, Malcolm Mac-Dowylt leaned forward, his voice a low, determined rumble, as if he fought to keep his emotions in check. "What do you mean, *no possible*?"

Funny. That was pretty much the same thing Dani wanted to know. That and how she'd gotten here in the first place. Lord knew she'd racked her brain try ing to remember anything that might give her some clue to that one.

She'd awakened on the floor this morning, neck stiff and back aching, to find a beautiful young woman standing over her. There'd been a brief dis cussion about how the woman, Elesyria she'd called herself, had managed to get into the room, since Dani had been sure she'd put the bar in place before going to sleep. Brief, because Elesyria had refused to answer, instead fluttering a hand at what she'd called the irrelevance of Dani's concern.

There'd been an equally futile discussion over the clothing she'd brought Dani to wear, a complicated mixture of baggy underdress and jumper-like overdress, all tied together without benefit of zippers or snaps or anything the least bit sensible.

Sitting here now, her stomach ready to heave, Dani regretted not having had more backbone when she'd first met Elesyria. She should have insisted on getting her answers right then and there before leaving her room.

But no. She'd ignored her better instincts and allowed the lovely Elesyria to lead her downstairs where, she was assured, breakfast and answers would be served up.

"Answer me, woman!" Malcolm demanded, emphasizing his displeasure by pounding his fist to the table.

Dani jumped at the noise, only mildly reassured that she wasn't the only one whose patience wore thin.

Next to her, Elesyria smiled, first at him and then at Dani, before daintily placing a bite into her mouth. "Your cook does such a nice job seasoning this porridge."

Malcolm rose slowly to his feet, his weight braced on his arms as he leaned against the table, glaring at the woman next to Dani.

He was even more impressive in broad daylight, fully clothed, than he had been last night. And that took some doing, because, for a fact, he'd been pretty impressive in the glow of the firelight, less than fully clothed. Much less.

The memory brought an unwelcome heat to Dani's cheeks and she fastened her eyes on the bowl in front of her. A bowl made from bread.

"Cease yer games, Elf, and answer the question."

Dani turned her attention to the man seated at Malcolm's side. He looked so much like Malcolm, she had little doubt that they were related. Elesyria, on the other hand, looked nothing like either of them, and yet they all seemed to know each other well enough, as if they were family. Well enough that that this one had used a nickname for her.

What was it he'd called her? Elf?

"Hold yer tongue, Patrick." Malcolm didn't bother to look at the man next to him, keeping his focus on Elesyria. "Why is it no possible for Danielle to go home?" Malcolm asked the question slowly, emphasizing each of the words, his voice laced with a dangerous edge.

If he'd spoken to her in that manner, she'd be telling him everything she knew right now. If she had the answer, that is.

Beside her, Elesyria made a sound, low in her throat, as much growl as sigh. Her gaze fixed on Patrick, she spoke directly to him, ignoring Malcolm as if he'd never spoken.

"Had my ancestors remained under the dominion

of your ancient gods, I might well be called Elf. As they did not, I would thank you to use the correct appellation for me. I am Faerie, Northman. Not Elf, Faerie. I'd thank you to get it straight."

Faerie?

Dani's already sensitive stomach lurched. Elf hadn't been a nickname at all but an accusation of what she was.

Faerie. It couldn't be true. Couldn't be.

She reached for the mug in front of her, squeezing her fingers tightly around the pottery as if to save herself from drowning.

But if it were true, it would explain so much.

Elesyria dusted her hands together and then wiped her fingertips on the cloth covering the table before turning her attention to Malcolm and his question.

"Dani can't go home because the Goddess sent her here for a purpose." She lifted her mug, catching Dani's gaze over the rim. "A boon granted cannot be rejected."

"A boon . . ."

The whisper escaped from Dani's lips without conscious thought. She'd always believed in her heart that the Faeries had some higher purpose for her. And the last thing she could remember before waking up here was standing in the little circle of stones she'd built, insisting that the Faerie Queen set her on the path to find that higher purpose.

"Oh my God."

After all those of years of believing, of waiting for some sign, any sign at all, she finally had her proof.

She'd been right. Faeries did exist. They were really, truly real.

She hardly noticed she'd risen to her feet. Faeries were real and they had answered her at long last.

"I was right all along. It's all true, isn't it?"

"What purpose?" Malcolm demanded, his voice drowning out her whisper. "By whose request?"

His words dissolved into an angry buzz that filled her ears even as the room around her darkened.

Be careful what you ask for, little girl, because you just might get it.

It was her aunt's voice fluttering through her thoughts just before her knees gave way.

THE COLOR DRAINING from her face was his first clue.

Malcolm sprinted the length of the table, taking Dani's weight from Elesyria's arms. Even as he lifted her against his chest, her eyes were beginning to flutter.

"My fault," she murmured. "Sorry."

"You've naught to apologize for, lass."

It galled him no end that this confused young woman should be claiming responsibility for a situation clearly brought about by the old Faerie who even now stuffed her face at his table.

"How did she get here?" he demanded of Elesyria.

The annoying Faerie had the nerve to look irritated at his question.

"You already know the answer to that, Malcolm. My Goddess brought Dani to your time for your benefit. She even sent you the dreams that allowed you to find her in the stone circle. She's been brought here as a result of your actions and put into your keeping."

There had been the dreams. He couldn't deny that. But how could this be because of him? There was no reason, unless . . .

Punishment, perhaps? Punishment for his having failed to protect Elesyria's daughter. Punishment for Isabella's death.

The woman in his arms pushed her hands against his chest, pulling his thoughts back to the present. Reluctantly, he lowered her to her feet, keeping a hold on her elbows. Just in case. Though her color had returned, she seemed prone to swooning.

"Wait a minute." Dani pulled her elbows from his grip and leaned her body toward Elesyria. "'His time,' you said. What's that mean exactly? What time is this?"

Elesyria paused, her hand halfway to her mouth with another bite. "Twelve . . . ninety-two? Ninety-three? I have trouble keeping up with how you Mortals delineate time."

"Twelve ninety-four," Patrick interjected. "November, twelve ninety-four, to be precise."

Dani paled again and Malcolm grabbed for her elbows, but she shoved his hands away, instead dropping down onto the seat she'd earlier occupied, her hands splayed open on her cheeks.

"Holy shit," she breathed, turning her eyes on the Faerie. "Holy. Freaking. Shit. What were you people thinking? I can't be here. I'm like seven hundred years away from where I belong."

"Be that as it may. This is where you must be to fulfill your purpose, my dear. That was what you wanted, wasn't it?" Elesyria shrugged and popped another bite into her mouth. "*This* is where you belong."

Malcolm flickered his gaze between the two women, feeling as if they shared some enormous secret that they were willfully withholding from him.

It didn't matter. All that did matter was getting this woman back to her own home so he could turn his attention to all the other problems plaguing his life. It was time he took charge. Secret be damned.

"Who are her people? Where are they? She's obviously no from around here."

Dani snorted in a most unladylike fashion. "Give the man a blue ribbon for understatement of the year."

He decided to ignore her nonsense, continuing to address his questions to Elesyria.

"Where is she from?"

"*When*, Malcolm, not *where*. Don't be obtuse. *When* is she from," the Faerie corrected, smiling up at him as if it were all some wonderful jest.

"When," he repeated, having no clue what the woman meant.

"When!" Dani asserted. "Unbelievable. I wait fifteen years for these damned Faeries to pay the slightest bit of attention to me and then when they do, they send me seven hundred years into the past."

"Into the—" Malcolm caught himself repeating her words and clamped his lips tightly together as understanding washed over him. "Yer trying to tell me they've brought you here from the future?"

Dani gave him a look, her lips pursed and her eyebrows raised. "So it would appear."

He sat down hard on the bench next to her, sparing a thought as to whether her tendency to swoon might not have transferred to him.

Eleven

"WHY ARE WE wasting our time doing this when Elesyria's already told us it won't work?"

The question had been circling around in Dani's thoughts from the moment she and Malcolm had first mounted the horses on which they rode. The Faerie had told them that the Goddess had brought her here to serve out her purpose. That she belonged here, so there was no way she could go back home.

And yet, here they were, wrapped in woolens and furs, traipsing hours through the frigid wilderness, headed for a stone circle where Malcolm claimed to have found her.

"I canna claim for a fact that Elesyria speaks the truth. This is something I must try."

"But she's Faerie."

"All the more reason to doubt her," Malcolm muttered, lifting an arm to point toward the woods they were about to enter. "We're very close now. Do you remember any of this? It's just through these trees."

Dani shook her head in answer. She had only a vague memory of awaking in this man's arms and feeling frightened and very, very angry. As if in response, a twinge of pain rippled through her right hand and another memory shimmered into being.

A memory of her drawing back her fist and connecting with his jaw.

Her gaze slid to his face, studying the strong chin covered in a day's growth of beard. The shadow of whiskers was dark against his skin, but the stain of color beneath was unmistakable.

No wonder he was so anxious to be rid of her. He'd ridden all this way out into the middle of nowhere to save her life and what was her response? A little gratitude? A hearty "Thank you for not leaving me out here in the cold to die"? No, not her. She'd tried to clean his clock.

An apology would probably be in order. And she'd give it to him, too. Just as soon as she could figure out how to word it while leaving his male dignity intact. He didn't strike her at all as a beta kind of guy who might not mind admitting a woman had bruised him.

Besides, riding single file through the trees staring at his horse's rear end didn't seem the appropriate time to give it a go even if she'd figured out how to approach him.

"Here."

His announcement preceded her horse pulling around his, revealing the forest opening and the circle of stones.

"I do remember this." It was like entering the scene of a recent dream.

"So do I," he answered, stroking his fingers absently over his jawline.

There was her chance. The perfect moment to apologize. She opened her mouth but closed it again, letting the perfect moment slip away, feeling acutely unsure of herself as he dismounted and walked over to her side.

He lifted his arms to her, offering to help her down.

She considered refusing. The thought, along with a thousand others, flitted through her mind.

There was no real need for his help. It wasn't like she hadn't ridden before. She had. She'd practically grown up in a saddle, albeit one vastly different from the one on which she now sat.

Still, it was a long way to the ground, and she was hampered by the outrageous layers of clothing she wore. Not to mention that the chances were good he'd be insulted if she refused his assistance.

It was for those reasons only that she leaned into his grasp. Sound, logical, compelling reasons all.

Or so she tried to convince herself when his hands slipped under the fur and woolens to fasten around her waist.

Over and over, she repeated the reasons in her mind, like a litany dedicated to sanity.

His grip was warm and strong as he took her weight. Though no more than a second or two passed before her feet touched the ground, it felt as if time had slowed, dragging out those seconds, leaving her disoriented and a little breathless when he stepped away from her.

She'd never imagined getting down off a horse's back could be such a sensual experience.

"We found you lying there in the center of the stones, on that green bit. Like as no, that's where you'll need to do it."

If this whole experience weren't odd enough, the patch of greenery at the very center of all this dry brown would have drawn her attention without any urging from him. If there were any magic to be found in this circle, it certainly looked as though it should be there.

Not that she had any idea what the "it" was he expected of her.

"What exactly is it that you want me to do?" Did he think she had some magic ritual that would send her winging back where she belonged?

He shrugged and picked up the reins to lead his horse to the edge of the circle. "Whatever it was you did to get here. Do it again."

"I didn't *do* anything," she muttered, as much to ease her conscience as to respond to his ridiculous directions.

She turned her back on him, trying hard to swish her skirts in a manner she hoped relayed her irritation as she moved into the circle of greenery.

"You must have done something. Yer here."

A surreptitious glance in his direction found him walking the perimeter of the circle, seemingly studying the ground at his feet. He stepped into the woods and back into the circle before speaking again.

"What's the last thing you remember before you woke up here? Describe it all for me."

The last thing?

Somehow she didn't think he'd consider constructing her own magical stone circle to be the "nothing" she claimed.

"Well, it was Halloween. Samhain," she corrected when he cast a quizzical glance her direction. "Since everything I read indicated that was the easiest time to make contact with the Faerie Realm, I called out to the Faerie Queen."

Something sounding suspiciously like a snort came from his direction.

"Yer first mistake, that. Most of us spend the entirety of our lives hoping to avoid the Magical Folk, no going out of our way to call down their attention, aye?"

Considering what had transpired, Dani was beginning to suspect the sensibility of his views.

It was her turn to shrug her response.

"That's it then. Do that same again. Call on yer queen. Tell her to send you back to where you came from. Tell her there's no a place for you here and none to watch over you so she must return you to yer home."

Dani cleared her throat, stalling, wondering what on earth she could possibly say. Not that it mattered. It wasn't Samhain, so the curtain between the worlds was thick and firmly closed. And, even if the queen did somehow hear her, it still wouldn't matter.

Elesyria had been clear on the subject. The Goddess herself had decided this was where Dani belonged. And, novice though she might be at dealing with Faeries, she was pretty sure a Goddess outranked a queen.

Still, if it made him feel any better about this . . .

"Can you hear me, Your Highness? You win. You sure showed me." A tight, nervous twitter of laughter bubbled up from her throat. "So . . . you can send me home now. Okay?"

As silly as she'd felt standing alone in her little room calling on the Faeries, it was nothing compared to how preposterous she felt right now with Malcolm MacDowylt as her audience.

They waited, silence surrounding them in the circle, as if even the creatures of air and land held their breaths right along with them.

After several minutes, Malcolm broke the uncomfortable silence.

"Do it again. Perhaps she dinna hear you. Make sure to mention her mistake in putting you somewhere you dinna belong."

As if telling the Faerie Queen she'd made a mistake was a smart thing? Maybe Malcolm didn't know Faeries as well as he claimed.

Dani reined in the impulse to share that thought with Malcolm. As miserable as she was out here in the cold, standing around arguing would only delay things more.

"Send me back, please," she called out to the forest. "To where I belong." Not that where she'd come from had been where she belonged.

Again they waited, staring at one another in silence.

"Try something else."

"Like what?" It wasn't as if she had some magical bag of tricks up her sleeve. "I don't know anything else to do. That's what I did before. I spoke to her. Out loud, just like now. And then all these little lights started flying around the room and that's all I remember."

Again they stared at one another across the clearing for fully a minute.

"If that's all you did then, why do you suppose it's no working this time?"

"Oh, let's see." She held up her hand, ticking off reasons on her fingers. "Maybe because it's not Samhain, so she can't hear me? Or because it was supposedly the Goddess who sent me here, not the queen? Or, like Elesyria said, because I'm supposed to be here?" Running out of reasons before she ran out of fingers, she crossed her arms in front of her. "I don't know. You tell me, since you seem to think you know everything. Elesyria said it wouldn't work. But you wouldn't listen."

What else could she say? It wasn't going to work and they both should know it at this point. Only he seemed determined to keep at this exercise in futility, no matter how miserable it was out here, all because he wanted to be rid of her. That much was clear, and though she hated to admit it, even to herself, the knowledge stung. After a lifetime of not feeling like she belonged anywhere and years of waiting for the Faeries to send her where she did belong, not being wanted when she got there just plain hurt.

She pulled the woolen tighter around her, shivering for good measure. Not that she needed to pretend that one. It was so cold she was simply grateful it wasn't snowing.

As if on cue, the first flake fluttered into the clearing, followed by a host of others.

"Perfect," she groaned. "Just freaking perfect."

Malcolm lifted a hand, pressing his fingers against the upper bridge of his nose, like a man with a vicious headache. She'd seen him do the same before and doubted he was even aware of telegraphing his frustration. When he dropped his hand, it was to gather up her horse's reins and start toward the spot where she stood.

"Yer right. An act of pure foolishness on my part, my lady. I apologize for yer discomfort and for wasting yer time. It's best we get you mounted and out of this weather."

As he drew close, she snatched the reins from his hand, fitting her foot into the stirrup to pull herself up onto her horse's back. She lifted her skirts, tossing them over her arm, and pushed up into her seat, ignoring his offer of help.

Decorum be damned. The last thing she needed was his hands on her again. She was cold and hungry and frustrated beyond belief to be trapped in a place where she wasn't wanted. His touch could well be enough to send her over the edge into a rare crying jag, and that was simply not happening.

Not in front of him.

With a tug to adjust her woolen, she kicked her

horse and started off, stopping only when she heard him clearing his throat behind her.

"What?" she demanded, forcing a level of irritation in her response to hide the humiliating threat of tears.

"Yer headed in the wrong direction, my lady."

She jerked her reins again, turning her horse to follow when he mounted and urged his horse forward. But she refused to make eye contact.

Damn it all. A perfect exit ruined by her crappy sense of direction.

Twelve

THE ELF SPOKE the truth.

The thought wound and circled its way through Malcolm's mind, over and over again, slithering like a snake across exposed rock in a field of heather.

He glanced over his shoulder to where Dani rode, her cheeks a mottled red, her eyes much too shiny, as if one wrong word from him would be all it would take to send her into a fit of blubbering. He'd seen just such a look on his younger sister's face when she'd taken all the teasing she could bear from her brothers. He knew all too well what came next. Tears.

The Elf spoke the truth.

No tracks marred the soft ground inside the ancient stone circle save for those he and Patrick had left. Not even a single animal had strayed into the area, let alone another human.

However Dani had gotten there to begin with, her visible frustration made it clear she had no idea how to return to where she'd come from. As clear was the fact that neither she nor anyone else had walked into the center of that circle from the outer ring. It was as if she had been dropped into the circle from the sky above.

Though nothing explained the tracks outside the circle. Tracks as if someone had waited there. Waited and watched.

The Elf spoke the truth.

About everything, it would appear.

He should have known that from the beginning. The old legends taught that the Magical Folk didn't lie. They might not tell a man the whole of the truth, but what they did say was spoken in accuracy. Even if what they disclosed was shared for their own nefarious purposes.

That would likely be a more profitable use of his time, trying to figure out Elesyria's purpose in telling him as much as she had.

"Do we have any water?"

At least he thought that was what Dani had called out, her words garbled as she tugged the plaid up over her mouth for warmth.

He pulled up on his reins, waiting until she drew her mount close to his.

She peered out of the hood of woolen and fur wrapped around her, her face drawn with exhaustion and discomfort.

Little wonder. Immersed in his own concerns, he'd lost all track of how long they'd traveled. Lost all track of his companion. Snow, which had fallen steadily since they had left the circle, clung to her garments like a second cloak.

"You wanted water?" he asked, making sure he'd heard her correctly.

"Really thirsty." Her lips quivered as she spoke, another reason why he'd had difficulty understanding her earlier.

He dug in his pack for the wineskin he carried and offered it to her, mentally amending his earlier assessment of her condition to include cold.

One sip and her face scrunched into a mask of displeasure.

"What is that? Beer? Seriously?" she asked, handing the container back to him.

"Honey ale," he corrected, and took a drink for himself before returning the container to his pack. "Ale is what we have with us to drink."

"No." Finality layered through the word. "Look, I'm tired and I'm hungry and I'm cold. I've sucked it up all day and followed along, agreeing to whatever you decided without unreasonable complaint. But this is where I draw the line. I've spent the whole day on horseback and I want some damn water to drink. Is that too much to ask?"

Guilt prickled uneasily under Malcolm's emotional armor. It was as she said. She hadn't really complained. And he, like some half-addled excuse for a man, hadn't once thought of her comfort or needs. Hadn't once considered how much of the day's light he'd squandered in the stone circle, forcing her to try again and again to send herself home.

As a result, it was approaching nightfall they faced now, along with hunger and cold.

More proof, if he'd needed it, that he was unfit to see to any woman's safety and well-being.

"As you say, my lady. It is indeed not too much to ask. There's shelter no far from here where we will see to yer water. And a meal."

Their current path carried them close to the high pastures where the flocks summered. There he could locate one of the scattered shelters the shepherds used. Huts, really, no more than a thatch-covered roof and four walls. But he could build a fire to warm her, and there were a few provisions Cook had sent along with them to eat. And nearby, a stream where she could get all the water she wanted.

"YOU'RE KIDDING ME. right?"

Dani looked from the stream she squatted beside back up at Malcolm. He stood there, beaming from ear to ear like some idiot who'd just led her to a treasure.

"You said you wanted water and it's water I give you."

"To drink." Surely he didn't really expect her to drink from this stream. They'd just ridden their horses across it, not five feet from this very spot. "I want water to drink. Do you have any idea how many germs are in here?"

His blank expression assured her he did not. Lord, did he even know what a germ was?

"Okay, fine. I need something to put this in so I can boil it."

Without a word he disappeared into the ramshackle structure he'd brought them to, reappearing with a disapproving frown and an iron pot that had obviously seen better days.

"You dinna say you wanted yer water hot."

He leaned down and scooped the pot full before turning his back on her to head into the hut.

Dani scrambled to her feet to follow him inside through the small opening.

Four walls, no windows and a hard-packed dirt floor greeted her. The only two features in the building, if she could even call it that, were the opening that served as a doorway and a small protrusion in the far wall that was meant to be a fireplace.

Malcolm worked over whatever materials were stacked there and within minutes a tiny flame flickered to life, quickly growing into a crackling fire.

Now that was better. Much better.

She huddled close to the fire, holding her hands extended toward it, surprised to realize how badly her fingers ached with the cold.

Next to her, the iron pot hung over the fire, flames licking up around the bottom of the metal.

"Give me yer wraps."

Dani did as asked, too tired to argue over the obvious cold in the room. Instead she scooted closer to the fire, turning her back to it to watch as Malcolm shook the woolen and furs just outside the doorway, sending droplets of water flying.

When he stepped back inside, he stretched something over the doorway, looping one corner over a hook in the wall.

"Tanned hide," he said when he caught her watching. "It will keep the better part of the weather out."

Offering to help as he bustled around the little room might have been the proper thing to do but she simply sat, watching while Malcolm unpacked the contents of the bag he'd carried on his horse.

As her hands and feet warmed, they swelled and tingled and every movement shot burning needles through the skin. Even the ring she wore felt as if it was cutting off her circulation. Clumsily, she twisted the band, working it round and round to get it off her swollen finger in an attempt to remove it before it was too late. When at last it gave way, it flew from her grip and she pushed herself to her knees, feeling around the dirt floor, hunting for her treasure.

"What are you doing?" Malcolm paused in his chores to stare at her.

"I dropped my ring. It has to be here somewhere." A flicker of panic formed in her stomach at the thought of losing the only physical reminder she had of her old life.

Malcolm dropped to his knees beside her, helping her search, and a moment later, he was successful.

"Here it is." He held the ring up toward the fire to examine it before handing it over to her. "I've no ever seen the like of this delicate jewelwork. It must be very valuable."

"Only to me," she said, accepting the ring and placing it on her little finger for safekeeping until the swelling in her hands subsided. "Thank you for helping me find it. It was a birthday gift from the aunt who raised me. It's not worth much money, but it means more to me than anything in the world."

Aunt Jean had been the only mother Dani could really remember, and the ring was her only tie to her memories of her aunt.

Silence reigned in the little hut as Malcolm spread a small cloth between them and laid out bread, cheese, and bits of hard, dried meat.

By the time he offered her a carved wooden ladle filled with water, she felt too guilty to even question how dirty the implement might have been. He had dipped it in the boiling water, after all, so maybe that had killed the majority of whatever nasties might have lived on it.

She blew across the surface of the liquid, concentrating on the little ripples that formed before she tested her first sip. Warmth filled her mouth and trickled down her throat, and for the first time in hours, she began to feel almost normal.

Malcolm sat cross-legged across from her, eating quietly, his gaze fixed on her face.

"What?"

He shrugged, a smile tugging at one corner of his mouth. "Thinking about the fine work on the jewel you wear, my mind runs to fancy, I must confess, contemplating the differences in yer world and the wealth of knowledge you likely possess, coming from the future as you have."

"So you believe it, now?" She wasn't at all sure he had before.

"The Elf said—"

"Faerie," she corrected. "Elesyria said that she's a Faerie, not an Elf. She seemed pretty emphatic about it, too." And more than a little bit irritated as well, but Dani didn't add that.

"Faerie," he conceded. "She said it was so and I've no longer any reason to doubt her word."

Apparently their day's adventure had precipitated quite a shift in his thinking. Only this morning he'd insisted she join him on this godforsaken quest precisely because he *didn't* believe Elesyria. Though why he'd need to verify the word of someone who lived in his home made almost as little sense as his quick switch in attitude.

And the fact that neither Malcolm nor his brother seemed very enamored with magical beings, period, regardless of what name they called them, made Dani even more curious.

"From the sound of it, you don't seem to think too highly of Faeries. So how is it you have a Faerie living with you, anyway?"

"No by my choice, I can tell you that." Malcolm's brows knit together in a frown, a fleeting expression that he quickly wiped away. "Elesyria is mother to the woman I married. I have no right to turn her away, no matter what I may think about what she is."

A small lump formed somewhere in Dani's chest, a hard blockage around which she suddenly found herself struggling to breathe normally.

The woman I married.

A wife? Malcolm had a wife? No one had ever said anything about a wife.

"I didn't realize you were married." There were likely many, many things she didn't know about this man, so why that one tiny piece of information should bother her so much made absolutely no sense at all.

But bother her it did.

"My . . ." He paused, like a man unwilling—or unable—to speak the next word. "Isabella is dead."

His statement sounded bitter, final, as if he wished to end the discussion.

It absolutely was not relief she felt at his declaration. It was more along the lines of some detached sense of sympathy, skewed by her physical discomfort. That had to be it. No other emotional response was even close to reasonable.

Dani inhaled, slowly, deeply, attempting to clear her confused emotions, nodding in what she intended to be a show of real sympathy.

He didn't sound as if he wanted to discuss it anymore. And she meant to drop the subject right there. Aunt Jean had always told her you didn't go picking at the scabs of someone's emotional wounds. Truly, she didn't want to make him deal with a painful past.

Only, try to let it go as she might, his story just didn't quite jell, and curiosity drove her to continue.

"Your wife must have been young. Really young." Like maybe twelve or thirteen, if even that. Because Elesyria didn't look to be much older than Dani, and if she'd had a child when she was barely a teen, that still wouldn't make her child more than, well, twelve or thirteen at the oldest.

And even if this was the Middle Ages, the idea that a man clearly in his twenties would marry someone that young added a whole new "ick" factor to their conversation.

His head cocked to one side and his brow furrowed as if she'd just commented on painting his face purple. "No, I dinna believe that to be the case. In fact, I'd reason Isabella to have been older than you. What would make you think otherwise?"

"Because you said Elesyria was her mother. And Elesyria can't be much older than me right now." If even.

That brought the smile back. Along with a laugh. "Are you daft, lass? That *Faerie*," he emphasized the word with a raised eyebrow, "is well advanced beyond yer years. You've only to look at her to ken that. Her hair is grayed, her face is wrinkled. Though she may not yet be a crone, her days as a maiden are long gone.

Was he blind? Or was there some mental defect there she'd just totally missed?

"Are we even talking about the same woman? Elesyria's young. And beautiful. There's not a gray hair anywhere on her."

Malcolm nodded thoughtfully, his fingers absently stroking his chin. "That's what you see when you look at her, is it? All the more proof that is of her Faerie blood, as if I still needed proof. Which I do not. It would appear she wears a spell for our benefit. But is it a spell that canna fool you, or one that canna fool us? Interesting, that is. I wonder why it's so?"

A spell? "So . . . you mean to tell me that you actually see her as old?" And if he did, why didn't she?

He shrugged and pushed up to stand. "It's the way of the Elves." Catching himself, he held up a hand to forestall her correction. "Yer pardon, my lady. Faeries. All the legends speak of it. The Magical Folk can appear to mortals in any way they choose."

Which still didn't answer why she didn't see Elesyria the same way he did. That question, along with any others she might have, was left on hold when he stepped outside, dropping the skin down to cover the opening behind him. Moments later, when he returned leading their horses through the opening, any questions Dani might have thought up completely fled her mind.

"What are you doing?"

She'd earlier considered the interior of the hut close quarters for perhaps five or six men. The thought of how many horses might fit inside would never have been on her list of size comparisons.

Middle Ages, she reminded herself, scooting to the far side of the fireplace.

"These lads have fed and watered—directly from the stream," he turned to look at her, one eyebrow raised. "And without the need for boiling. They'd fare little better overnight in the cold snow than yerself, my lady. And, to our advantage, having them inside with us will only add to the heat of the room."

Could be. She was pretty sure their being inside was going to add to the fragrance of the room, too. And not in a pleasant way.

"Okay, then. In that case, I guess I won't have to share my freshly boiled, pretty much germ-free water with them. Wait." His whole comment penetrated at last. "Overnight? We're staying here?"

"That we are, my lady. With the time we spent at the circle and our stop here, we've lost the light. There's no even a sliver of moon showing out there and I've no taste for forcing you on in both snow and dark."

So it was because of her they stopped for the night.

Dani briefly considered pointing out that she could continue on if he could. Very briefly. The short time he'd had that flap open had confirmed that it was much warmer in here than it was out there. Besides, the rest would do them both more good than harm.

He settled the horses where they'd entered, directly between them and the door.

Glancing first to the fireplace and then to the lack of an easy exit, Dani felt it was no more than her duty to point out the obvious hazard.

"You know, if we have a fire or an emergency or something, getting out of here in a hurry is going to be really difficult with the doorway blocked."

"Aye, you've a point there, lass." He tossed his pile of woolens and furs to ground at his feet, an equal distance between the horses and her, and then dropped down to sit on them. "On the other hand, if it's difficult for us to get out, it's equally difficult for anyone else to get in, aye?"

He was right. Apparently she needed to start thinking more medieval.

He leaned across to the fire, pulling and pushing bits about until the flames burned low, and then, with a muttered "Sleep well," he rolled into his plaid and grew silent.

Dani fussed with her own pile of woolens and furs, finally getting as comfortable as possible, her back to Malcolm and the horses.

He lay two and half, maybe three feet from her, at most. If she rolled to her side and stretched out her arm, she could touch him.

Not that she would.

Still, the knowledge was unsettling. Almost as unsettling as the vision that danced through her mind of him on her first night in this world: his dark hair falling loose at his shoulders, his skin gleaming bronze in the firelight, that mark over his heart that had captured her attention, highlighting what she'd admit was one very impressive chest.

She'd been mere inches away from him then. Close enough she could have traced that mark with a fingertip. Traced it over skin she had no doubt would be warm and solid and—

Stop it! Right now, before she started to breathe heavier than the damn horses.

She tried to fill her mind with the stone circle and, when that failed, with the faces of all the people she'd met at MacGahan Castle.

Each try failed, fading back into that flickering room and the expanse of decorated muscle that even now lay within easy reach.

"What's that mark on your chest mean? That

round tattoo thing?" She blurted out the question, desperate to distract her thoughts from the path they were on.

"A family mark," he said after a moment, his voice deep and rumbly. "Protection for the House of Odin. Now go to sleep. We'll need to be up and on our way at first light."

She rolled to her back, considering what he'd said. *Odin.* These guys were descended from Vikings? She'd read somewhere about Vikings invading Scotland, hadn't she? Which would also explain Elesyria calling Patrick a Northman.

Her mind raced as she tried to concentrate on the mark, but each attempt simply filled her mind's eye with flexing pectoral muscles.

She rolled to her side and found him staring at her.

"Go to sleep," he said again, more like an order to an unruly three-year-old this time.

With a tug on her blanket and an audible huff, she rolled to her other side, her back facing Malcolm.

Sleep? Not likely. Not now. Not unless counting ripples on his chest would work as well as counting sheep, because chest ripples were all she was able to envision when she closed her eyes.

It was shaping up to be one very long night.

Thirteen

WITH THE SUN little more than a promise in the sky, Dani stood in the doorway, surveying her surroundings. Sometime in the night, the snow had stopped, leaving only a light covering on the ground. It was still cold, but hopefully that would improve as the sun actually made its appearance.

A few feet away, Malcolm stood next to her horse, as if waiting to help her mount.

Right, then. New day in her new world. According to Elesyria, this was her reality now, so she might as well make the best of it with a fresh start. After so many years of feeling as if she merely existed on the sidelines of other people's lives, waiting for whatever it was the Fae had planned for her, she was more than ready to jump into this life with both feet.

She simply wanted to make sure that when she landed, those feet were firmly planted, and the best way she could see for that was to start off with a clean slate. No regrets, no secrets.

Especially since the man in whose home she'd ended up didn't seem to want her here very much. If this was where she belonged, she needed to make sure nothing interfered with her being here until she could determine exactly why it was she belonged here.

Besides, there was another, more personal, reason for making sure she started off right with Malcolm. Maybe his wanting to get rid of her was why she was so obsessed with him. She always had found the unattainable more interesting than the freely offered. If she could only set everything straight between them, then he might not be so intent on getting rid of her.

Maybe then she could stop dreaming about his body.

Face already heating, she hurried over to where Malcolm waited. As he grasped her waist, she placed a hand on his chest, thinking to stop him.

Now was the time to talk it out.

"I have a couple of things I need to get off my chest."

Malcolm, however, appeared in no mood to stand and talk. He responded with a frown and lifted her to her saddle as if she were no more than a sack of feathers.

"You'd best be keeping everything on yer chest, my lady. Though the sun promises to shine on us this day, it will no be so very warm for a good many hours."

"No." She shook her head, waiting for him to mount his horse next to her. "I meant that there are things I need to say to you. To clear the air between us."

She sighed at his confused look. "Fresh new start"

would need to include her thinking about what she said before she said it.

"There are those at the castle who will fash themselves over our not having returned last night. We need to be on our way. But certainly you are free to speak as we ride, my lady." Another little frown. "Into the clear air, if it pleases you."

She deserved that one.

With a click of his tongue, he pulled his horse ahead of hers, leading the way. That was okay. She could talk loud if she needed to.

"First thing, let's start with this whole 'my lady' business. I have a name, not a title. It's Dani. I'd appreciate your using it. We're not real big on royalty where I come from."

"We have a few issues of our own with royalty."

Of course they did. She'd seen the Braveheart movie. "So you understand, then. You call me Dani, I'll call you Malcolm. Deal?"

He slowed his horse, waiting for her to pull up beside him. "As laird of the MacGahan, I'm usually addressed as—"

"Look, I'm a cook and a waitress, but I don't want people using my job title to talk to me. You might be the laird, but you're also Malcolm. It *is* your name, right?"

They sat in silence for a short time as he appeared to contemplate her argument.

"I concede yer point, my . . . Dani."

He tugged at his reins, starting his horse forward, and she followed his lead, staying close to him. She wasn't finished yet. In fact, she was working her way through a mental list. She might have missed the perfect opportunity for the next item, but oh well. His ego would just have to deal with her apology.

"Good. Second thing is, I feel bad about that bruise on your jaw. I'm sure it was just a lucky punch and had everything not been so . . . weird, I never would have been able to hit you that hard."

His fingers stole up to his jaw and when he turned to look at her this time, his face broke into a grin that took her breath away.

"You've a good arm, Dani. A fine, strong hit that would have surprised any man."

Maybe he wasn't so arrogantly alpha as she'd thought. She was on a roll. Two down and one to go. Saving the hardest for last.

"Okay, so, I know you're not happy about having me here, and I'm sorry that I've caused a problem for you."

She paused for a breath and he slipped into that space.

"I told you before, you've no blame on that count. You canna control what actions the Magical Folk take. They've their own way of thinking and their own intent. Yer but a pawn in whatever game Elesyria thinks to play. You've no call to apologize to me for being here."

It would be so easy to leave it at that. So easy to let him believe as he did rather than to confess what she suspected to be the truth. But easy now would lead to complicated later on, and she would not be responsible for starting her new life off on the wrong foot.

"No, I am sort of to blame. Not sort of. I am. Remember Elesyria saying something about not being able to reject a boon and you asked who had requested something?" She waited for a response, picking back up when he said nothing. "That would be me. You see, I've always believed in the Fae. Always believed they had some higher purpose for me. I've been waiting forever for some sign of what that purpose is. So when I called on the Queen at Samhain, I asked her to send me to do whatever it was the Faeries wanted of me."

Again she waited, holding her breath that he wouldn't just ride off and leave her here.

"Fifteen years, aye?"

"What?" She kicked her mount, forcing it to reach Malcolm's side.

"It's how long you told Elesyria you'd been waiting for them. Fifteen years."

"That's right. Since the summer of my eighth birthday, when I read my first book about them."

His eyebrows drew together, but he kept riding, staring straight ahead.

"You've no call to take this responsibility on yerself, lass. Waiting fifteen years should tell you that. It's of no matter that you asked the Fae to set you on yer path. They'd have ignored you for another fifteen years lest they had good reason of their own to send you now." He turned toward her at last, his gaze an intense blue framed by his dark hair and whiskers. "Of that you can be sure. I give you my oath on it."

It could be truth. After fifteen years of hearing absolutely nothing from the Fae, it certainly wouldn't surprise her.

"And what do you think their reason is?"

He shook his head, turning away to stare into the distance before he answered. "I suspect it's Elesyria's way of punishing me for what happened to her daughter. You've no part in it, other than getting snared in their spiderweb of schemes."

His accusation felt like a punch to the stomach. Here she was spending her nights battling some physical obsession with this man, and he viewed her as nothing more than punishment from the Fae. Having him angry with her couldn't have been any worse.

He sighed, rubbing his thumb and forefinger over his eyebrows. "If yer to stay, I suppose we'll need to find something to do with you. Have you any skills?"

"Skills," she squeaked, clenching her teeth together to keep in what she actually thought. Skills. Like sleeping on dirt floors? Or riding around in the wilderness? Or putting up with arrogant, thoughtless men?

"Aye. Any abilities or talents we could use?" He spoke calmly, as if he had no clue as to her real feelings.

Which, obviously, he didn't.

"I'm a pretty good cook. I could do that. I'm also a waitress. I could do what your serving girls do."

"Castle MacGahan has a cook and yer a wee bit long in the tooth to be a serving lass."

"Long in the tooth"? She'd seen that phrase before, in the historical books she loved to read. He was calling her old! Again she clenched her teeth together. She was actually sorry she'd bothered to apologize for slugging him. In fact, if given the chance right now, she'd kind of like to punch him again.

"Dinna fash yerself over it. We'll find some use for you."

No "probably" to it. Definitely. Her fist actually ached just thinking about it.

Their conversation ended, they rode for some time in silence while Dani fumed.

"It's true, then, you come from seven hundred years in the future?"

After such a long silence, the question seemed to wing in out of left field. "Yes." Freaking-scary true.

"In that case, perhaps we could take advantage of yer knowledge to aid my people. You can tell me if we need to prepare for the English to invade again, or if Edward will be satisfied with having his man sit on our throne."

It took a minute for Dani to realize what he was asking. He wanted the history of his country. At least, what to her would be history. To him it would be fore-knowledge.

And that, somehow, didn't feel right. Her aunt Jean had always cautioned about people who knew just enough to get them in trouble. This seemed like a perfect moment for that adage. The idea that she might be responsible for somehow changing what was to come rattled her.

Fortunately, at least to her way of thinking, she didn't know all that much.

"Who's your king right now?"

"John Balliol sits on the throne of Scotland."

Not ringing any bells. Good. She could be honest in her response.

"I'm guessing you're in for more changes." Everything she'd ever read certainly pointed to it. "But, in fairness, pretty much all I know about the history of Scotland I learned off the trivia notes printed on the napkins in the diner where I worked." She'd actually learned a lot of useless information off those napkins.

"What are these napkins of which you speak?" He'd reined in his horse, once again waiting for her to catch up, a spark of curiosity in his expression.

"They're paper things that people use to wipe their hands and mouths on when they eat."

"Paper . . ." He repeated the word, his brows drawn together in confusion. "And this paper is . . . ?"

"Paper." Dani struggled to find a good explanation. "Like what you write on, or like they print books on. You know, paper."

"Parchment, you mean?"

"Like parchment, I guess," she agreed. Unbelievable. She was so far out of time, they didn't even have paper, for crying out loud.

"This I find hard to believe. Parchment is too costly for wiping one's face and hands." He shook his head from side to side, in obvious rejection of her information as he set off again ahead of her. "How careless the people of your time must be to waste in such a manner."

She couldn't help but smile at Malcolm's back. If he thought using napkins to clean your hands and face was wasteful, she couldn't help but wonder what he would think of toilet paper.

Fourteen

THE SUN, BLESSEDLY warm on this day, hung high in the sky by the time Malcolm reined in his horse to wait for Dani to reach his side. One look at his face told her something was wrong.

"What is it?"

"Riders approach." He pointed ahead of them. "You'll stay behind me, aye? And if there's trouble, you'll break for the trees and follow a straight line toward the setting sun, riding as hard as you can. You're no to turn back or slow for anything."

She stared into the distance, squinting to make out the tiny figures.

"You expect trouble? There's only two of them. Maybe I could help."

She wasn't completely worthless if it came down to it. All she'd need was a weapon of some sort—a branch, a rock. Surely there was something on the ground she could find.

"You'll stay behind me, Danielle. Out of harm's way. The course I've set will lead you straight to the gates of Castle MacGahan if need be. I'll no brook yer arguments on this point."

Ride away and let the bad guys chase her down? Not freaking likely. Dani shook her head but said nothing; Malcolm's attention was already focused on the little figures in the distance. No, she'd feel safer staying right here with him and taking her chances.

Malcolm pushed back the fur he wore, allowing it to pool on the saddle behind him, revealing a sword and scabbard strapped to his back. His hand briefly caressed the hilt, a move Dani would bet was more instinct than conscious movement. He looked back at her and held out a knife he'd pulled from the belt he wore at his waist.

"Take this."

Dani accepted his offer, grateful to have something to concentrate on other than the approaching men. The knife was small, but it looked wickedly sharp. Sharp enough to do some real damage.

She only hoped she didn't have to test that theory.

As Malcolm had instructed, Dani dropped back behind him, but tried to keep no more than a horse-length between them. Everything she'd ever known about fighting said you didn't get separated from your partner. You closed ranks. Kept your backs together. Of course, all she knew came from books and movies. Scripted and well choreographed.

This, on the other hand, was real.

Tension knotted in her stomach as they continued forward, each step on their path carrying them directly toward confrontation with the mounted figures.

Only when the riders drew close enough to see their faces did Malcolm seem to relax his guard. Patrick led out in front, followed by a younger man Dani hadn't seen before.

"Thank Freya!" Patrick pulled his animal to a stop in front of them. "What happened to you? Even the Elf was worried when you dinna return."

"Faerie," Dani muttered under her breath, completely ignored by both men.

"We delayed too long at the circle and lost our light. Spent the night in one of the high country shepherds' huts. Any word of Eric?"

Patrick opened his mouth to answer but stilled as the younger man arrived.

"Where have you been, Colm? The whole castle was in a tizzy last night. And who's this?" The new arrival jerked his head toward her, his face riddled with curiosity.

"This is our guest, Lady Danielle. She'll be staying with us for a time, under my protection. Lady Danielle?" He turned his head toward her, his expression unreadable. "This is my brother Dermid."

Another brother. This one she never would have guessed belonged to the same family. While Patrick and Malcolm were obviously related, this young man looked nothing like either of them. Somewhere in his late teens, he was the exact opposite of his brothers. A soft, fair-haired cherub bookended by two hard, dark-haired devils.

Genetics in action.

Their parents must have been an interesting match, a pairing of light and dark, much as she and Malcolm would be.

Not that *that* was ever going to happen.

Suddenly uncomfortable, she straightened in her saddle to find three sets of eyes turned on her.

With all three staring her direction, she discovered the one feature that betrayed the blood connection between them—their eyes. Each a blue so oddly deep in hue that if she were in her own time, she'd have sworn they all wore the same colored contact lenses.

"Is that where you've been, then? Off to collect her?" Dermid's head swiveled between Malcolm and Patrick. "Why dinna you tell me that was the case, Paddy? You ken I was worried, did you no?"

Patrick shrugged, his face returning to its usual emotionless mask. "It's Colm's place to tell you what he will of his own personal business, no mine."

"Personal, is it?" Dermid looked past Patrick, fixing his gaze on her again. "Am I to be the last to learn yer bringing home the woman who's to be our new sister?"

Sister? Surely he didn't think that she and Malcolm . . .

"Hold on there a minute."

"Mind yer manners, lad!" Malcolm snapped, cutting off anything else she might have said. "The good lady is to be a guest in my home. I expect you to treat her as such, no to badger her with yer blether. Is that clear?"

"But . . ." Dermid's face hardened into a stubborn frown, as if he intended to pursue the discussion in spite of Malcolm's rebuke.

"Best you ride on ahead, lad," Patrick intervened, likely preventing an argument. "Carry word to those who wait at the castle that we've found our laird."

"But I've no had a chance to speak with Colm for any length since I arrived." Dermid's expression quickly flickered from stubborn frown to innocent distress. "And I've certainly no had a chance to acquaint myself with her."

Patrick held firm. "You claimed you want to be one of the men defending Castle MacGahan, did you no? A soldier in our ranks? If yer to find yer place here, Dermid, you'd best be about following orders when they're given. Without question."

Distress morphed to anger, and with a snap of his reins to his horse's rump, Dermid galloped back in the direction from which he and Patrick had traveled.

"You ken I've no desire to risk our brother's life to the ways of soldier, aye?" Malcolm set his horse in motion, holding it to a walk even as spoke over his shoulder. "And I'll certainly no have him take his first battle against Torquil's men. He's too young."

Patrick drew his mount up beside his brother's. "Need I remind you, we've call for every man who can wield a weapon? And our brother is years beyond what either of us was when we left for our first battles."

Dani dropped back behind the two of them, not wanting to eavesdrop on their conversation. It wasn't her fault they spoke so loudly she could hear everything.

Almost everything.

She moved a little closer.

"I want him kept out of this, Paddy. All of it. I task you with that responsibility."

"You ken it'll no be easy. Dermid's curiosity is no small thing. Already he questions the activity at the keep. His groomsman acts like a deerhound on scent."

"Bollocks," Malcolm swore, lifting a hand to the bridge of his nose. "Then we need a way to put both him and Dermid off the scent."

"A distraction." Patrick nodded to himself as if considering the idea.

None of her business. This was most certainly a conversation she should stay out of. And yet, they were both missing the obvious.

"What about me?"

Malcolm glanced over his shoulder, irritation evident. "We'll find a spot for you, lass. I've told you that already. You've no need to fash yerself over it. We've time to figure out what useful skill you have."

Oh, good lord. Arrogant one-track alpha brain on display. If it weren't for the both of them trying to keep their younger brother safe, she wouldn't even bother.

But they were and, grudgingly, she admired that.

"I don't mean what to do with me, Malcolm. I mean what about using me as the distraction you need? Your brother already thinks there's something going on between us. What if you were to let him continue to think that, without ever actually confirming it? You wouldn't be lying to him, but it would give him a mystery to search out to keep him busy.

Perhaps he'd even suspect the activity at the castle was because I've arrived."

"She's a good point," Patrick conceded. "Give him a trail to follow. A trail we don't mind having him pursue."

"Since there's naught there to hurt him. Aye." Malcolm nodded, a corner of his mouth lifting in what threatened to be a grin before it faded away. "It could work. Do you think Elesyria would go along with us in it? There's no a need to burden him with the knowledge that the Magical Folk have had a hand in any of this."

"You leave the Elf to me." Patrick's face broke into a full-fledged grin. "I can deal with her."

"It's settled then." Malcolm slapped his brother on the back and urged his mount into a trot.

Dani didn't bother to correct Patrick's misuse of Elf versus Faerie this time. She was too busy wondering what she'd just gotten herself into.

So that was what she'd "do" in this time. She'd be a fiancée. Sort of. A mystery fiancée.

Apparently, she'd discovered a useful skill all by herself.

ℱifteen

"ᴇʀɪᴄ ʜᴀs ʀᴇᴛᴜʀɴᴇᴅ."

Three simple words that sent a chill to the depths of Malcolm's soul.

Patrick's expression gave no hint as to whether his captain of the guards carried good tidings or ill.

"He awaits you in the stables. I've informed him of the need for discretion in this matter." A simple cough and Patrick almost imperceptibly tilted his head toward the entrance doors of the great hall.

Malcolm traced the direction his brother indicated, spotting the object of Patrick's interest immediately. Their younger brother stood just inside the room, back to the wall, his groomsman a shadow at his side. Dermid's gaze scanned the great hall, reminding Malcolm of a hawk in search of prey.

It was Dermid's presence here that forced his need for caution. If it were to come to war with his elder brother, Torquil, he would not have Dermid involved. He would not put his younger brother's safety in jeopardy.

"Best you go before he makes his way to yer table and yer forced to come up with some excuse for leaving."

"Aye. It's as you . . ."

Whatever he'd intended to say, the very thought itself diffused into the air around him. His feet refused to move, the wisdom of his brother's words lost in the vision stepping through the door and into the great hall.

Danielle. *Vision* was hardly a strong enough word. Her hair cascaded around her shoulders like a golden waterfall of curls, framing her face. She lifted her chin, and he could almost swear he felt her determination as her gaze swept the room, stopping when her eyes met his.

For an instant it was as if his heart beat against his chest in a wild attempt to escape his body before the connection was broken and they both looked away.

One deep, shaky breath brought the self-control he had briefly lost and, with it, the ability to rationalize his response to his guest.

More likely the discomfort he felt could be directly attributed to the Faerie at Dani's side. He wouldn't put it past Elesyria to try casting some sort of Faerie Magic over him. But he wouldn't so easily fall prey to any such attack from her.

"Colm?"

Patrick's hand on his shoulder brought him fully back.

"I go now to see to Eric and hear what word the MacKilyn has sent. You make sure Dermid disna follow me, aye? And keep watch over what passes between our brother and my . . . intended."

He shared a grin with Patrick over their subterfuge and made his way quickly from the hall.

It took longer going the back way, but there was no help to be had for it. The direct path would have led him past Dermid and into the questions he wished to avoid.

A few twists and turns through the dark hallways into the kitchens and then he was out, into the night. Once there, with no need to keep up appearances, his measured steps broke into a run, carrying him swiftly to the stables.

One of the guardsmen who'd accompanied Eric sat on the ground at the doorway, head down, looking as if he napped to any but a trained eye.

Malcolm knew better. Eric had set a guard to make sure there were no interruptions when he delivered his report. He would have expected no less from his trusted friend.

Stepping through the door, Malcolm wasted no time getting to the heart of his business.

"You bring word from the MacKilyn?"

"Aye, Malcolm. The MacKilyn stands ready to send men to aid in our cause at yer request."

Hearing the words was a gift, loosening the grip of anxiety that had fettered him for so long. It was as he'd hoped. MacKilyn would send the men he needed to enable him to confront Torquil and demand his sister's release.

"You've done well, Eric."

"Thank you, my laird. The MacKilyn did ask that I convey to you his intent to seek a boon from you as repayment for his allegiance."

Malcolm nodded his understanding. He expected no less.

"Go now. Make sure yer men are tended to. And yerself as well. You've earned a good night's rest in a soft bed."

"A soft bed and a full tankard, aye? What more could a warrior ask for?" Eric passed him with a grin, headed toward the castle and likely to find the tankard he'd mentioned.

Malcolm waited, not wanting to set tongues wagging by entering with Eric. When he did step out into the night a few minutes later, the beginnings of his campaign to free Christiana were already taking shape in his mind.

How had he disappeared so quickly?

Dani swiveled her head, scanning the room, certain she must be missing him somewhere.

But no. Malcolm was gone.

She followed Elesyria to the head table, refusing to accept the disappointment welling at the back of her throat. So what if he'd chosen to leave after seeing her arrive? It didn't matter. After all, she was only an actress, allowing his younger brother to believe that she might be important to Malcolm. It was her only useful job here. Pretending to be something she wasn't.

Considering she'd spent her whole life doing that, it should be an easy enough task.

"This way, my lady."

Patrick held out a chair for her and she sat, grateful that Elesyria was seated next to her. More grateful that their places hadn't been switched when she realized Dermid sat on the other side of Elesyria.

Not that the young man bothered her so much. It was the older man who shadowed his every move that made her uncomfortable, standing there behind Dermid's chair, as he did now. Watching everything, his eyes darting around the room as if he were soaking up everything with a single look.

"Creeps me out," she muttered under her breath, earning an imperious look from her dining companion.

Unlike her, the Faerie had no problem addressing the issue to Dermid.

"How am I to eat with your man hanging over me like some bird of prey? Must he do that?"

"Rauf is my groomsman. It is his responsibility to guard my person. What else would you expect of him, good woman?"

Though Dermid seemed a tad offended by the complaint, Rauf's expression remained unchanged, as if he neither heard nor cared what transpired in the conversation at the table.

"I expect him to guard you from his own seat, young man. Are you incapable of defending yourself against an unarmed woman?"

Dani swallowed hard, hoping to avoid spitting the drink she'd just sipped back into her cup. Unarmed woman, indeed. Unarmed Faerie, more like it. And who knew if even the "unarmed" part was true.

Though, to her surprise, it seemed to work on Dermid.

"You may leave me, Rauf. Take yer spot at the table there." He pointed to one of the tables in front of them. "You can reach me soon enough if I have need of you."

"As you will it, good sir." Rauf dipped his head respectfully and made his way around the long table and off the dais, taking a seat at the table in front of them.

Dani wasn't sure the change was much of an improvement. Standing over the top of them or staring directly at them from a distance, the man still creeped her out.

"Well, I've done all I can," Elesyria whispered as she lifted her cup in acknowledgment to the man. "You'll simply have to deal, my dear."

Dani set her own cup back on the table, unsure whether the guard's stare or the Faerie's apparent ability to read her mind unnerved her more.

"Begging yer pardon, miss."

Dani shifted in her seat to allow a young girl to set a large wooden tray in front of her. On it was the big bread bowl she'd come to expect, filled with a dark, thick, meaty stew.

She watched as the girl—child, really hurried away from the table and another young girl placed a similar tray in between Elesyria and Dermid. Other children carried similar trays in between all the tables stretching out in the great hall in front of her.

Little wonder Malcolm had rejected her offer to wait tables by telling her she was too old for the job. She doubted any of those girls was a day past twelve.

"Perhaps Danielle would be better suited to answer that question, wouldn't you, dear?"

Dani jumped at hearing her name and turned to find both Dermid and Elesyria staring at her expectantly.

"I'm sorry, I was distracted. What question is it you think I can answer?"

"Dermid here is wondering whether you don't find it a tad bit uncomfortable to have the mother of your betrothed's deceased wife serving as your companion?"

"I never said that," Dermid attempted to deny, but Elesyria was having none of it.

"Perhaps not those very words, but that was your question, was it not, young man?"

"The mother of my betrothed's deceased—" Dani stopped midway through the tongue-twister, buying time to think of an appropriate response by dipping a small chunk of bread into her stew. "I find it—"

"She finds it as annoying as I do to have you badgering my guests, little brother."

Malcolm!

Rarely had Dani been so glad to be interrupted by someone.

"I'm no badgering, Colm. Only asking a logical question of the woman who is to be my sister."

"And what makes you think that's the case? Have I told you as much? No. Have I done anything to make you think it's so? No."

As he finished speaking, Malcolm grasped Dani's hand and brought it to his mouth, capturing the morsel of food she held between her thumb and forefinger, even as his eyes captured and held hers.

His lips were soft against her fingers and his breath was warm where it feathered over her skin. Warm enough as he lingered over the bite that her own temperature spiked a degree or two. Or ten. Warm enough that she felt the excess heat flood her face.

Her stomach flip-flopped like a novice launching off the high-dive board, landing somewhere close to her ovaries, if the resulting shimmer that felt suspiciously like need was any guide.

"There! You see?" Dermid slammed his tankard to the table like he'd discovered a new planet. "That's exactly what I'm talking about."

"I've no idea what yer talking about," Malcolm replied with a grin, gently releasing the hand he'd held before turning to engage Patrick in a quiet discussion as if nothing at all had just passed between them.

Maybe nothing had.

Dani glanced to her hand, slowly lowering it to the table, feeling as if it were a foreign object. Only when she noticed the obvious tremble did she quickly draw her fingers into a tight fist and move the offending appendage into her lap.

Maybe it was only her.

Damn it! There was no reason for that kind of reaction. Not at all. She didn't respond to men in that way. Ever. And it certainly wasn't as if she'd never had guys flirt with her before. They did. All the time.

It was a fact of life. And yet, for some strange reason, this one particular man seemed to have the ability to get under her skin like no other.

"You should eat what's put in front of you, lass. Starving yerself is no way to keep up yer strength."

Once again she stared up into those intense blue eyes, unable to look away.

Fine. She had no choice but to accept the fact that maybe she couldn't control how her body reacted to the overbearing Scot. But there was no way in the world she was giving him the satisfaction of knowing she felt that way.

"Perhaps if I had something other than my fingers to eat with," she grumbled, searching for something, anything, other than his touch as the culprit in her inability to eat.

"You've a knife, aye? As we all do. What more could you want?"

"What about a fork?" she answered, warming to her deception. "Like any civilized person would use."

"A fork," he repeated, one eyebrow rising. "As you wish, my lady."

He raised a hand, summoning a young girl to his side. After a short conversation in which, presumably, he instructed the child to fetch a fork, she hurried from the great hall. But not before casting a confused look over her shoulder in Dani's direction.

Within moments, the girl returned, bringing with her what, at first glance, Dani would have sworn was a long stick. She handed the object to Malcolm, who turned to Dani, placing it on the table between them.

"As you requested, my lady. Perhaps now you will finish yer meal."

"You're not serious."

The two-pronged monstrosity, carved of wood, must have been nearly two feet in length.

Malcolm's brow wrinkled in obvious irritation, but he held his thoughts private while he tore a small chunk of bread from their shared loaf and dipped it into the stew.

"I dinna question whether or no you were serious in yer desire to have a cook's tool at the table, did I? No. You asked for a fork and I had one brought to you."

"I meant that I wanted a dinner fork." At his questioning frown, she continued. "A miniature version of this. Perhaps the length of your hand. It's what polite society uses to feed themselves where I come from."

He nodded as if he considered her argument, then took her breath away by leaning in close enough to whisper in her ear.

"And then you wipe yer mouths upon the parchment, aye? Polite society, my arse. That's no how we do it here."

She shivered at the proximity of his lips to her ear, his warm breath trailing down her neck as if his fingers traced across her skin, raising chill bumps in their wake.

Her lungs felt as if they might explode from lack of oxygen and she opened her mouth for a deep shaky inhale.

Immediately, Malcolm popped the bite he held between her open lips.

"Now eat yer food and dinna force me to feed it to you as if you were a wee bairn."

Her face heated, as much from Elesyria's quiet laughter behind her as anything. Embarrassment, surely, though her hands still shook, even tightly fisted as they were in her lap.

If she hadn't accepted it before, she'd certainly received quite the lesson in the last few moments.

Malcolm MacDowylt, laird of the MacGahans, was one powerfully dangerous man.

Sixteen

HE'D DREAMED OF her again last night. No misty, shrouded portents of things to come, these. No. Full-on dreams, filled with Dani dressed in the thin, frilly shift she'd worn the first time he'd laid eyes on her.

Dressed in it until it slipped off her shoulders and floated to her feet.

Malcolm leaned back in his chair, propping his feet on the table in front of him, allowing the woman of his dreams to fill his waking thoughts while he waited for Patrick to join him in his solar.

By Freya, but the woman made him smile.

"Care to share what's put that grin on yer face?" Patrick leaned against the open doorway.

Share? No, Malcolm thought not. Not this. Better to steer his brother on to the business at hand. "What did you want to see me about?"

"After I left our strategy session last night, I bumped into the Elf. She asked what yer plans for Danielle are once this business with Torquil is finished."

He'd not thought that far ahead, concentrating his energy instead on the task at hand—leading an army to march on his half brother to demand his sister's freedom.

"None, eh?" Patrick shook his head. "I told the Elf as much, though it dinna please her to hear it in the least."

"Aye, well, Elf or no, we've more important worries than keeping my mother-in-law happy."

Patrick shrugged but did not appear to be satisfied with Malcolm's response as he moved into the room, shutting the door behind him. "She asked that I deliver a message to you. A warning, if you will."

Now there's what he needed. Though, in truth, Patrick as messenger was better than a visit from Elesyria herself.

"And that would be?"

"She says to warn you that the woman was sent to you by the Goddess herself."

As if he hadn't figured that out already. "So it would seem. As a test, no doubt. To see if I fail in protecting her as I failed Isabella."

His brother's jaw tightened. "I've said my piece on that, Colm, and we'll no argue the point now, but no. No as a test. As a gift, she says."

A gift? Not likely. Not unless it was as a gift meant to test. To punish his failures. He knew the stories of the Magical Folk all too well to believe anything else.

"Consider yer message delivered." Malcolm lifted his feet from his table, placing them firmly on the floor. Where they belonged. "Make sure I'm notified when MacKilyn's men approach."

Patrick nodded, heading toward the door again. "I'll see to it that all is in readiness. We will be prepared to leave as soon as our allies have a good night's rest."

Before Patrick reached the exit, the door burst open and Dermid presented himself, the ubiquitous Rauf close at his heels.

"I thought I'd find you here."

Their youngest brother was persistent, if nothing else.

"Now that you've returned from yer"—Dermid slid a knowing glance from Patrick to Malcolm—"*personal business,* I'm assuming yer ready to deal with our brother's demands. I'm offering myself as messenger to carry the tribute demanded back to Torquil."

"We're no going to—" Patrick began, but Malcolm held up a hand, stopping him midsentence.

He had no intention of disclosing to Dermid the fact that there would be no tribute, especially not in front of Rauf. There was something about the grooms-man he simply didn't trust.

"We're no going to allow you to return to Tordenet Castle. Yer here with us, safe and sound now, and I intend to keep it that way."

As he'd expected, Dermid bristled.

"There's no risk to me in returning to Tordenet. Torquil trusts me. And it only makes sense to send me as I'm the one who kens his movements and his thoughts like no other you have here."

That Dermid could ever think he had their half

brother's trust proved more than anything else his youthful lack of judgment.

"We've enough to worry over with finding a way to convince Torquil to release Christiana into our hands. I'll no allow him to hold you hostage as well."

"All the more reason to send me. I could convince him to release our sister."

"No." Malcolm rose to his feet, hoping the lad would accept the finality of his decision. "My decision is made, Dermid. We'll do this my way."

Though his brother might not understand the danger he would be in if he were to return to Tordenet Castle, Malcolm had no illusions about it. Torquil was possessed of all that was most evil in their bloodline. He cared for naught but power and wealth, and Malcolm would not expose his youngest brother to that risk again, no matter that Dermid was older than he had been on his first campaign. Dermid was still his youngest brother.

He moved across the room and into the doorway, deciding as he did that he would be the decoy to throw Dermid off the scent of their true plans.

"And where do you think yer off to now?" the lad demanded, obviously not yet satisfied with the way things would be.

Since they'd gone to all the trouble to convince Dermid that Dani was here as his intended, he might as well make use of their duplicity. Keeping the lad busy spying on him would free up Patrick to see to all the arrangements necessary to ready their men to prepare for battle against Tordenet Castle.

"I'm off to see to some of that *personal business*." With a grin and a wink he walked out, closing the door behind him.

He decided not to put too much thought into why the idea of finding Dani and spending the day with her kept the grin he wore for Dermid's benefit from fading.

Striding purposely toward the great hall, he reached his destination only to realize that he had no clue where Dani might be this time of morning. The hall itself was unusually quiet, with not a single person to be found.

No one tending the fires or working in the room at all.

He continued on, his footsteps on the smooth stone the only sound, heading through the small door in the back and down the dark maze of hallways leading to the storage rooms and kitchens.

Stranger than the eerie quiet of the great hall was the scene in the kitchen, with the better part of the women who worked there gathered at the back door, all jostling for position as if to watch some sort of great sport.

His sinking stomach alerted him it would be Dani at the center of that spectacle even before he pushed his way through the women and out the door.

"I dinna think I'd live to see the day when Cook herself would be skimming the ale," the woman ahead of him confided to another at her side.

"Or carrying her own risen loaves to the ovens, aye?" the second returned, to the vigorous nodding of the first. "There they are!"

Two figures emerged from the alehouse, heads huddled together in conversation. Dani and the head cook.

"What's going on here?" he asked at last, his curiosity no longer waiting to be satisfied.

"Laird Malcolm!" The woman who had been speaking earlier jumped, obviously surprised to see him here, and surrounded by the women of the kitchen at that. "We tried to discourage her, but she'd no hear of it, that one."

She nodded her head so hard he wondered if she might not injure her neck.

"Discourage her from . . ."

He had no time to pursue his questions. Dani had spotted him.

"Malcolm!" She hurried toward him, a radiant smile on her flour-smudged face, two clay pots tightly clutched in her arms like battle prizes. "They use the skimmings from the ale for their leavening agent."

She babbled, so overpleased with her discovery, her eyes glistened with happiness.

"What have you done to yer hair?"

It appeared to be wadded onto her head somehow, with a stick protruding from a spray of golden curls.

"I stuck it up out of the way." She shook her head, dismissing his question. "The whole concept is brilliant in its simplicity. I should have guessed. It totally explains the tang I tasted in the bread. Here I was thinking sourdough. I can't believe I wasn't able to identify it."

"I'll take those, lass." The old cook reached for the pots Dani carried, tucking them close to her chest. "You've had yerself a busy day. Best you go grab a bite to eat now, aye?"

"I *am* hungry," Dani agreed, her wide grin belying any discomfort she might have felt.

"Lady Danielle and I will adjourn to the gardens. Have one of the serving girls bring something to her there. And send along a wrap as well."

Though the weather had cleared, there was still a bite of chill in the air.

"Aye, Laird Malcolm. Right away." The cook agreed with a dip of her head before hurrying inside, shuffling all the gawking women ahead of her like a mother hen with her chicks.

"Thank you, Ada!" Dani called out as she took the arm he offered, allowing him to direct her toward the gardens.

"Is that Cook's name? I don't believe I've ever heard it used before." No one had ever dared address the woman as anything other than Cook, so far as he knew, not even in the days when she'd served in his father's home.

"We've had this discussion before, haven't we? You really need to get over the whole call-you-by-your-job-not-your-name thing."

Yes. He should have remembered. If there was anyone out there who could convince Cook to use her given name, it didn't surprise him that it would be Dani.

He led her to the garden, bidding her to take a seat

on the bench in the corner while he relaxed on the ground, his back against a tree.

"So." She had clasped her hands tightly together in her lap, looking everywhere around her except at him. "What do you grow here in your garden?"

He didn't really know. "Whatever is needed in the kitchens, I suppose. Herbs, greens."

It was impossible to tell now, with the first frosts of autumn already past. All that remained were dead brown stalks and stems.

She turned to look at him at last, a hint of a smile in her eyes. "You're more forager than farmer, huh?"

"So it would seem. And you? What were you doing in the kitchens so early?"

At this she laughed, as if he'd said something amusing. "Early is the only time to be in a kitchen if you want to find out how things get done. And if I'm going to stay in this time, as Elesyria says, I need to learn how things are done."

"You'll no be working in the kitchens, Dani. You've my word on that."

Since she'd been taken from her own world and sent here because of him, he'd never see her spend her life as a servant. He'd marry her himself before he'd allow that.

The thought flittered through his mind, shocking him even as it did.

He'd sworn he'd never marry again, never be responsible for another woman. But, as he already seemed to be responsible for her, he could think of worse things than to spend his life with a woman such as this.

She leaned down toward him, lowering her voice almost to a whisper. "That man of your brother's is watching us. You know that, right?"

Rauf. He had expected as much when he'd left Dermid with Patrick.

Flour smudged her nose and cheek and, this close, it felt only natural to wipe it away. He reached out a finger, stroking it down her nose, cleaning the powder from her skin.

The dark centers of her eyes enlarged like those of a doe he'd happened upon in the forest and he was sure he heard her breath catch.

With his thumb, he gently stroked the fine dust from her cheek, his fingers resting at the base of her jaw where her pulse beat against his skin like a drummer in the heat of battle.

Before he knew it, he was on his knees, his mouth lightly covering hers. She made no move to pull away and he deepened the kiss, his tongue running across the contours of her lips, sampling the taste of her.

She might have groaned, but he couldn't be sure; the rhythmic pounding of his own blood echoed in his ears, driving out all sound.

All sound save that of a throat clearing as a young maid arrived with a basket of food.

Dani launched herself away from him, back up onto the bench she'd somehow slid off of, her hands splayed across her pink cheeks.

Oh, yes, at this very moment he could think of many things worse than spending his life with a woman like this.

WHAT THE HELL had just happened?

Dani ran her hands over her hot cheeks before lacing her fingers together in her lap.

One minute she'd been warning Malcolm about that creepy groomsman spying on them, and the next she'd been about to eat his face.

Good Lord. When the Faeries had transported her over, she must have left her self-control on the other side. At least any self-control where Malcolm Mac-Dowylt was concerned.

He accepted a basket from the young woman who had—thankfully!—interrupted them, and spread out a selection of bread and cheese on the bench next to her. When he leaned in close to wrap a plaid around her shoulders, her heart beat so loud she was amazed he couldn't hear it.

Perhaps he did. The lopsided grin he wore had been put there by something.

The breeze blew a curl across her face and she realized that somewhere along the way the stick she'd used to hold up her hair had failed her.

Probably about the same time her good sense had.

She lifted a shaking hand to remove the stick she'd threaded through her hair, wincing when the bark tangled.

"Allow me." Malcolm stood and leaned over her, carefully separating the hair from around the stick.

Only when he stepped away, once again seating himself on the ground with his back against the tree, was she able to fully fill her lungs.

"Our watcher seems to have disappeared. Perhaps the serving girl frightened him away."

Or perhaps he'd just had an eyeful.

Which would have been Malcolm's intent.

Dani wanted to slap a hand to her forehead. What a dunce! It was as if she'd completely forgotten they were trying to convince Dermid that they were an item. No wonder he'd kissed her right after she'd told him they were being watched.

And here she'd allowed herself to think he might feel . . .

She seriously needed to get a grip. After all, the whole idea of using her as a distraction had been *her* idea to begin with. She must have spent too long breathing in those fumes from the vats of ale this morning.

Hopefully, he'd assumed she was acting too. But just in case he hadn't, she needed to keep it light and breezy now.

"Do you want some of this?" She held out a piece of bread, willing her hand to stop shaking. "Sitting out here with our meal is just like having a picnic on a date, isn't it?"

He refused her offer with a shake of his head, his hands busy with his knife and a small stick. "Picnic?" His brow wrinkled in confusion as his eyes darted up to hers and back down to the idle whittling of his hand.

"Picnic. It's when you pack up some food to take with you to eat outside. For enjoyment."

"Hmmm," he responded, as if he were trying to understand the concept. "And for this you set a meeting. A date, you called it."

"Meeting? Not exactly." Even though the Faerie Magic had done something so that she could communicate with people in this place and time, there were still many differences in their understanding of individual words. "Where I come from, a date is when two people spend time together to help determine if they really like each other. Sort of a bonding experience. To help you find the person you want to marry. Or just to have a good time."

"And this . . ." He lifted his chin, motioning around them. "This is what a date is like?"

"More or less." It was certainly uncomfortable enough to qualify as first-date territory.

"Well then . . ." Malcolm pushed up to his feet, straightening his plaid and replacing the small knife he'd used into the bag he wore at his waist. "I've work to do today, lass. Work that'll no get done as long as I sit and enjoy yer company. Here." He held out the stick he'd been carving. "To catch up yer hair. Without the bark to snag and pull."

She accepted the token, surprised that he'd thought to do something like that for her. "Thank you."

He shrugged and started off, stopping a few feet away and turning to look back. "I propose we picnic another date in the spring. With the plants coming up. So you can see what grows here, aye? Since yer curious about it."

Picnic another date? She held back the laughter that threatened. Laughter that had nothing to do with his mangling of her terminology and everything to do with the intent behind the words.

"I would love to picnic another date with you in the spring."

No question but that it was she who put the smile on his face that time. With a nod of his head, he turned and strode away, leaving her to stare after him, even after he'd turned the corner.

"It's lovely to see the two of you coming together so nicely. Though of course it couldn't be any other way." Elesyria wandered into the garden and dropped to sit next to Dani. "Not that I was eavesdropping, you understand."

"There's no coming together," Dani denied, irritated at having been caught staring after the man. "And you were too eavesdropping."

Elesyria shrugged, her face a picture of happiness. "Perhaps I was. But you can hardly blame me. True love is hard to resist, and for a Faerie? It's like honey and bees. Like fish and water. We're drawn to it."

"True love?" Dani laughed aloud. "I'm afraid you have your wires crossed, my friend. There's nothing going on between us. Just the pretend thing I offered to do to help him with his brother. I already told you all about that."

"Danielle." Elesyria made a little clucking noise with her tongue. "Perhaps you can fool yourself, girl, but you've no hope of fooling me. I sense how you feel. And even if I didn't, I asked the Goddess to send Malcolm's SoulMate and here you are."

The Faerie's admission, so blatant, so matter-of-fact, weakened Dani's knees, making her grateful she hadn't attempted to stand.

"That was what you meant when you told him I'd been sent here for his benefit."

Elesyria, poking through the leftovers in the basket, nodded her head. "Exactly. I'm still boggled that it took you both so long to realize it. As a result of his attempt to help my daughter, Malcolm deserved to be rewarded. You wanted what was intended for your life. Nothing is more intended or a better reward to the Fae than that they should find their other half. Their SoulMate. It's what we all want most. And you, lucky girl, you've had it given to you."

Dani didn't feel very lucky. Though what Elesyria shared with her certainly explained why she felt the way she did, it didn't explain Malcolm's lack of reciprocation.

"Maybe you should explain all this to Malcolm. I'm not sure he's feeling it."

Now it was Elesyria's turn to laugh. "Oh my dear, he's . . . how did you say it? 'Feeling it.' Most definitely feeling it."

For the first time in days, Dani felt as if a weight had been lifted off her chest.

She could find a place for herself here. Things weren't really so different. She'd proven that to herself this morning in the kitchens when she'd made friends with Ada and helped with the day's bread baking. The moment she'd laid hands on that dough, she'd felt like she was where she belonged. She'd even offered to share her favorite recipes with the old cook, in trade for help in figuring out their conversions into current ingredients.

And now Malcolm. Learning that he felt about her the same way she felt about him?

It was like the old television commercials had claimed.

Priceless.

Seventeen

As you directed, Eric has established the encampment on the site where Isabella's cabin stood. There's fresh water and natural shelter, all within a half day's ride of the castle."

Malcolm nodded his approval of the actions taken by Patrick and their captain of the guard.

"Have Eric bring their senior men here to meet with us for a final review of our plans."

Plans that fell far short of satisfaction. Too many lives at risk for his taste. He would go forward, but stay vigilant for any opportunity that might present itself that would allow him to avoid open warfare.

Patrick waited at the door, eyes on the floor, hands behind his back, every fiber of his being radiating an unspoken dilemma.

"Something troubles you, brother?"

The pause before he spoke, before he even looked up, concerned Malcolm as much as any words his brother might have to say.

"In all the years I've followed yer lead, I've never questioned yer decisions and you've never failed to deliver. You've taken us from vagabond warriors to where we are today, with a home and a people to call our own."

"But?"

The unspoken word hung in the air between them.

"Our timing on this is wrong, Colm. We place our army at a grave disadvantage with winter so close at hand. Once more I'd ask that you reconsider holding off until spring. Should the snows overtake us in the mountains, we risk losing many men."

They risked losing many men even if they reached Tordenet Castle ahead of any snow. Unless he could figure out another way before the battles began.

"We canna wait, Paddy. It's what Torquil will expect of us. You ken his powers and his strength as well as I do. Our best hope is to arrive with surprise on our side."

"As you say." Patrick nodded, all expression wiped from his face.

His brother understood the risks and the necessity as well as he did. But, as a good second should, he played the part of devil's advocate well. It was one of his traits Malcolm appreciated most.

"I am but a tree in a din of spears," Patrick continued, reverting to the ancient way of speaking. "Yours to use as you will."

Malcolm waited until Patrick closed the door behind him before propping his elbows on the table and rubbing his hands over his eyes.

The kenning his brother had used was not lost on him. *A warrior in battle.* It was, as it always had been, the perfect description for Patrick.

Malcolm only hoped that in this quest to save their sister he could prevent his brother from becoming a felled tree in a din of spears.

When he heard the door open, he assumed Patrick had returned.

"Do you want to talk about it? Whatever it is that's causing you such worry?"

Not Patrick. Danielle.

"I've no worries." None that he would share with her. She didn't deserve such a burden.

"Right." She pushed the door halfway closed before she crossed the room and seated herself in one of the chairs at the table, propping her arms in front of her and leaning forward to meet his gaze. "Let me guess. You're a lousy gambler, aren't you?"

"Gambler?" He shook his head, in no mood to try to decipher her odd words.

"Games of chance. For silver. I'm guessing you're not very successful at it. Am I right?"

"I do no risk my people's silver on games of chance." It was a foolish waste of time.

"Because you're not good at it. Am I right?" she asked again.

"No man is," he countered, unwilling to admit more.

She chuckled, a broad smile on her face, and leaned back in her chair. "It's because you have a tell. Someone would only need to observe you for a little while and they'd figure it out. You telegraph your feelings. I could tell you were worried when I walked into the room."

"A tell," he repeated, lifting his hand to his forehead. He had too much on his mind this day to even attempt to understand her comment.

"That's it!" she all but shouted, leaning forward again. "You do that every time you're bothered. You rub your hands across your face like a man with a headache. You couldn't send a clearer signal if you climbed up on the table and complained out loud. That's what you were doing when I walked in. That's why I asked what was bothering you."

He started to deny it but realized even before the first word left his mouth that she was correct. Instead he responded by laying his hands flat upon the table in front of him.

Dani stood, a grin spreading over her face. "Oh, I do like a man who listens to good advice. I know you have stuff going on, so I won't keep you any longer. I just stopped by to make sure you planned to be at tomorrow's midday meal. Ada is allowing me to fix something special and I want to make sure you're there to try it."

Had he not yet made it clear to her that he did not consider her a servant here? Obviously, he had not. He rose to his feet and moved to where she stood, catching up her hand when he reached her side.

"Yer no one of the kitchen staff, Dani, and you've no a need to learn to be one. Yer a lady, aye? My lady. You can spend yer day in . . ." He paused, realizing as he spoke that he wasn't exactly sure how the lady of the castle might spend her time. "In pursuit of a lady's activities," he finished somewhat belatedly.

"A lady's activities?" she echoed, her smile lighting her eyes and lilting in her voice. "Oh, Malcolm, I have no idea what those might be, but please understand, I love to cook. It's a pleasure to me to create good food, and a whole new challenge here. It's something I want to do, not something I think you expect me to do."

As if he could deny her anything that brought her pleasure when she looked at him like that. He would have told her that very thing, too, but a flicker of movement caught his eye. The door, almost closed a moment earlier, was less so now. Someone had moved it, ever so slightly.

His guess was that Dermid or his man Rauf stood just outside. Listening.

One look at Dani and it was clear she suspected as much. Her back facing the door, she cut her eyes in that direction and back to him again as a slow, mischievous smile lifted her lips.

With a waggle of her eyebrows, she lifted her free hand to his neck, twining her fingers in his hair.

"So you'll be sure not to miss tomorrow's midday meal, right? I want to surprise you." Stretching up on tiptoe, she pressed her lips close to his ear. "Dermid, you think?" she whispered.

He could only nod his answer, his body reacting too intensely to having her so close, the scent of fresh flowers filling his senses. His free arm tightened around her, pulling her against him, and he bent to her, his mouth finding hers.

Her lips were soft and pliant, opening to him, her

tongue dancing against his. She tasted of mint and cinnamon, like an end-of-meal sweet he found himself desperately craving.

Both his hands were at her back now, sliding down, lower, to capture the perfectly rounded curves of her buttocks, lifting her from her feet and pressing her against his heated, hardened desire.

She groaned into his mouth, and both her hands tangled in the hair at the base of his neck, sending shivers down his spine.

When she lifted one leg, hooking her foot behind his thigh, it was all over. Desire spiraled into a rage of need, beyond his ability to understand.

In two long strides he backed her into the hard slab of wood and pressed against her, crushing her against the heavy oak door.

The partially open heavy oak door.

Clasped together, they stumbled against the solid surface behind them as it gave way, slamming the door shut as their bodies fell against it.

A yelp from the other side hit Malcolm's ears like a bucket of cold water tossed onto a randy dog.

He stared into Dani's eyes, huge liquid pools, a languid green he wanted nothing more than to immerse himself in, as he fought to calm his breathing.

A scratching at the wood and he looked down to see a wiggling fold of plaid caught in the closed door.

Dani's gaze had followed his and a strangled little huffing noise escaped from her as she stared at the twitching material.

Pray Odin he hadn't made her cry! How he could have so lost control of his actions, he could not say.

Desperation invaded his heart as the noise continued, her whole body trembling with it as she clamped a hand over her mouth.

With a tentative finger, he raised her chin, his desperation washed away with the relief of what he found.

Her eyes sparkled as her lips pressed together in a vain attempt to hold in the sounds she made. No tears. Laughter!

"Lord, Malcolm," she whispered, even as she fought the giggles that threatened to overcome her. "If you don't open that door, do you think he'll just abandon his plaid and make a run for it? I can already picture him. . . ."

Another scratch at the wood and she gave up all pretext, covering her mouth with both her hands as she leaned her head against his chest.

The vision she suggested was enough to bring a smile to his face as well.

One deep breath to regain himself and he was ready. With his hands on her shoulders, he directed her away from the door and pulled it open to greet a red-faced Dermid on the other side.

"There was something you wanted, little brother?"

Dermid opened his mouth and closed it just as quickly, once, twice, his eyes darting every direction except straight ahead.

Their spy had apparently gotten more than he'd bargained for.

"Well, I'm sure you boys have plenty to talk about, so I'll be leaving you to it." Dani, having recovered, pushed between them, stopping at the last minute to blind Malcolm with another brilliant smile. "Don't forget, now. I'm preparing a surprise for you tomorrow."

Forget? Not likely.

Though he sincerely doubted there was anything she could prepare for tomorrow that would surprise him more than she had here today.

Eighteen

LIFE WAS GOOD. Not just good. It was right next door to perfect.

Dani shook the long piece of linen she held, snapping it in the air in front of her with a satisfying crack. The cloth the kitchen girl, Jeanne, had brought to her would serve as a wonderful apron.

She wrapped it around her middle, tying the ends behind at her waist. Later she'd see if she couldn't work with the seamstresses in the castle to come up with a proper apron, but for now, this would work just fine.

She twirled in a tight little circle, feeling more than a bit like a fairy-tale princess. She was making friends in her new home, and yesterday her fairy-tale prince had all but declared his intention of marrying her. *My lady,* he called her. And not in the vernacular of time, but as in "You are my lady." Little wonder she hadn't been able to sleep in more than catnaps all night.

With another twirl and one last reassuring pat to the coil of hair she'd fixed in place, she was out the door and hurrying through the dawn-gray halls to the stairs and beyond.

To her surprise, even as early as it was, the castle was already astir, with young boys and girls bustling about in the great hall. She passed through the cavernous room with its great fireplaces set at either side, wondering at all the activity.

Maids scuttled down the normally empty hallway, smiling and nodding in greeting as they passed, relieving some of Dani's anxiety. It almost felt as if she'd passed some entrance exam over the past few days in the kitchens and was now accepted as someone who belonged.

She paused at the entry to the kitchen, squaring her shoulders. Though she had yet to carry off a dish on her own, today would be her true test, at least for her own sense of self. From start to finish, from baking the bread this morning to putting together the dessert she planned for the midday meal, today she would put her newly acquired knowledge to work.

With both hands, she pushed open the door and was very nearly run down by a young boy, his arms filled with wood scraps.

"Beggin' yer pardon, my lady," he called breathlessly, racing past her.

Lord. She'd thought the great hall was busy, but by comparison to the activity in the kitchen, it might as well have been deserted.

Right in the center of all of it, she located Ada. The old cook, her hair covered with a tightly wrapped scarf, her sleeves rolled up beyond her elbows, appeared to be in her element, directing the rush of bodies.

A rush Dani had *not* expected.

She'd taken care to make sure she hadn't over-slept. In her excitement and determination not to be late, she'd swear she'd awoken every hour on the hour throughout the night. And yet, these people had clearly been hard at it for quite some time.

"I thought you said we'd begin at sunrise." She was, in fact, positive that was their appointed time to begin.

The old cook looked up from the huge pot she stirred, a look of surprise sweeping over her perspiration-dotted brow. "Och, lassie, we'll no be spending our time on a midday meal on this day. We've a feast for this very night that needs preparing, we have."

Dani ignored her twinge of disappointment and summoned a smile. "Then tell me how I can help. I'll do whatever you need."

Whatever it was that drove this beehive of activity, obviously it was important to all these people. And since they were her people now, it was important to her, too.

"Good on you, lassie. All hands are welcome on this day, what with so little warning to prepare. Jeanne!" She waved the dripping wooden spoon in her hand, summoning the young maid who'd become Dani's right hand in her kitchen adventures. "Lady Danielle has offered her help. I'm putting her in yer care, aye?"

Jeanne's head bobbed up and down and, with a grin, she clasped Dani's hand in her own and led her to the end of a table piled high with stacks of vege-tables.

"All we need to do is cut them into pieces and toss them into the buckets. One of the lads will carry them over to where Cook needs them."

Dani worked in silence, establishing a rhythm with Jeanne until the buckets in front of them began to fill.

"What's this feast for? I hadn't heard a word about it until I walked in here this morning."

"Nor any of us, either, until Cook came round in the middle of the night, rousting us from our pallets. The Feast of Odin, she called it. I hear they'll even be uncorking the Berserker brew." The young woman's grin spread across her face, lighting her eyes. "I've heard tell of what it does to a man, aye? I'm looking forward to seeing for my own self what effect it has my Eymer if Cook's tales are true. It could be quite an evening."

"And I as well," the woman working at the next table over added. "Though not on yer lad, Jeanne. I only hope I'm no too tired to reap the benefits."

"I dinna think it possible for you to ever be that tired, Matildis," another woman chimed in to a ripple of muffled giggles.

"True," Matildis replied with a little shimmy of her shoulders. "There's naught like a hardened stallion to renew a woman's energy, lest it be a roomful of them."

Muffled giggles turned to outright laughter.

"Matildis!" one of the older women admonished. "Watch yer tongue. There's wee lassies about."

"Wee lassies need to hear the truth of it as well,"

Matildis replied with a shrug. "And if that bog myrtle brew works as Cook says, you'll do well to keep those wee lassies safely tucked in their rooms tonight with their doors bolted, along with any others who've no enjoyment for the ride."

The buzz of happy conversation filled the air and Dani laughed along with the others, enjoying the comfortable camaraderie of the group as her buckets filled. A boy of perhaps eight or nine dashed in and swooped up those buckets, returning a minute later with empty ones for them to fill again.

Dani's curiosity was piqued. History had never been one of her strong points, but actually living history? That was turning out to be much more enjoyable than any dull class filled with names and dates to memorize.

"Obviously this Feast of Odin is a big celebration. What's it about?"

Jeanne shrugged one shoulder without looking up, her knife chopping expertly through the row of carrots in front of her. "It's meant to bring victory in battle or some such. I've heard Cook tell stories from her old home about it, but I dinna ken much more meself. Only that there's to be all the food we can eat and drink aplenty this night."

"Meant to bring victory in battle?" The knife in Dani's hand stilled.

That didn't sound at all like a celebration of some long-remembered battle out of history. Besides, if that were the case, they would have known that it was coming and would have been preparing for days. This big party, whatever it was for, was something no one had expected.

Meant to bring victory in battle.

No, that sounded suspiciously like something yet to come.

It also sounded suspiciously like something she didn't think she was going to like.

Not at all.

And everything that anyone knew about this feast came from the cook's stories.

Setting her knife down, she turned and made her way over to the center of the room, straight to the old cook.

"Ada? This Feast of Odin, can you tell me why we're celebrating it now?"

"Feast *to* Odin," her friend corrected. "To honor him. Tonight we petition the God of War to protect our warriors when they march off to battle tomorrow. It's long been a tradition of the MacDowylt to placate their testy ancestors, aye?"

Dani had been correct. She didn't like what she was hearing. Not one bit.

"Where are they—wait. Why? Why are they going into battle?" And why hadn't Malcolm said a word of it to her?

"Because our good laird Malcolm kens his responsibility to rescue his sister before it's too late to save the poor lass. Their half brother holds her prisoner at Tordenet Castle." Ada beat the air with her spoon as she spoke, her eyes narrowing as she got into her story. "I've no a doubt but that Laird Alfor's ghost is walking the halls of his beloved castle over that one, though he's none to blame but himself. Serves him well enough, it does, naming his firstborn to succeed him as laird. Torquil was an evil, sneaky arse from the day he was old enough to take his first steps. It was the idea of serving him what sent my Ulrick following after Malcolm when his father first sent him off to fight his battles for him."

Oh, hell. All the movies she'd ever seen, all the books she'd ever read, all of them spoke to how the Scots couldn't get along with one another. She'd always just thought it was storytelling.

"Where's Malcolm now?"

"In his solar, I'd say." Ada stuck her spoon back into the big pot, stirring in sweeping wide circles. "Likely with the MacKilyn's men, who arrived in the night."

She had to talk to him. She couldn't let him ride off into battle. Not now. She couldn't bear the thought of losing him when she'd only just found him.

She couldn't very well be a fairy-tale princess if her fairy-tale prince went off and got himself killed.

"THEN IT'S SETTLED, William." Malcolm clasped the forearm of the man across from him, slapping his shoulder as he did so. "You and yer men will join up with us tomorrow at first light. We meet where the trail to yer camp reaches the main road."

"It will be so," William answered, his hand to Malcolm's shoulder in return of the earlier gesture.

Malcolm stepped back, his arms crossed at his

chest, waiting as the three MacKilyn warriors made their way out of his solar.

"One last thing." William paused at the door. "Our good laird bids me remind you that by our being here, you've a debt of honor you owe to him. Due and payable upon his request."

"Due and payable upon his request," Malcolm echoed.

"My laird then bids me inform you of his intention to collect upon said debt before Yule. In one month's time, he will arrive, accompanied by his daughter, expecting to be welcomed in the fullness of yer hospitality. This is agreeable?"

"It is."

Malcolm did not hesitate in his response. He could not. He could not risk losing the support of the Mac-Kilyn, no matter the personal cost to him.

Patrick stepped back as the MacKilyn men disappeared out into the hallway, to slump down into a chair close by.

"You ken what you've just agreed to, aye? It's no secret that this is no the first time the MacKilyn has exercised this ploy on an ally."

Malcolm understood. All too well.

"It is nothing more than the artifice of a desperate old man."

"A desperate old man with no sons, mayhap. But lacking in honor, Colm, you ken as well as I do. There's no honor to be found in forcing a man to wed yer daughter to obtain the alliance he desperately needs. It's the sale of yer soul he wants."

Malcolm nodded his agreement, refusing to allow regret to poison his heart. He had no choice. His sister's life depended on his securing the MacKilyn warriors to his cause.

They'd heard the stories of the MacKilyn's trickery from the time of their first visit to Castle MacGahan. Stories about the wily old laird with riches and land, but no sons to pass them on to. No sons, but a dozen daughters, it was said.

A dozen daughters, each in turn to be married off to an ally of the MacKilyn in return for a pledge of their father's alliance.

Now he, too, would be one of those stories.

"And what of Lady Danielle?"

Malcolm shook his head, unable to meet his brother's gaze, his tongue too thick to answer.

"Based on what you told me yestereve, I had thought I would be welcoming a new sister into the family."

Perhaps it was the work of the Norns, the vile fate-bringers of Asgard. He should never have confided his plans for Dani to his brother. Now they would never be. For a man who had wanted no entanglements with women, his life had become as a web of spiders.

"You *will* be welcoming a new sister into the family, Patrick. A daughter of the house of MacKilyn."

"The Elf will no be well pleased," Patrick muttered, thumb and forefinger stroking his chin.

"No, I dinna suppose she will be, though in truth, her feelings are no my first concern."

It was the feelings of another woman that troubled him now. Another woman with eyes of green and skin so soft and fragrant, he could lose himself in her for a lifetime.

A noise in the hallway had Patrick on his feet, sword drawn, and at Malcolm's shoulder as he approached the door.

"Dermid?" Patrick silently mouthed Malcolm's suspicion.

With a flick of his wrist, Malcolm set them both in motion, toward the opening where he expected to find his brother waiting. Even as he took the last step, he prepared to lecture Dermid about his penchant for spying at half-open doorways.

With Patrick in place to his left, he flung the door open wide.

It was not Dermid standing in the hallway, but Dani, her face an expressionless mask.

No words passed between them, and for half a heartbeat he deluded himself into believing she had not heard the discussion that had passed between him and Patrick.

In that half a heartbeat, his world held still as he stared into her eyes. Hoping against hope, even as her fingertips lifted to her lips, as if only by physical restraint could she hold back her words.

Half a heartbeat only before hope died a wicked death.

And then she was gone. Racing away down the hallway, her skirts lifted high to give her more speed.

Patrick's hand to his shoulder kept him from running after her. That was as it should be. Even if he had pursued, even if he caught her, what could he possibly say? He'd said too many words to her already.

Once again he'd failed a woman entrusted to his care.

Nineteen

"I TOLD YOU ALREADY, I don't care how my hair looks, Elesyria. It doesn't matter."

Nothing mattered now. Dani sat with her back to the Faerie, patiently allowing her friend to pick at her hair. All she really wanted was to climb into the big bed behind her and draw the covers up over her head, shutting out the world of pain.

"Are all women without guile in your time, or is it only you? Don't be such a simpleton. Of course it matters when you're dealing with a man. Men are simple creatures. They sample you with their eyes first, whether that man be Faerie, Mortal, or something else."

A twinge of irritation elbowed its way into the pain.

"I have no intention of being sampled by anyone, thank you very much. Especially not one particular anyone who's getting ready to marry someone else." The thought sent a brand-new stab of pain zinging through her heart. "And what on earth is a 'something else'? I mean, we have Faeries and Mortals. What else is there?"

Elesyria moved to stand in front of Dani, hands on her hips, issuing forth a clucking noise that rivaled any chicken Dani had ever heard.

"You are robbing me of my faith in the women of the future. I am no longer so sure that I am comfortable with having my daughter live there if women have so lost their ability to reason."

"I reason just fine."

"Very well. If, as you say, reason isn't lost, it certainly isn't highly utilized, is it? There are more Others walking your world than you can imagine." Elesyria rolled her eyes and leaned forward. "Obviously, more than *you* can imagine, in any event."

"That's it." Dani rose to her feet, turning to face the Faerie. She was done with this ridiculous primping and the insults accompanying the activity. "My problem isn't lack of imagination. My imagination is as good as anyone else's, thank you very much. Maybe my problem is that my Faerie godmother is just totally inept. Maybe said inept Faerie dragged my ass seven hundred years into the past to dump me in the lap of a guy who's going to marry some. Other. Woman."

"First off, I am not your Faerie godmother. Let's get that straight right now. I am Faerie, true, but the whole godmother thing is a myth. Wishful thinking on the part of envious Mortals." She patted her hair and walked toward the door. "And, second, I'm not sure you even deserve to be with the man into whose lap your Mortal ass was dropped. You've no idea the trouble the Goddess and I went to in order to find *the* perfect woman for Malcolm MacDowylt, laird of the MacGahan. You obviously have no idea how incredibly rare a coupling between SoulMates is. Or that every Fae's life dream is to achieve such. We've handed this precious gift to you on a gilded platter and you, ungrateful child that you are, you're not even willing to exert the smallest effort to secure the union."

Ungrateful? At the moment, Dani regretted every drop of milk she'd ever set out for Faeries. Regretted every single minute she'd wasted reading books about them. Regretted ever having heard of them.

"Well, I'm just oh so sorry that you find me ungrateful for this once-in-a-lifetime opportunity you've given me, but maybe you missed the last news flash. Malcolm is marrying someone else."

Elesyria huffed out her breath, looking every bit the irritated Faerie. "Once in a lifetime? You wish. We all do. No, child, it's more like once in a millennium. Once in a thousand lifetimes, and only then if you're very, very lucky. You may never see this opportunity again, and what do you do with it? *Pffft.*" Her hand flittered above her head like a butterfly in flight. "You fritter it away as if it has no more value than a cup of dirt. If you place no more value on true love than this, you don't deserve true love."

With a flounce of her skirts and a slamming of the door, Elesyria was gone.

"Fine!" Dani yelled at the closed door. "I'm glad you're not my Faerie godmother, because you suck!"

She sat down on the foot of the bed, head in her hands, rubbing her face with her fingers.

Just like Malcolm did when he was stressed.

"Damn it," she whimpered, giving herself over to self-pity.

It was all so unfair. She'd just begun to feel accepted here. To feel as if she really belonged. As if these were the people she'd searched for her whole life. As if Malcolm was the one she'd searched for her whole life.

And now this. This other woman that he was going to marry simply to secure an alliance.

Elesyria was wrong. It wasn't her turning down true love. It was Malcolm. She'd been receptive to his overtures. She'd made every effort.

"Ha!" she snorted, rising to her feet to pace back and forth.

Receptive? Oh yeah. She'd definitely been receptive. And it hadn't required any effort at all on her part. Hell, she'd been all over the guy. If his brother hadn't interrupted them yesterday, she'd probably have had him on the floor, and had her way with him.

Like that had required any effort on her part. If anything, the effort was to *not* wrestle him to the floor.

No, Elesyria wasn't wrong about her.

She'd been a fighter her whole life, willing to go after whatever she'd wanted, grabbing hold and hanging on for dear life. And now that she faced maybe the most important fight of her life? Now she was just rolling over and giving up.

"Oh, no, I'm not."

That had never been her and it wasn't going to be her now. The Faeries had handed her a chance at the perfect life. Her SoulMate. Her true love. And she was by God going for it. She'd been successful for years in *discouraging* men's interest. Now it was time for success at *encouraging* it.

With a tug at the neckline of her dress and a push to her breasts, she exposed a little more of herself. A flip of her hair and one long curl dangled down on the bare skin.

If she ended up losing Malcolm to another woman, it wasn't going to be without a damn good fight.

With new determination she flung open the door and found herself face-to-face with a grinning Elesyria.

"I knew you'd come around once you thought about it."

The Faerie linked her arm through Dani's, pulling her forward toward the revelry awaiting them one level down.

Midway down the stairs, the music began, slowly at first, picking up in tempo and volume. By the time they reached the double-wide entry to the great hall, the drums were echoing through the cavernous rooms and throbbing in Dani's chest.

If she were going to describe the scene before her, the one word that came to mind was *Valhalla*.

Delicious aromas wafted to her, reminding her none too subtly that in her pouting, she'd skipped all meals today. The huge fireplaces on either side of the hall burned brightly, an enormous carcass roasting slowly on a turning spit in each one of them.

The tables were filled with more people than

she'd even realized inhabited the castle, all laughing and shouting, trying to be heard over the music. The young girls who normally served at midday were nowhere to be seen, replaced tonight by the women she'd worked with in the kitchens this morning. They laughed and shouted right along with those they served, splashing a dark amber bubbly from the pitchers they carried into the tankards held up as they passed.

The musicians themselves held sway in one corner, three men on drums and one playing a bagpipe. Their rhythm pulsed through the crowd, punctuated by the occasional primitive scream and bellow. The piper's face was a bright red and the cords in his neck stood out like lines of rope in response to his exertion.

It was shaping up to be some amazing party.

Presiding over it all, seated at the middle of the great table set upon the dais, was Malcolm.

Their eyes met across the room, locked to one another like iron filings to a magnet. Slowly, as if he weren't even aware of his actions, Malcolm rose to his feet.

"Showtime," Dani whispered and stepped into the room.

DANIELLE!

She stepped into the great hall, her eyes boring into Malcolm's very soul.

As if a great warhorse sat on his chest, he struggled to fill his lungs with air, even as his feet moved him toward her of their own accord. The noise around him dulled to a dim roar even as the path ahead of him narrowed like a tunnel, focused on a thing of beauty at the end.

He met her halfway down the aisle separating the two halves of the enormous room, aware of nothing more than the way she looked this evening.

Most of her hair had been piled up upon her head in a most artful manner, but a couple of curls fell carelessly loose, trailing onto her bare skin, tracing a path downward, leading his eyes toward the swells of her breasts.

He met her gaze again to find her smiling, a soft, seductive turn of the lips aimed directly at him. And good that was, too. He had not a single doubt that he'd draw sword and skewer any other man she graced with that look.

She held out her hand and he took it, leading her back to the dais and behind the table to the seat next to his. On the morrow he might well owe his soul to Angus MacKilyn, but for this one night, he would enjoy the lady of his own choosing at his side.

One of the women stopped at their table, her large pitcher held high on her shoulder. He lifted his tankard and she streamed the battle brew into his cup.

Dani held her cup aloft when the woman offered, but he placed his hand over it.

"This is no the normal ale we drink with our meals, my lady. This brew is from an ancient recipe, made potent with the strength of the bog myrtle."

Dani grinned and pushed his hand away. "I had

no trouble with Guinness back home, so I doubt your bog myrtle beer will do me in, either."

She touched the rim of her tankard to his and took a sip before leaning her head close to his in order that she might be heard. "Interesting flavor. Is it true that your men drink this before battle to turn them into berserkers?"

Someone had been filling her ears with the old stories.

"It is the custom of my people."

He spoke into her ear as she had into his, breathing her in, reveling in the tingles shooting through his body. Whether it was her loose hair tickling his face or the effects of the battle ale, he could not say. Did not care. It only mattered that his senses were alive with her.

Another small sip and she set her cup down to lean close again. "I never heard of that custom. Never read about any such Scottish tradition, never saw it in a single mov—well, let's just say, it's not a Scottish tradition I was familiar with."

"I never said it was, my lady." It was all he could do to keep from taking her earlobe between his teeth. "I said it was the custom of my people. My father's people. He came to these shores long ago, a Viking raider. After defeating the MacDowylt in battle, he settled in as their laird, bringing his wife and son from his homeland to join him. When his wife passed on, he married my mother, and though he committed himself to this land to raise his family, he raised us in the ways of our ancestors lest we forget who we were."

"Thus the Odin feast," she said, sweeping her hand to encompass the activity in the room.

"Thus the Feast to Odin," he confirmed.

Food was brought to them course by course, each served in a trencher he shared with Dani. Pottage, soups, roasted meats, and sweet creations all made from the MacDowylt's meager storage of supplies. Every dish accompanied by a seemingly endless supply of the ale and served to the soul-searing beat of drums and pipes.

While the feast itself was a custom of his father's people, the music belonged to his mother's world. Primitive, ancient, it stirred his blood.

At intervals the music would pause long enough for the players to rotate, allowing each group of four musicians to rest until it was their turn to play again.

During one such interval the old cook, Ada, appeared at his side, a cloth-wrapped box held reverently in her hands.

It was time.

He accepted the bundle, laying it on the table in front of him. Peeling back the soft linen he exposed a box, hand-carved in generations past from the wood of the sacred rowan tree. He lifted the lid to reveal three large drinking horns, each engraved with the symbol of one of their gods.

He stood and poured a draft of ale from his tankard into the first horn, lifting it above his head.

A hush fell over those gathered in the room, many of whom had followed him for years. The warriors among the assembled lifted their tankards above their heads in a duplication of his move.

"For victory and power," he called out.

"For victory and power," they echoed.

"For Odin," they all yelled in unison with him, downing their drinks even as he swallowed the contents of the drinking horn.

He laid it back on the table and picked up the second, once again pouring a swallow from his tankard into the horn before lifting it above his head.

"For faith in yer own strength and power," he called, waiting until the room had once again filled with the echo of his words. "For Thor," he yelled above the noise, leading the room in the toast before downing that drink as well.

A third time, he picked up a horn and poured the remainder of his ale into it before lifting it above his head to lead his people in the final blessing.

"For good years and peace." He waited until the echo died to lead the chant of "For Frey."

He downed the last of his ale and sat, carefully replacing the three horns in their box while the room reverberated in shouts and cheers that were quickly drowned out by the resumption of the pounding, pulsing music.

"Did you think to keep this from me? Did you no think I'd be smart enough to recognize the purpose of this gathering?" Dermid shoved his way to the table, his fair skin mottled with anger and too much ale. "Patrick says I'm to be left behind on the morrow. I want to go with you, Colm. You need me there."

Malcolm had known this moment would come, just as he'd known his answer would be a blow to Dermid's pride, no matter how he might try to position it. All the same, he would not see the young man's life at risk.

"I'd ask yer understanding. I leave you behind to see to my castle. To see to my people."

"Do you take me for a fool? It's horse dung you think to rub my face in now. I'm no a youngling. I've a right to go with you. Christiana is my sister too."

If Dermid wouldn't accept an excuse, he'd have the truth, though Malcolm doubted it would satisfy him any better.

"Yer my brother, Dermid. As I'd have Christiana safe with me, so, too, I'd have you safe. You stay behind."

"Patrick is yer brother too, but he trails along, sniffing yer butt like a dog on every campaign, does he no?"

Beside him, Patrick rose to his feet.

"Patrick is a seasoned warrior, fighting at my side as my right hand. You've no his experience." Malcolm reached out, laying his hand over Dermid's. "Yer my brother. I love you. I'd no ever place yer life in jeopardy."

Dermid slapped his hand away, staggering back at his own exertion. "Love me? Ha!" He spit on the floor at his feet. "Torquil was right about you. You care for nothing but yer own glory."

"Dermid . . ." Malcolm thought to soothe, but his

brother stormed away, weaving a path through the crowd.

"He'll be fine." Patrick reclaimed his seat, shaking his head with a grin. "Well, fine once the ale-sick passes. He'll come to his senses when his head clears. He's no one to hold on to an anger."

Malcolm nodded, hoping his brother was right. But angry or no, Dermid would remain behind. He might be angry, but at least he'd be alive. More than many in this hall would be able to say in a week's time.

Ada leaned in and swept the box away and Malcolm looked out over the hall, an enormous regret filling the hollow between his shoulders.

The Battle Sorrow, he and Patrick called it. The knowledge that these warriors stretching out in the hall before him would ride into battle on his word. The knowledge that not all of them would return.

A soft touch to his shoulder and he turned to find Dani leaning close.

"What's wrong?"

He shook his head to dismiss the conversation. He could not speak of this now.

"We should probably talk." She stood up and reached a hand out to him. "Come on," she yelled over the commotion in the room.

They did need to talk, though he dreaded the words he would have to say.

He rose to his feet and took her hand, allowing her to lead him out of the hall and through the narrow hallways to the kitchen and beyond, out into the dark.

Out here, with the moon shining brightly in the cloudless sky, the music was but a faint beat in the night. The early snow that had plagued their journey back from the stone circle had fallen only lightly here and melted into the thirsty soil almost as soon as it had touched ground.

Dani's steps slowed and she glanced up at him, a shy smile perched at the corners of her lips.

"I didn't exactly have a destination in mind. Only out. Away from the smoke and the noise."

"And good timing it was to be out of there, too." Warriors whose senses were heightened by the free-flowing ale and pulsing music were already pairing off with eager women, their bodies swaying together to the beat of the drums. Another hour and they'd have been forced to step over the writhing heaps on the floor. He didn't fancy the idea of Dani's seeing that part of the celebration. "This way."

He took the lead now, holding tightly to her hand as he directed their path out to the glory he would one day complete. As they approached the half-finished building, he tried to imagine it through her eyes, wondering what she would think of his project.

The site straddled a small stream, which had been part of his reason for choosing this spot. Stone walls jutted up on all four sides, though they'd only reached a height equal to his chest. The roof was yet a dream, but one day he would complete his design.

"What is this place?" she asked when they stopped.

"In my father's homeland, most settlements have a bathhouse. It was one of the first additions he made to Tordenet Castle when it became his. It is my intent to construct one here as well."

"A bathhouse," she repeated, smiling and stretching up on tiptoe for a better look.

"This way," he encouraged, drawing her toward the side where a door would one day stand. "The entrance."

She walked through ahead of him, stopping just inside. "Oh, Malcolm."

Her voice, thick with disappointment, stopped him where he stood.

Again he tried to see it as he thought she might. An unfinished set of walls, surrounding a piece of meadow.

"I've much yet to accomplish before it's done, but one day the world will see it as I do in my mind."

"I don't doubt that," she responded quickly, walking toward the center of the enclosed space. "It's just such a shame you'll have to cut down this tree. It feels as if it belongs here on the bank of this stream, its little branches stretching out over it as they do."

She was a king's ransom indeed that he was giving up in order to save his sister's life.

"The tree will stay." It, more than the stream, was the impetus for choosing this site. "The rowan is sacred to my people. When I finish construction, the roof will open to the sky at this point, allowing this rowan to live on." Exactly as in the atrium room his father had built at Tordenet Castle.

"Oh, good," she said, nodding as she reached out to run her fingers down the tree's trunk. "That's so good. I'd like to see that when it's finished." A pause, almost as if she were marshaling her courage to continue. "But I wonder, will I get to see it, Malcolm? Or do you plan to send me away when you return?"

And there it was. That which needed to be spoken aloud. The words that would rip his heart from his chest, but which must be said.

"This is yer home now, Dani. I've told you that. You've no a need to doubt yer future."

"But you'll be wed to another." She leaned against the tree, her arm outstretched, her fingers still laced with his.

The pale skin of her breasts rose and fell with each breath and, in the moonlight, her skin seemed to glow as if her life spirit radiated a light from within. So delicate and sweet, yet her words cut like a freshly honed blade.

"When I return with my sister, I must wed the MacKilyn's daughter. But I'll see to it that both you and Christiana are well cared for. I'm sure you'll get on well with her and become great friends. You'll have shelter and food such as we have and the freedom to spend yer time as you wish. You'll want for nothing as long as I draw breath. You've my oath on that."

She filled her lungs, slowly, deeply, and blew the air out again before meeting his gaze.

"Don't give an oath you can't keep."

"There's none that can stop me from keeping that oath." He would build an entire section onto the castle if he had to. No matter the cost. No matter how long it took. This would be her home.

"No." She shook her head, the gleam of tears shining in her eyes. "You can't promise I'll want for nothing because the one thing I want, the only thing I want, you won't be able to give me."

He opened his mouth to refute her claim, but she pressed one delicate finger to his lips.

"You can't, Malcolm. Because the only thing I want is you. And no matter what happens, I lose you after tonight. Whether you're lost in this battle you go to fight or you're lost to another woman, the end result is that I can't have you."

There should be blood to accompany pain such as he felt now. Copious amounts of bright red blood. Enough to cover the largest of battlefields. But no, a broken heart did not bleed as a wound of the flesh would. Nor, he feared, would it heal as a wound of the flesh would.

"I . . . I have no choice." He held her hand, grasped it tightly within his own, willing her to understand. "Skuld wove the skein of our lives long ago. What is to come after this night is not in our power to control."

"Maybe not," she conceded, taking his other hand in hers and pulling him toward her. "But what is to come tonight is completely within our control."

She leaned into him, rising up on tiptoe to press her soft lips against his, dropping his hand to twine her fingers in the hair at the base of his neck.

He could push her away. Should push her away. But he couldn't seem to find the strength for anything more than lifting his lips from hers.

"I will not ask you to be my mistress." He would not dishonor either her or the woman he would marry in such a way.

"That's a good thing, because I have a very strict, no-exceptions policy about not dating married men."

She caught up his hand again and pulled him with her as she sank to her knees under the rowan tree.

He joined her willingly, though Freya knew, he should walk away.

Instead he caressed her face, running his thumb over her cheek. "One night, love. Can you live with the knowledge of only one night?"

She kissed him again, fiercely this time, breaking the kiss to capture his face in her hands. "I'll have to. Because what I couldn't live with is the knowledge that you're the one man in the whole of time for me and I let you slip away without sharing even one night with you."

Her fingers tugged at his shirt, freeing the cloth to slide underneath against his bare chest.

"Yer hands are cold."

"All of me is cold." She hooked her fingers in the waist of his plaid and urged him toward her as she lay down on her back. "Come heat me up."

He wouldn't make her ask him a second time.

MALCOLM'S BODY WAS warm and large and even had he not supported his weight on his elbows as he did when he covered her, Dani wanted him so badly that she wouldn't have cared.

Cold air skittered along her skin as his knee

nudged the edge of her skirt up along her leg, even as his fingers worked at the laces covering her breasts.

Need coursed through her body. Desperate, mind-numbing need.

She pulled at the sides of his plaid, crumpling the cloth in her fingers until at last the coarse hair of his legs brushed against the backs of her hands.

The drums in the distance beat in time with her need, a heady background of *now, now, now,* thrumming in her mind, until she moaned with her impatience.

His tongue playing a game of hide-and-seek at her ear, stilled, and a puff of air wafted over her lobe as he chuckled his response.

"Easy, love. We've this whole night for ourselves. We'll take it slow and enjoy one another."

"Like hell we will," she panted.

They lay, for all intents and purposes, in the man's backyard, a party in full swing well within earshot. Not to mention she was pretty sure she could see her breath out here.

Oh, she had every intention of enjoying the whole of the night, but act 1, "Love Under the Stars," would be only a prologue. A short, quick prologue.

She pushed her body against his, and he rolled with her, grasping her waist with his hands as she sat on his midsection.

The erection pressing against her leg was every bit as good as she'd hoped.

Maybe it was more appropriate to think of this as an appetizer to a banquet.

She covered his mouth with hers, letting her tongue dance across his lips before sitting back up astride him and opening the laces he had been fumbling with.

Cold peaked her nipples instantly. Cold or want. Not that it mattered which. His hands covered them immediately, the pads of his rough thumbs tracing circles of heat.

She was ready. She was more than ready.

Rising to her knees, she gathered her skirts out of her way before leaning forward to drive herself down on his jutting manhood.

"For the love of Freya," he groaned, and flipped her to her back.

They stared into one another's eyes for a long moment, his body poised above hers, him buried within her heat.

And the need overtook her again. The searing, driving want of him, pushing her over the edge. He tightened his grip as, beyond her control, her muscles pulsed in rhythmic contractions around his heat as if her very soul sought to draw him deep inside her for keeping.

His panting echoed hers and, as their eyes locked together, he began a slow withdrawal and reentry.

Slow at first, but his need matched her own, evidenced by his increasing tempo. She lifted her hips to meet him and he drove into her, crushing her against him, burying his face in the curve of her neck as he buried his pulsing shaft in the folds of her body.

They lay together, each breath a short, hard little pant, neither willing to move.

So this was what it was like making love with your SoulMate.

"Once is definitely not going to be enough," she confided, tracing a finger over the contours of his cheek.

He kissed the tip of her nose, her forehead, and both her eyelids before pulling away to brush a curl away from her face.

"Yer right, it's no, to that I will confess. But we agreed. Only this once."

She shook her head, forcing a smile much brighter than she actually felt. "No. We agreed on only this one night. Surely a powerful warrior like you, descendant of the mighty Odin and the gods of Asgard, is good for more than just one time a night."

He stared at her for a moment before throwing his head back, laughter bubbling up from his throat.

"Oh, aye, lassie. I'll gladly be about proving my endurance to you."

Twenty

How wrong was it to pray for an eclipse?

Dani lay in Malcolm's arms, head on his chest, willing the sun not to rise and bring an end to her one night with him. But even now the abundance of candles they had lit in their exuberance to explore one another's bodies burned low. And the fact that he'd been a man of his word, repeatedly proving his "endurance," only made the approaching end of their time together that much harder to accept.

Her fingertip tingled as she traced the line of the tattoo over his heart, a perfect circle of what appeared to be spears, with runic writing at its center. Perfect except for a small bump of a scar across one of the spokes. It was meant for protection, he'd told her, a sign of Odin, from whose bloodline his family claimed descent. As the moment he would leave her to ride off to battle approached, she sent up prayers to her god and all of his that the protection ward would be effective.

"Would that the sun might slow its arrival this day. You were right, my love, I canna see how once will be enough."

She smiled as his voice rumbled in his chest and tickled her ear, unwilling to allow herself to waste her last hours with him drowning in sorrow and self-pity. Instead she chose to concentrate on the wonder that allowed them both to have shared a single thought with regard to the sun's arrival.

There would be time for sorrow after he'd gone.

"Losing you tears at my heart as wickedly as the knowledge that I canna countenance so much loss of life if I am able to prevent it."

Not a concern she'd ever thought to hear expressed by a medieval highland warrior.

"My aunt Jean used to say that, instead of sending men into battle, if they made the leaders square off against one another, there'd be way fewer wars."

His fingers combed through her hair, tracing the shape of her earlobe, sending a shiver of delight sparking down her spine.

Until his hand stilled.

"It occurs to me you present a possibility I'd no even considered."

"What?" she asked lazily, waiting for his hand to move again.

"Yer aunt Jean sounds to be a wise woman, love. She may well have had the right of it. Two leaders meeting face-to-face might well avert a battle."

He kissed the top of her head and slid out from under her, out of her grasp, out of the bed.

Dani's body tensed as she rolled over to watch him slipping into his clothes. What had she done? It had only been idle chatter. She hadn't been talking about him personally. Of all the things she didn't want, his risking his own personal safety was right at the top of the list.

"You're not thinking of doing something stupid, are you? You don't need to get dressed yet, you know. We still have a good hour or so before first light."

First light. When he'd leave her to join his men on a journey that would end in battle. With him as the leader.

Her stomach flip-flopped, forming a hard, sour knot as she anticipated what was going through his mind.

"Malcolm? Tell me you're not going to do what I think you are. Tell me you're not that foolish."

He finished knotting the leather around his waist before he came to her, gathering her in his arms to draw her close.

"It's no foolish to attempt to gain yer ends without sacrificing the lives of others. Those men are my friends, my kinsmen. They've women who care for them every bit as much as you do for me."

"Don't do this," she whispered, knowing even as she spoke he'd already made up his mind. "Those men won't thank you for leaving them behind, you know. It's not worth risking your life just because you're worried some of them might be harmed."

He cupped her face in his hands and placed a kiss on her forehead.

"It's no just their safety, love, though that should be enough in its own right. Think." He pulled her to him, covering her lips with his for a brief kiss. "If I've no call to use the MacKilyn men, I've no debt to the old laird. I'll be free to return to you. To many more nights such as the one we've just spent together."

Another kiss and he stood to retrieve his sword and sling it onto his back.

"If you return at all," she whispered, giving voice to her greatest fear.

"Here, now. None of that. The gods hear and favor confidence." He grinned as he leaned down to rummage in a wooden chest, standing up with a cloth roll he tucked under his arm. "I'd ask you to act as the warrior's woman you will be soon enough. Will you do that for me?"

Dani slid to the edge of the bed, her lips still tingling from his last kiss, wrapping the blanket around her body as she stood. "I'll try."

What else could she say? She wasn't about to send him out that door with more on his mind to distract him than he already had.

"Good. I need you to dress and station yerself in front of Patrick's door. It's yer best chance to catch him there before he goes to make ready the men. I need you to tell him what I'm about and to pass along to him my orders. He's no to follow me, but to wait here for any word I send. I hold him responsible to see that Dermid is kept here where he'll be safe, even as I hold him responsible to see to the safety of all our people here. I must do this on my own, to avoid unnecessary bloodshed. To reclaim my own life. Will you carry that word to him for me?"

She nodded, feeling too close to tears to attempt words.

Again he pulled her close, bending to kiss her. She fastened her arms around his neck, returning the kiss as if she might never feel his lips on hers again.

Fearing as he walked out of the room and closed the door behind him that indeed she might not.

Twenty-one

IF HE WERE to slice her throat now, to bleed her dry as she lay helpless in the thrall of her visions, he would never again suffer the vexation of her stubborn resistance.

He also would never learn the content of those visions. That knowledge alone stayed his hand.

Torquil of Katanes, laird of the MacDowylt, chosen son of Odin, looked out on the sparkling stars dotted across an inky night sky and roared in frustration.

At his feet, his half sister, Christiana, lay on a bed of cushions, lost in the visions that even now danced across her face in shadows he was at a loss to interpret.

That power had been denied him.

Delicate and fragile, she was the exact image of the dark-haired Tinkler whore his father had married after his mother's death. That the blood of his ancestors, the mighty Gods of Asgard, ran through her tainted body sickened him. That the power of the ancient *seid*, the magic of their ancestors, lay in her hands infuriated him. It was a power that should have been his.

The half-breed abominations his father had

spawned with the Tinkler were a stain on the world, an insult to the purity of their bloodline, for which he would never forgive his father. He had no doubt that Odin had never forgiven the old man, either, as evidenced by Alfor's recent death. It was Odin's punishment, as much as the potions he personally had prepared for his father, that had been to blame for Alfor's final days of suffering.

Now, as it should, it fell to him and him alone to redeem the family line and reclaim the greatness of their destiny. Before he was finished, the world would answer to him as it once had to his mighty ancestor.

Christiana moaned, tossing her head from side to side as if attempting to escape the hold of the gods' visions, and he nudged her side with the toe of his boot.

Another moan and her eyes fluttered open, a blue so darkly vivid, they were almost violet. Framed in a thick lace of black, the eyes of the old gods stared out at him.

Perhaps when she reached the end of her usefulness, before he tossed her body to its final indignity in the ground, he would carve out those eyes and give them the honor of the pyre their bloodline deserved.

"What did you see?" he demanded, stepping away from her. "Does Dermid yet return with the tribute from my southern holdings?"

She pushed herself up to sit, every movement a study of grace and fluidity, belying her filthy heritage.

"You haven't long to wait, Torquil. Even now I see my brother making preparations for his return to Tordenet Castle."

"Are his pack animals laden heavy with the Mac-Gahan silver?"

He wanted every coin in Malcolm's possession. He wanted his prideful half brother broken in spirit and, one day, in body. Oh, he knew of his father's wish to give the MacGahan holdings to Malcolm to possess for his own; he simply didn't choose to honor that wish. He and he alone deserved it all.

"My brother travels with no silver."

"What?" he yelled, pleased to see her flinch.

Pleased with her fear. She should fear him. And obey him. As long as she shared her gift of vision with him, he would allow her to live. Though he trusted her not, he knew that in the matter of relaying the visions, she was incapable of speaking anything but the truth, and therein lay her value.

"Why does he not carry my tribute with him?"

"The visions have not shown me this, my laird. Only that my brother makes preparations this very night for travel to Tordenet Castle."

"Without any silver," he added.

"Without any silver," she confirmed.

"Leave me," he ordered, turning his back when she lifted a hand for his assistance.

When she had gone from his tower, he leaned against the open window, hands fisted against the cold stone ledge, staring sightlessly into the black night.

Though she claimed Dermid only now prepared for his trip home, he wanted to see for himself. To know that his envoy had not yet set foot on his lands.

Only by verifying with his own eyes could he reassure himself that Christiana was incapable of trickery.

He stripped out of his clothing, folding each piece into a neat square and placing it carefully on the table beside him before stretching out on the cushions Christiana had vacated. A fleeting impression of heat left behind by his half sister's body skated over his skin, gone almost as quickly as it had appeared.

Breathing slowly, deeply, he closed his eyes and called on one of the powers of Odin that he did possess. It was necessary to concentrate on the attributes he required for his task. Accurate vision in the dark of night. Speed of travel to cover his land and view it from above.

A shape began to form in his mind.

The trance that had once taken him hours to accomplish was as child's play now, settling upon him in mere minutes. That which was the essence of him floated from his body, up, hovering near the ceiling to look down on himself where he lay. From here it was easy to admire the beauty and strength that housed his essence in the form of the body that lay below him, naked, open to his inspection.

Only a few hours until dawn.

Great wings flapped, stretching his muscles and propelling him forward to dive through the open window. The air caressed his feathers in an almost sensual experience, boosting him like a helping hand into the night sky. Soundlessly, he circled and dove, instinctively finding the currents to speed him on his way.

Below him, as Christiana had predicted, nary a single mortal trod his land other than those who had pledged him their fealty.

Through these eyes he saw everything in details of black and gray. But what he couldn't see, he could hear, targeting in on the tiniest of movements. Something small scurried for cover and he gave himself over to the need, death on a silent wing. The strike made, one sharp squeal from his victim, and then a mind-obliterating orgasm of pleasure as fresh, warm blood sprayed down his throat and across his face.

He left the corpse behind. He might inhabit the body of an owl, but he had not the beast's taste for rodent meat.

Instead he once again traveled the air currents, lifting and diving until, as the first rays of light lit the eastern sky, he reached his own window. Once inside, he cast off the form he had chosen, to settle back into his own body.

Opening his eyes, he stretched his limbs, the excitement of the evening's kill still thrumming through his body, exhibiting itself in a much more human form now. A much more human need.

He wiped a hand across his face and it came away streaked with blood. The need to clean himself wasn't unusual after one of his shifting trances. He relished it. It only enhanced the experience.

Pushing himself up to stand, he strode across the floor to throw open the door, and called out to his personal guard.

"Have a tub and hot water brought to me." When

the guard's eyes flickered down toward his swollen manhood, he laughed. "Yes, Ulfr, I'd have one of the maids sent up as well."

"Brenna, my laird?"

"Yes," he replied but was struck with another thought. "No! One of the dark-haired lasses, Ulfr."

"Aye, my laird," the man replied, hurrying away.

Torquil strolled back into his room, stopping at the bed of cushions on the floor, smiling as he rubbed his hand over his chest.

He would take the little dark-haired maid there. There on the bed where Christiana had lain.

Twenty-two

HAD IT BEEN only this morning Malcolm had wished the sun could delay its assent into the sky, allowing him time to linger with Dani in his arms? Now, at the opposite end of day, he wanted nothing so much as for the sun to hang where it was, forgoing its inevitable disappearance.

Perhaps the biggest disadvantage of a late-autumn assault was the shortness of the days.

Though he'd ridden since before daybreak, both he and his mount had miles left in them. Miles, perhaps, but not the light to cover them safely.

Ah, well. At least he'd made better distance traveling by himself than he could have at the head of an army. And without the worry over the well-being of his men.

At the crest of the next hill, he slowed his mount, stretching his legs and scanning the distance ahead for a likely campsite. Ahead lay a valley, where the setting sun already cast shadows of purple over the land. A stream ran its length, disappearing into a stand of trees.

Cover and water together in one place. That was

where he would make his camp for the night. As if his horse sensed his intent, the animal gave the run its all, reaching the trees in short order.

One look at the spot close up and Malcolm knew it had been as much fate as fortune that had led him here. A rowan tree, old and gnarled, spread its limbs out over the stream. Surely a good sign.

With a little effort, he was able to build a fire and set up camp all before the last rays of light deserted him. The moon, which had shined down on him the night before, hid herself this night, concealed in a cloud-filled sky.

Wrapped in his plaid for warmth, Malcolm sat under the rowan, too awake to even consider sleep. He caught up a small piece of branch from the pile he'd gathered and pulled out his knife, idly whittling at the wood to occupy his hands and pass the time.

Fire flickered in the pit before him, and as he stared into the flames dancing to the music of hissing wood, thoughts of Dani spun through his mind. Her eyes, her laughter, her body—they comforted him. Regardless of what fate Skuld had woven for him, he vowed to all the old gods of Asgard he would return to her when this was done. He would claim her for his very own in front of clan and kin.

With a sigh, he allowed his memory to fill with the woman the Fae had sent to him.

If he closed his eyes, it was almost as if he could relive their night together. He felt her as she'd lain beneath him in the shelter of another rowan tree, her eyes filled with want. Want of him.

He heard her laughter as they'd tumbled into his bed after lighting every candle they could find.

He saw her, her breasts heaving as she panted, her skin aglow with the exertion of their love-making.

He smiled at the memory of how he'd very nearly disgraced himself the first time he'd taken her, with no more ability to control himself than an untried lad on his first go at a woman. But he'd recovered, and quite nicely, too, redeeming himself throughout the night. Repeatedly.

And Dani!

He dropped the wood to his lap, giving up all pretense of work to immerse himself entirely in the memory.

The woman was amazing. Fearless. Adventurous in more ways than ever he could have guessed. He'd no doubt she could teach the strumpets of Edinburgh a trick or two. Hell, he'd no doubt but that she could teach the strumpets of London a thing or two. She'd certainly managed to satisfy his lusty appetite.

With a sigh, he returned to the piece of wood in his lap that was already taking shape. He would carve for her a fork, a small one, exactly like the one she'd asked for all those days ago.

He concentrated on the wood in his hands, trying to imagine her pleasure when he returned to her, bearing this gift.

Out beyond the light of the fire, a dry twig snapped, ending Malcolm's pleasant reverie. Though he was instantly alert, he didn't move at all. No sense in alerting whatever, whoever, watched that he was aware.

Animal? Possible. But man was equally possible, especially considering the tingle around the mark on his chest.

He sensed no imminent danger. This was different. Simply a watcher, and not of the forest animal variety.

His position was strong enough. The rowan and stream at his back, a mound of rocks to his left. By instinct he'd considered defense when he'd made camp. It was a place he could well defend if the necessity presented itself.

With the situation fully assessed, he rose to his feet, drawing his sword as he did, making no attempt to disguise its distinctive metallic ring.

"I ken yer out there. Come in to the fire and show yerself."

Whoever it was, he'd prefer to confront them now rather than wait until they could become a threat.

A short silence was followed by a general crunch of undergrowth, his mystery watcher no longer making any effort to conceal himself as he and, from the sound of it, his horse approached.

It should have been more of a surprise when Dermid stepped into the circle of light.

"And what is it you think yer doing here?" And after he'd made it perfectly clear the lad was not to come with him.

"I followed you."

"Alone?"

From the moment Dermid had arrived at Castle MacGahan, he hadn't taken two steps outside the shadow of his guardsman Rauf.

"Aye. I was sleeping it off in the stable and I awoke to find you readying yerself and yer horse. I waited until you left and then I followed. I'd no time to tell anyone I was going." Dermid ducked his head sheepishly, casting a glance to the fire. "I dinna suppose you've an extra morsel? I've no had anything to eat since last night." His stomach growled loudly as if to corroborate his story.

Malcolm resheathed his sword and squatted next to his pack. In short order he'd pulled out a sampling of the food he carried to hand over to his brother.

"I thought I made it clear you were to stay behind."

Dermid nodded, eagerly stuffing a chunk of bread into his mouth. "Aye, that you did, Colm. But that was when I thought you planned to lead an army against Torquil. Since you go alone, I'm thinking you've decided to take him his silver after all?"

Malcolm tossed a skin of ale to the lad, fearing he might choke on the dry food he stuffed into his face.

"I carry no silver."

Hand midway to his mouth, Dermid paused. "Then what do you think to do? Surely yer no about stealing Christiana from under his very nose? You ken the enormity of such a task, aye?"

More or less, that was exactly his plan, if a plan it could be called.

"I go to counsel with our brother. Torquil's an intelligent man. I've faith he'll see the reason to my argument."

Dermid snorted his disbelief. "You canna expect me to believe what you say. We all ken there's no love lost between you and Torquil. It's a good thing I followed you. I can help you."

Malcolm should have realized his brother wouldn't be so easily dissuaded. "I spent as many years at Tordenet Castle as you have, lad. I've no a need for you to guide me about the passageways."

"Mayhap." Dermid shrugged. "But I've been there more recently than you. I ken the habits and the practices of our brother. I can show you the weaknesses in his underbelly. You need me, Colm, even as I need to go with you."

Malcolm studied his youngest brother. Maybe the lad was right. Maybe he did need to go along. To prove something of his manhood to himself. So be it, so long as he stayed out of harm's way.

"You can come along on one condition. I'll have yer promise that you'll no enter the castle gates. I want yer word that you'll remain outside, where you can make yer escape if it comes to that. Will you swear to it?"

Excitement danced like the reflection of the flames in Dermid's eyes as he shook his head up and down, his mouth stuffed overfull with the last of the meat and bread Malcolm had given him.

Malcolm sent up a brief prayer to Odin that he might not regret the decision he'd just made.

Twenty-three

I'VE A FEELING I don't like. A bothersome gnat of worry pestering away at the back of my mind."

Dani glanced to the woman at her side as they hurried down the hallway, her stomach fluttering with its own share of pesky gnats. She was stressed enough about Malcolm and his stubborn-headed plan all on her own. But having the Faerie confirm her concerns? That was enough to push her right over the edge.

Elesyria patted a hand to her hair as they approached the carved wooden door of Malcolm's solar.

"I'm sure I'll feel better once we've had a talk with Patrick."

Dani wished she could muster the same kind of confidence in Patrick that Elesyria demonstrated.

Though the door itself stood ajar, it was the angry voice blustering out of the opening that stopped them a few feet away.

"What do you mean, you canna find him?"

Dani pushed aside Elesyria's outstretched arm to step closer. Close enough, in fact, to allow her to see who was on the receiving end of Patrick's tirade.

Rauf.

"What kind of sorry excuse for a groomsman are you that you've lost my brother? Yer only task as far as I can see is to watch over him."

Not that she should care that Dermid's grooms-man was getting royally reamed. The man absolutely gave her the creeps, always showing up at every corner she turned, like some cartoon spy.

But from here, observing his face, it was obvious the man was utterly distressed.

"Dani!"

Elesyria's whisper of caution went unheeded. Damn, but she hated always feeling sorry for the underdog. Rauf might be a weasel of a man, but there was no way she was going to stand here and allow this browbeating to continue while the man in there visibly shivered in discomfort.

"What's going on in here?" she demanded, pushing the door open and stalking into the room, Elesyria at her heels.

Patrick arched an eyebrow in their direction. "Am I to believe that in yer homeland, my lady, people dinna knock before they enter?"

Snide was so not going to work with her.

"Oh, we knock." Dani moved fully into the room to stand at Rauf's side. "But we're not kept out by bullying blowhards. Now, how about we have this discussion without all that yelling."

For a moment she wondered if Patrick might not turn his anger her direction, especially when Elesyria reached out to clasp her hand.

Instead, he sat down at the table and steepled his hands in front of him, his usual mask devoid of emotion firmly back in place.

"Though I dinna recall having invited you to be part of this discussion, perhaps you can assist Rauf here in explaining how he's managed to lose track of my brother's whereabouts. Especially considering that Dermid's whereabouts were the only thing he was tasked with keeping track of."

His mask appeared to have a crack or two in it.

"As I've already tried to explain, Master Patrick, I searched the entirety of the castle when I awoke and realized yer brother had no slept in his bed. It was near sunrise by the time I found his horse was gone as well."

"What?" Patrick was on his feet again, his fist pounding down on the table.

No mask at all now, only raw emotion on display.

Elesyria dropped her grip on Dani and skimmed around the table to place a hand on Patrick's shoulder. "More flies with honey," she murmured.

Once again, mask in place, Patrick took his seat. "You dinna share the news that my brother's horse was missing as well."

"I tried, Master Patrick, but . . ." The man's bravado seemed to fail him under the burn of Patrick's glare.

"Maybe if you hadn't been yelling at him," Dani interjected. "Perhaps then he might have gotten the whole story out."

Patrick's glower fell on her before turning back to

the original target of his displeasure. "You've done what you can for now, Rauf. Come to me immediately if you learn anything else. Begone with you now. And close the door behind you. Firmly."

Dani crossed her arms in front of her, holding her tongue as the groomsman scurried out.

"You realize Dermid has likely gone after Malcolm, do you no?" Patrick tapped one long finger against the tabletop. "You realize as well, that being the case, Malcolm will no be pleased in the least."

She nodded her agreement. Of all the things Malcolm would be if Dermid caught up with him, pleased was not one of them. Especially considering that an admonishment to see to Dermid's safety had been part of the instructions he'd had her give to Patrick early this very morning.

Looking at it from that perspective, Patrick's reaction made a lot more sense.

"I dinna suppose you showed up here solely to rescue poor old Rauf, now did you?"

"Hardly. The man makes my skin crawl." Elesyria began to pace, much as she had in Dani's bedchamber before they'd come down here. "I suppose it could be possible that this was what I felt," she murmured, as if to herself.

"Well then, since it's no Rauf you came for, do you plan to tell me what brought you here or am I to guess yer purpose, Elf?"

"Elesyria's worried." Dani chose to leap into the void, none too comforted by the flash in the Faerie's glare.

"About?" Patrick prodded.

"About your brother." Elesyria stopped her pacing to face him. "I awoke early this morning to a nagging disquiet. I can feel something is wrong, something evil on the move, though I cannot tell what or from where it originates. I know only that it stalks your brother."

"By the gods!" Patrick was on his feet and across the room in three strides, grasping Elesyria by the shoulders. "Tell me all that you see, Elf."

She jerked her shoulder from his grasp and backed away. "I *see* nothing, you foolish Northman. I have no gift of vision. I simply have a feeling. And my feelings are rarely wrong."

"Forgive me, Elesyria." Patrick dipped his head in an obvious show of apology. "It's no you what's earned my anger. Only myself. Bad enough it is that I failed Malcolm's instructions. But to have you confirm the truth that my brother is in danger, that's the rub of it. I should have locked Dermid in the dungeons. That would have kept him safe."

"Dermid?"

The expression on Elesyria's face set a knot of panic rising in Dani's stomach.

"You misunderstand what I'm trying to tell you, Patrick. Dermid is not the brother of whom I speak. The evil I sense stalks Malcolm."

Twenty-four

THERE WOULD BE no fire to warm them this night.

Malcolm glanced across the clearing to where Dermid huddled into the curve of the great stones, his furs completely obscuring his head and body.

"Rest well, little brother. We move at first light."

Dermid's reply drifted back to him, barely intelligible from under the layers of fur covering the lad.

For days now, they'd traveled long and hard to reach the MacDowylt lands as quickly as they had. With a little luck, exhaustion would take its toll and his brother would fall asleep quickly.

Malcolm tightened his furs around him, refusing to think upon the pleasures of a fire even as he shivered with the cold. His new life of comfort was taking its toll, turning a warrior soft. And everyone knew a soft warrior was a dead warrior.

Fire was a luxury he could ill afford this night. Torquil was too close.

Well enough he knew the potential of his half brother's abilities. His father, who himself had possessed the talent to send his enemies running from the battlefield in abject fear, had often alluded to the wealth of Odin's power that resided in Torquil's hands.

No sense going out of their way to draw his eye to their presence.

Across the clearing, the mound of fur that was his brother rolled over and curled into a ball.

"Sleep, little brother," Malcolm whispered into the wind, sending the words like a prayer to be heard by the gods.

Or at least by one god. Well he could use Odin's favor this night.

In spite of the plans he'd gone over with Dermid as they'd eaten their cold meal, he had no intention of risking his brother in his attempt to free Christiana. He would not sacrifice one sibling for another. Instead, he would wait until he was sure the boy slept and then he would be on his way to do what must be done.

Though he'd shared the scope of his plans, he had intentionally misled his brother on the timing. That Dermid believed they would begin their assault on Tordenet Castle at first light further served to convince Malcolm that his brother was no warrior. Only a fool would forgo the cover of a moonless night.

Nose cocooned in the warm furs, he waited, his mind drifting to thoughts more pleasant than what he would face in but a few hours.

A sparkle of colors shimmered and coalesced in his mind, forming itself into a vision of Dani. Her visage wavered across the backs of his closed eyelids as if he watched her moving directly in front of him, as if he were looking through a hole into his own chamber at Castle MacGahan. She stood by his bed, gently gliding her hand across his pillow before she shouldered out of her robe and climbed under the covers.

It was as if he could feel the warmth of her body next to his, stretched out against him, one slender foot tracking its way up and down his calf.

He kept his eyes closed tightly, fearing the sensation would fade at any moment.

In the vision, he pulled back the blankets covering Dani's body and grasped the hem of the gown she wore, lifting it up and over her head and tossing it to the floor. He skimmed his lips down the soft skin of her cheeks and neck to bury his face between her firm, rounded breasts. Her breath caught with a gasp and her back arched even as tiny shiver bumps arose on her skin.

Never would he tire of her body's instant reaction to his touch.

Willingly she opened to him as he slid a hand across her belly and down to the juncture between her legs. A soft moan was his reward when his thumb began a lazy circle against the small, hard nub that inflamed her desire. A soft moan that inflamed his desire as well.

One finger and then two he dipped inside her heat, continuing the motion he had begun.

Her hips lifted from the bed and the walls of her sheath clenched rhythmically around his fingers, even as she grabbed for his hands.

"Now, Malcolm," she panted as she pulled him to her. "Now is the time."

His head jerked forward and his eyes flew open.

A moment of panic assailed him as he realized he'd foolishly allowed himself to drift off, dreams of the woman he wanted holding him captive in the arms of sleep.

A quick scan of the sky reassured him that he'd dozed for a thankfully short time. Obviously, Dermid hadn't been the only one to taste the exhaustion of their strenuous journey.

He stood, allowing the night air to cool the heat that throbbed through his body. Heat that had nothing to do with the furs he'd wrapped around himself.

A check across the clearing showed no movement from the mound of furs that covered his brother. It was the moment he'd awaited.

As quietly as possible, he gathered his sword and his pack and slipped away from the circle into the sheltering cover of the night.

He was close enough now not to need his mount. He'd make better time on foot. The ground he covered as he neared his destination would be treacherous for the large animal, and he'd have nowhere to safely hide the horse when he did enter the castle.

Stealth was his ally this night. Stealth and the secret entrance to Tordenet Castle his father had shown him after a hunting jaunt on his twelfth birthday.

Since Dermid had been unaware of the entrance when he'd mentioned it as they'd gone over their plans, he had reason to hope no others would know of its existence either.

Time would tell.

The outline of Tordenet Castle loomed ahead of him and he circled to the north, keeping to the cover of stone and brush as he made his way to the rock face at the water's edge. Slipping and sliding on the gravel, he lowered himself over the rim to hunt for the brush-shrouded entry to the tunnel his father had shown him.

Nothing had changed, allowing him to locate the well-hidden entrance without much effort. The underbrush had the weathered appearance of undisturbed growth—all the more reason to feel confident in his plan.

If only he could muster the actual confidence all the signs would seem to indicate was warranted.

Instead, the mark on his chest burned a warning of friction as if a million midges beat their wings against his skin.

Worry about the brother he'd left behind, no doubt. Worry about the sister residing within these walls.

He pushed the old growth aside to crawl through the narrow entrance. When he was a child, it had seemed so much larger to him. Pitch black awaited him as he dropped down inside and began to edge his way up the slope, one hand braced against the side of the confining passageway. He moved slowly, following the curve of the wall until the faint shaft of light behind him was no more than a memory.

Ahead of him stretched an unnatural dark he had been spared before by his father's torch.

There was no torch this time.

The passage narrowed here; he remembered even as child feeling hemmed in. His shoulders touched the walls on both sides and he was forced to dip his head to continue forward.

A few more steps and a light flashed in the tunnel ahead of him, blinding him with its brilliance after so long without his vision. He would have drawn his weapon but there was no space. He barely had room to lift a hand to shield his eyes from the blinding glow.

A figure stepped into the light, the radiance surrounding him like a golden halo. In his hand he held aloft a shining sword.

Torquil.

"And so the prodigal son returns. But why, I wonder, would he choose an entrance such as this rather than the front gates?"

A flash of movement where Torquil had stood and a fire of pain consumed Malcolm's chest, all but doubling him over in its intensity.

Torquil had moved in, not two feet separating them, the hilt of his sword flat out, the blade leading toward . . .

Malcolm's head dropped forward, too heavy to hold up any longer. His gaze followed the length of his brother's blade to its destination, buried in his own chest, a ribbon of dark red blood flowing down where already it pooled on the stones at his feet.

"Welcome home, little brother," Torquil murmured, his voice somewhere nearby. "Be grateful I don't take yer head."

The sword was withdrawn from Malcolm's body and he crumpled, feeling himself falling forward into a void much blacker than even the tunnel he'd traversed this night, his ears assaulted by the sound of his brother's laughter until he could hear no more.

Twenty-five

DANI JOLTED AWAKE with a jerk, her pulse racing as if she'd had one of those awful nightmares of falling helplessly through space.

Only it wasn't falling that had awakened her. And it certainly hadn't been a nightmare.

She sat up in the big bed, gathering the covers around her that she'd apparently kicked away in the throes of her dream. Lord, she should have known better than to tempt fate by sleeping in Malcolm's bed after the things they'd done here less than a week ago.

Sliding to the edge of the bed, she swung her feet to the floor, realizing as she did that somewhere in the course of the dream she'd even managed to strip out of her nightgown.

Her body aching with unfulfilled need, she bent to retrieve her clothing and drop it over her head. Even as she slipped the long robe on over her gown, she knew there would be no more sleep for her tonight. Not with her heart pounding and her pulse racing the way it was.

If she were back home, she'd make a beeline for

the kitchen for some cookies and milk. A moment to consider the idea and, although there were no milk and cookies waiting, she decided to head for the kitchen anyway. There had to be something she could find to nibble on.

She lit a candle from the fire and slipped out into the hallway. At the top of the stairs she smiled in spite of herself at her foolish behavior. This running to the kitchen when she thought about Malcolm had better not become a habit or she'd weigh a ton by the time he returned.

The long stone staircase seemed even more intimidating than usual by the flickering light of a single candle, and she held a hand against the wall to steady her descent.

Rather than go through the huge gathering room, she opted to take the back halls. They were narrow and winding, but a less intimidating option. The great hall was depressingly cavernous in the light of day with both of the big fires burning. She didn't want to even consider what it would feel like to walk through there now with nothing more than the glow of embers to light her way.

When she reached the kitchen and slipped inside she was surprised to see another candle already burning. Elesyria sat on a bench, leaning over onto a small table in the corner, a clay bowl and a goblet in front of her.

"Your dreams wake you up, too?" Dani asked.

The Faerie shook her head and waved her arm, motioning for Dani to sit beside her.

"Would that I might be able to get to sleep to have dreams." She popped a bite into her mouth and sighed. "Tell me of your dreams, Dani. Perhaps a story will soothe my unease."

Elesyria might be the closest thing she had to a good friend here, but that still didn't mean Dani was comfortable sharing what she considered intimate details.

"Let's just say it was, bar none, the most realistic dream I've ever had and we'll leave it at that."

Dani sat down and reached into the bowl Elesyria offered, delighted to find it contained bits of dried fruit and nuts. It wasn't cookies, but it would do.

"Good dream or bad?" her friend prompted.

"Good," she responded without hesitation. "Way good. So good that I think my heart might still be racing from it."

Elesyria's back straightened and her eyes lit with interest. "Was it Malcolm you dreamed of by any chance? An intimate dream?"

Heat flooded Dani's face. "I thought I was pretty clear that we weren't going into details here."

"The Soul Bonding," Elesyria whispered, clasping her hands together. "You did not tell me you'd consummated your relationship before Malcolm left."

"Damn straight I didn't tell you. And I won't be telling you anything like that now either." Dani scooped up a handful of fruit but didn't eat. "Besides, what makes you think we did? And what's that Soul Bonding thing you were talking about?"

"I no longer have to think, my dear. I know." Elesyria chuckled and ran her finger idly around the edge of her goblet. "It's the 'Soul Bonding thing,' as you call it, that tells me, you see. Once you've bonded with your SoulMate, your senses function on a different level. I've even heard stories about Bonded couples who experience one another's emotions and some who can communicate by thought over vast distances. Still, Dream Mating is one of the rarest gifts among SoulMates."

Dream-Mating. Another bizarre experience she could lay at the feet of the Fae.

And since they were sharing . . .

"What about you? Did you ever experience any of those things with your SoulMate?"

"You mistake me, Dani. I've never had the good fortune to find my SoulMate. Not in this life, anyway. And let me assure you, this life has been a very long one by your standards."

"But you have a . . . had a child."

"Have. Isabella yet lives, just in a different time. You of all people should understand that. And as for my having a child, well"—a wicked little smile curved Elesyria's lips—"surely you don't need me to explain to you the mechanics of how that is accomplished."

"No." Dani felt the heat returning to her face. "But what about Isabella's father? You must have loved him."

"Of course, I did." Elesyria picked through the bowl, appearing to search for her favorite tidbits. "But love and true love are completely different creatures. Thom was good man and I did love him. But he was not my true love. The paths my SoulMate and I travel have not yet crossed." She shook her head, as if to clear away bothersome thoughts.

Dani refused the bowl when Elesyria offered again. It wasn't bad enough she was down here stuffing her face, all but gloating over her own good fortune. Now she'd depressed her friend with all her questions.

"So. We know why I'm here. What's brought you down to the kitchens in the middle of the night?"

Elesyria's eyes darted to the bowl in her hand. "Perhaps it's time we both make another try at sleep."

"No, I don't think so." Fair was fair. "I shared with you even though I didn't want to. Now it's your turn."

Her friend carefully set the bowl on the table, pushing it away from her before looking up to meet Dani's gaze.

"I cannot escape that which I feel is to come. Whatever evil stalks Malcolm's path, it has found him this night."

Dani swallowed, her throat tight and dry. Only moments ago she'd thought to ask for fairness, and fairness was now on evident display. First she'd managed to depress Elesyria with talk of SoulMates and now the Faerie had returned the favor by finding the one thing in the world guaranteed to depress her.

The threat of losing the SoulMate she'd only just found.

Twenty-six

AN UNRELENTING HAZE of pain fogged Malcolm's mind even as he struggled to open his eyes.

The room spun around him and he blinked, slowly, carefully, trying to determine where he might be. Vaguely, as if in a dream, he remembered a blinding light that, praise Odin, was no longer present. Only the dull flicker of a candle somewhere in the room served to illuminate his surroundings now.

His head lolled forward, his chin resting on his chest, and he breathed through the pain lancing across his shoulders. His arms felt oddly out of kilter, as if some giant attempted to pull them from the sockets where they belonged.

Once again he lifted his head and forced his eyes open.

In the corner lay a pile of blankets and furs, with what looked suspiciously like his pack and saddle tossed upon them. That seemed wrong somehow, though he couldn't quite remember why it wasn't possible for his things to be with him.

A wooden door on the far side of the room appeared the only means of entry or exit. At its very top, a small opening was blocked by a thick metal grate. No windows in the room that he could see. Straw covering the floor. Chains hanging from the walls.

Chains like the ones holding his arms above his head.

He stumbled to his feet and leaned his weight against the cold stone wall behind him, alleviating the pressure on his arms.

Less pain. Better.

He was a prisoner!

The realization surprised him, loosing whatever barrier had clouded his mind. Memories flooded back in short, broken scenes. He'd been in the tunnel entrance to the castle when white light had exploded around him, burning his eyes with its intensity.

"Torquil."

The name slipped from his lips like a curse and he dropped his head to study his chest. Dried blood colored his shirt where his brother had pierced him with his sword.

Not for the first time.

He'd been twelve when Torquil, seven years his senior, had goaded him into a practice round in the lists. Only Torquil hadn't used a practice sword.

His half brother had professed it had been an accident as Malcolm had lain on the ground, the world turning black around him as blood pumped from his chest. He'd awoken in his father's bed, his mother bending over him, wiping his forehead with a wet cloth, her face pinched with worry.

"It's the Alfodr's protection what saved you, lad," his father had claimed. *"See for yerself. He's marked you as one of his own warriors."*

His father had lifted the compress from his chest and there, covering his heart, surrounding the torn flesh of his wound, he saw Odin's Mark.

To this day, Malcolm had no idea how it had gotten there.

Through the Magic of Odin's protection, he had somehow survived that first attack. Apparently Torquil had thought to have another go at it.

Across the room, metal scratched against metal and the door opened just enough to allow a small figure to slip inside.

Christiana.

"So it's true," she said quietly, hurrying across the room to his side. "Oh, Colm. What have they done to you?"

She reached up and placed her fingers over the bloom of dried blood on his shirt, her face wearing the same pinched expression he remembered seeing on his mother's face all those years ago.

"No *they*, little sister. It was *him* what did this." He had no need to protect Torquil now. Not that he really thought she would doubt the truth of it.

"I know." She nodded her head, her eyes scanning over his body. "Yer wrists are raw around the irons. Shall I find a damp cloth for you?"

"No." She wouldn't be able to use it on him anyway. The top of her head barely reached his shoulder. Though she had grown in the time since he'd seen her last. "You've filled out, lass. Yer no so scrawny as you were."

"As well I should have, dinna you think? You've been gone long, my brother. I'll be twenty come Yule."

How negligent he'd been to leave her under Torquil's dominion for so long.

"I'm here now. I've come to take you away." As he should have done long ago.

"You shouldn't have come at all. You had to ken it would no be safe for you here. No with Father gone."

"It is what it is." Malcolm caught his breath, waiting as another pain lanced through his chest. Thank Freya, they seemed to be growing weaker at last. "I'm here to rescue you."

The corners of his sister's lips twitched and for a moment he wasn't sure if she were going to smile or cry.

"Aye, well, yer rescue seems to have run into a bit of trouble, from the looks of it. If we can but convince our brother to set you free, you must leave at once and never return, are you clear on that?"

He shook his head stubbornly, ignoring the wave of dizziness it caused. "You need to be away from this place, little sister. You need to be rescued."

"That I do, Colm. And I will be in time. But no by you. You must believe me in this. I've seen it." She snapped her head toward the door and then turned back, leaning in close to him. "Trust me on this, beloved brother."

His pride stung that his sister should feel the need to protect him with stories designed to send him scurrying away to his own safety. But there was no time for argument. Before he could respond, the door swung open wide, admitting Torquil, flanked by two men on either side.

"What a touching scene we interrupt," Torquil sneered. "A family reunion, is it? And you dinna think to invite me?"

Christiana turned to face her elder brother, lifting her chin as she did so. "I heard whispers from the servants that Colm had returned. That he'd returned as a prisoner in our own dungeons. I had need to see his condition for myself."

His sister was a MacDowylt through and through, brave beyond all good sense.

"And now that you've seen for yourself, go back to yer chambers, Christiana. Unless you fancy keeping Malcolm company on a more permanent basis." Torquil lifted a hand, motioning toward the wall. "We've chains and irons aplenty if that's yer wish."

"You must send him away, Torquil. Free him and send him away at once."

"You've seen this?" he asked, edging closer to her.

Malcolm recognized the hesitation on her face, as he was sure Torquil did. Christiana's gift allowed her glimpses of what was to come, but the knowledge came with a price. She could not utter a falsehood about what she had seen. Torquil knew that as well as he did.

"No," she answered on a sigh. "I have not seen this. But I believe it to be so."

Torquil chuckled, looking from one sibling to the other. "Your blind loyalty is admirable, Christiana. Too bad you give it to the wrong brother." He snapped his fingers and held one hand aloft. "Take her to her chambers and see that she remains there."

One of the guards stepped up to Christiana's side and, with a nod, followed her to the door, where she paused.

"Odin's blessing be upon you for a safe trip home, Malcolm," she called over her shoulder, before resuming her sedate pace through the door and up the stairs beyond.

When the door closed, Torquil began to pace back and forth, arms clasped behind him. Once, twice, three times he passed before he came to a stop in front of Malcolm.

"Return home? That, I can assure you, will take more than Odin's blessings to accomplish. Did you take me for a fool? Did you think I'd no realize you were here? That you walked upon my land?" He shook his head as if sorely disappointed. "I expected better from so great a warrior as you claim yerself to be."

"I seem to have grown careless in my ways."

Though how Torquil had known was another matter. The Mark of Protection prevented his brother from sensing Malcolm's presence, so there had to have been another means of discovery.

"Indeed, you have." Torquil nodded his head in agreement. "Too long spent in the easy life, playing laird of my new holdings. Well, we'll have to see if we can't change that. Ulfr, come! You remember Ulfr, don't you? He's captain of my personal guard now."

Torquil motioned toward Malcolm, and Ulfr approached, a large key dangling from his hand. The enormous guardsman, who had long been a favorite of Torquil's, jerked at the chains above Malcolm's head, sending a new fire of agony shooting through his wrists and arms.

Malcolm clenched his teeth, determined his captors would see no sign of his pain.

Even as the chains rattled to a noisy pile on the floor, another noise drew Malcolm's attention. A scraping of wood against stone in the corner of the room.

It took all the willpower at his command not to fight against what he knew was to come as two of Torquil's men dragged him across the room. Fighting now, with his strength not yet restored, would do him more harm than good.

His mind raced to come up with something—anything—that might keep him out of the death hole. But while escape from such a place was beyond unlikely, ending up down there with fresh wounds could only serve to hasten his demise.

He'd need to bide his time. Build his strength. Pray for an opportunity.

"You surprise me, Torquil. I dinna think even you

would stoop to so low as to toss yer own brother into the oubliette."

"And what a great pleasure it is to be able to surprise you yet."

The stench wafting up out of the hole was itself enough to gag a man. When he turned to face Torquil, his brother had already pulled a cloth from his pocket to cover his nose.

"There, there, little brother. Think on the advantages I am about to afford you. No luxuries here. Perhaps you'll regain that sharp edge you used to value so much." Behind the cloth he chuckled. "That or you'll rot."

Malcolm had only a second to prepare himself before the men on either side shoved against him and he pitched over the edge of the opening into the black hell below. He landed hard, knocking the air from his lungs as his shoulder took the brunt of the fall onto the slimy, straw-covered stones.

With an effort, he rolled to his back, staring up through the hole above him.

As if he'd already dismissed Malcolm from his mind, Torquil had turned his back.

"Have Dermid brought to my chambers. I would speak with him now."

The words echoed down to Malcolm seconds before the heavy wooden covering was replaced over the opening to the oubliette.

They'd found Dermid!

That explained why seeing his things in the room above had felt wrong. He'd left them behind at the campsite when he'd set out for the castle. Obviously, when they'd captured Dermid, they'd gathered up everything at the site.

Malcolm dragged himself to the wall and leaned his weight against it. His priority had to be regaining his strength if he was to have any chance at escape.

And escape was no longer just an option, but an imperative now, because the lives of both his sister and his brother hung in the balance.

Twenty-seven

WHAT DID IT mean when a Faerie wouldn't look you in the eye?

Dani doubted it could be anything good.

"Very little is known about Dream Mating. Not just because it's so rare, but also because when it does occur our people view it as an intensely personal and private event."

In spite of the cold, Elesyria had assured her a walk in the gardens would do her good. She claimed it had been one of her favorite pastimes when she'd lived at Castle MacGahan as a new bride.

For Dani it simply felt depressing to wander among the rows of dead plants. And if there was anything she didn't need right now, it was another way to depress herself. She was doing just fine in that regard all on her own.

"I can see how that would be the case." She certainly had no intention of sharing all the particulars of her experience. "But what do you think it means that for the past week I haven't been able to see Malcolm at all in my dreams? It's as if a door has been slammed in my face each time I close my eyes." As if he didn't even exist. A big black door. Or maybe a curtain. Or a shroud. "You've got to have at least a guess. Please, Elesyria. I need your honesty. I'm making myself sick imagining all sorts of horrible things."

They'd reached a bench at the far end of the garden and Elesyria sat, patting the spot beside her in invitation to Dani.

"As long as you understand this is pure speculation on my part." The Faerie's lips pursed as if she carefully considered the words she would say. "I can think of only two reasons. The first is very likely the one you've already considered yourself. That something has happened to Malcolm."

Yep. That was the big one that haunted her thoughts every single moment of the day.

"And the other?"

If there was any hope at all to hang onto, she was desperate for it.

"Perhaps Malcolm himself has shut that door. Perhaps he has reason not to want you wherever he is right now."

Not want her with him? But why would he—

"Lady Danielle!" Jeanne, the kitchen maid, scrambled through the brambles of dead plants, not taking the time to stay to the paths. "I've been searching everywhere for you." She held a hand to her chest, panting as if she'd been running.

"And now you've found her," Elesyria pointed out. "What is it you want, girl?"

"Laird Malcolm's brother has returned. Him and

his man both. I saw them enter into the bailey with my own eyes and I began my search for you."

"Malcolm?" Dani asked, knowing what the answer would be even before the girl shook her head.

"No, my lady. Just his brother and the man who rides with him."

"Where did you see them last?" Elesyria asked.

"Mounting the stairs to the keep."

Dani didn't wait to see what else Jeanne might have to say or even to see if Elesyria followed. She was on her feet and running. Since the men would most likely report in to Patrick before anything else, that was where she was headed, too.

The news the kitchen maid carried weighed heavily on her heart.

Dermid had returned to Castle MacGahan. Dermid and his man Rauf.

Without Malcolm.

There could be any number of explanations for that, she reasoned, forcing herself to slow the pace that already drew stares from those she passed.

Rauf had disappeared the same day they'd discovered Dermid missing. Perhaps the groomsman had simply hunted down his charge and returned him here. Perhaps they'd never even caught up with Malcolm.

Perhaps they carried news that Malcolm was dead.

Dani lifted her skirts and ran. To hell with what people thought. Right now she only cared about locating Patrick and finding out what had actually happened.

She'd be no trouble at all. Just discreetly slip into the room and wait quietly to observe what Dermid had to say.

Out of breath, she rounded the corner and skidded to a stop outside the laird's solar. She debated only a second before fisting her hand to knock upon the closed door.

"Dani! Wait!"

Ignoring Elesyria's call from farther down the hallway, she pounded once and then again before throwing her weight against the door, her plans for discretion completely forgotten.

Elesyria reached her side just as the door opened and she pitched forward, stumbling into Patrick's broad chest.

"And why am I not surprised to find the two of you here?" he asked, his hands at Dani's elbows to steady her.

"Where's Malcolm?" she demanded over his shoulder when she caught sight of Dermid and Rauf. "What's happened to him?"

"I dinna suppose you'd be willing to wait in yer chambers and leave this to me to handle?" Patrick looked from Dani to Elesyria and back again. "No. I dinna think so. Then I'll thank you to have a seat and be quiet while I get to the bottom of what my brother has to tell me."

Patrick held on to her elbow as he walked her over to a chair at the side of the room and she sat. Elesyria took the seat next to hers, catching up her hand to hold once she was seated, too.

"My apologies for the interruption," Patrick began with an annoyed look in her direction. "Perhaps you'd begin again at the beginning for the benefit of our . . . guests."

"Torquil demands twice the silver he originally required. One portion for homage to yer rightful laird and one portion to secure Malcolm's release."

Dani straightened in her chair. *Malcolm's release? Then he lived? He lived!*

"Ransom, you mean," Patrick interpreted.

Dermid shrugged. "I only deliver Torquil's words as they were passed to me. Yer to pay and I'm to return with the silver. He says to tell you that if you attempt to follow, Malcolm's blood will be on yer hands."

Patrick sank into a chair at the table, his finger tapping out a tattoo in the momentary silence.

"You've a hard journey behind you, Dermid. I'll have food sent to yer chamber for you. You'll need yer rest to recover yer strength."

"As you say, brother. A hard journey behind and another ahead." With a nod first to Patrick and then one in Dani's general direction, Dermid left, Rauf at his heels as always.

Dani had restrained herself as long as she could. "What are you going to do?"

Patrick shook his head, his finger still tapping. "I canna say as yet, though I'm no at all pleased with the idea of sending Dermid back into the enemy's nest. And I've little doubt that Malcolm would agree with me on that count."

No, Malcolm likely wouldn't approve of sending

Dermid back, either. But she didn't approve of leaving Malcolm to whatever it was that he didn't want her to see behind that black door.

"Then why don't you go ahead with your original plan. Lead the army you intended to use to save Christiana and free them both."

Yes, it would mean Malcolm would be indebted to the MacKilyn, but she would rather lose Malcolm to another woman a million times over than have him killed.

Again Patrick shook his head. "We might well have had a chance before. But Torquil is aware of our intent now and will likely expect that of me. He'll no be caught off guard to an army's approach as long as he holds Colm. I'll have to devise another plan, though at the moment, I'm at a loss as to how to get enough armed men in there to make a difference."

"You need to start with what it is Torquil wants." Elesyria had risen to her feet and was pacing the length of the room. "Your wealth, to begin with, since he's doubled the amount of silver he's asking for. What else?"

"Knowing my brother? As much as he can get. Money and fealty. And if he can humiliate and destroy Malcolm in the process, so much the better in his eyes."

Dani didn't need to meet this Torquil character to know he was someone she didn't like.

"Then best we appeal to his greed. Find some way to hide our strength and weapons within that which he wants."

"Too bad we've no the trickery of a Trojan horse at our disposal," Patrick muttered.

"Maybe we do," Dani said, the thin threads of an idea taking hold. "Sort of an inside-out one. The Greeks filled a gift with soldiers. But what if we just pack our gifts full of power? We're forgetting that we have access to the power of Faerie Magic. Let's use it."

After all, they did have a real live Faerie on their side.

"I would assume it's my Magic you're talking about." Elesyria stopped her pacing to face them. "And though I'm more than willing to do whatever I can to help Malcolm, I'm not at all sure my Magic is the answer."

"Of course it is!" Dani countered. "If you could zap me seven hundred years into the past, you've got to be able to do something to disable the people who are holding Malcolm and set him free."

"You credit me far too much." Elesyria sat down in the chair next to where she stood, heavily, as if her legs had grown weak. "Let's just worry with the obvious complications. We won't even go into the issue of my being prohibited by oath from using my Magic for anything other than what I came here to do."

"Obvious complications?" Patrick asked, leaning forward in his chair. "Name them."

"The Magic that guards over your family, for one thing. I sampled it when I touched Malcolm on the day I arrived. Though I recognize it as ancient Magic, I've not felt its like before."

"Odin's protection," Patrick explained.

"Wait a minute." Dani stared at the two of them. "That's not really true, is it? I mean, Malcolm told me that tattoo on his chest was there because your family claims to be descended from Odin, but that's just family legend stuff, right? He wasn't really serious about that. Was he?"

She could accept people believing in Norse gods. What she couldn't accept was that those gods might actually exist.

"Quite serious. He shared that with you, did he?"

Dani still wasn't ready to believe what Patrick was telling her. "Yes. But a tattoo doesn't prove anything."

"It's no a mark made by any man, Lady Danielle. It appeared when Odin chose my brother to be one of his own warriors."

Right. It just appeared. *Poof.* All by itself. Patrick might be that gullible, but she wasn't.

"And you believed Malcolm's story about that? You never questioned him about when he had it done or who did it for him."

"I'd no the need to doubt his story, as you call it. I'd a mark of my own appear shortly after my twelfth birthday."

Experiencing it for yourself was certainly one way to know for a fact.

And who was she, after all, to argue with mystical beings and Norse gods? She'd spent the better part of her life believing in Faeries. And here she sat, seven hundred years from where she belonged, as proof that they existed. Elesyria had told her there were more Magical beings in the world than she could imagine.

"Everyone in your family bears this mark?" Elesyria still had questions.

"No, only Malcolm and I." Patrick shrugged one shoulder as he continued. "Why us? No way to explain it, according to my father. Entirely a matter of Odin's whim. Christiana was gifted with Sight. She has visions of what is to come. It's because of her gift that Torquil holds her prisoner."

"What about Torquil? And Dermid?" Dani was ready to hear almost anything at this point.

"The Magic skipped over Dermid entirely. Whether that's because he was the last born or because, as our mother claimed, she prayed through her entire pregnancy that he might be spared, I canna say. And as for Torquil . . ." Patrick closed his eyes for moment, as if to prepare himself. "As firstborn, Torquil received the lion's share of our bloodline's gifts. None of us ken the extent of all that he can do."

"That explains much," Elesyria groaned. "I'm not at all sure I wield the power to combat Magic such as you describe."

Sure or not, the Faerie was still the best chance they had.

"Then it's time we find out, isn't it? You told me yourself that you came here to determine what had happened to your daughter and mete out reward or punishment. You're the one who decided Malcolm deserved to be rewarded. What better reward is there than helping to free him?"

"I already arranged for his reward," Elesyria grumbled. "As you well know, since you're it."

"So you're just going to let the man who did everything in his power to save your daughter—"

"And the man she loved," Patrick interrupted to add.

"The man who saved your daughter and the man she loved," Dani repeated, hoping against hope she was getting through to the Faerie. "You're just going to abandon him when he needs your help the most?"

Elesyria clasped her hands together on the table in front of her. "And what if I haven't the power? What if I fail?"

"Then at least you will have tried."

Elesyria remained very still, her eyes locked on the hands she clasped together as if she expected them to fly away.

"What would you have of me?"

"You and I must carry the silver to Torquil. We'll be the perfect Trojan horse. We'll waltz in there and distract them with the silver while you Magic them so we can grab Malcolm and make our escape."

"Why you?" Patrick asked.

"Because chances are good Dermid already told this Torquil about me. We'll use that. They'll never suspect a frightened new wife and her companion of being a danger to them. At least they won't until it's too late. And by then, well, it'll be too late."

Patrick's fingers tapped out a tattoo on the table while Dani waited for his response to her idea. When the noise abruptly stopped, she knew he'd made his decision.

"If the Elf is up to it, it could work," he admitted at last.

Of course it could. It had to. It was their only hope.

Twenty-eight

WHAT HAD EVER made her think she actually enjoyed riding horses?

Dani slid off her mount and gratefully handed the reins over to one of the guardsmen Patrick had sent along to accompany them to Tordenet Castle.

Every muscle in her body ached. And after the last few days on the road, she was pretty sure she'd discovered some new muscles she'd never even known existed.

Rauf, cradling a load of stones, kneeled to set about building their fire pit for the night. Dani circled the perimeter of their campsite, gathering sticks and dried grass for kindling before joining him.

"My thanks, my lady." Rauf nodded his head without turning his eyes from his work.

Dani had been opposed to having him join them in the beginning, but she'd been quickly overruled. As Patrick had pointed out, since there was no way he was allowing his younger brother to return to the dangers of Tordenet Castle, Rauf was the logical one to send. He not only knew the way, he also knew the people they would encounter.

More than once Dani had considered the suspicion that Rauf might be more danger than help, but in the past few nights around the campfire as they had their meals, she'd begun to view him differently. Only one of many surprises she'd already encountered on their journey.

"There is no substitute for getting to know someone," she muttered to herself as she made her way back around the edges of their site gathering more wood.

"Begging yer pardon, my lady?" One of the guards halted his steps as she crossed his path.

"Nothing, Eymer. I was just talking to myself."

"My Jeanne does that as well," the lanky young blond answered with a grin, continuing on past with the bedrolls they'd carried on their horses.

Of the three guards whom Patrick had sent along to accompany her and Elesyria on their journey, Eymer was her favorite. Though she'd met the man briefly at Castle MacGahan on a few occasions when he'd come to the kitchen to speak to his wife, she hadn't realized until the two older guards, Guy and Hamund, had teased him that he and Jeanne were newlyweds.

She carried her second armload of wood back and dropped it beside the fire where Elesyria was already nestling a large pot into the flames.

"Soup or porridge?"

It had been one or the other every night. Though whether it was hunger or the Faerie's cooking skill, she'd been surprised each time by how good it tasted.

"Porridge," Elesyria answered with a tired smile. "I haven't the energy to prepare a proper soup this night. Will you watch over this for me while I see to the blood ransom?"

"Of course I will."

Dani accepted the spurtle and stirred circles in the watery oats, watching as her friend checked on the six small bags containing the silver they carried to Torquil.

Each of them carried one of the bags during the day to prevent too heavy a load on any one of their animals that might slow down their progress.

Not that there was that much silver to begin with. Certainly nowhere near the amount Torquil had demanded. The MacGahans had suffered through a hard year, and there was precious little coin in their coffers.

Dani and Elesyria had organized a small army of maids to search every room in the castle, stripping it of any treasures they might bring along with them. Candlesticks, cups, even a small bag of jewelry they'd found that Elesyria claimed had belonged to the old laird's wife, all of it resided in those six bags.

Each evening when they'd stopped, Elesyria spoke some prayer over the pile. A blessing of protection, she claimed.

Dani was hoping that, when the time came, the Faerie would have a similar blessing handy for them.

When Elesyria returned to her side, Dani shooed her away to rest with the assurance that she could handle a pot of porridge. Cooking calmed her, like a little slice of normalcy in a world gone bizarre.

"That's the end of the bread," she announced as she served their meal, dividing it equally among the six of them.

"I've a loaf my Jeanne sent along, rolled in my bedding." Eymer grinned as his two fellow guards began to chuckle. "Aye, well you should laugh. It's Jeanne's ma what baked it, but I freely offer to share, with a note of caution. She's no as careful with her ingredients as Cook."

"And you've proof of that, have you no, Eymer? Show 'em."

The young guard laughed along with his friends, pointing to a missing front tooth as explanation.

"We've no need to risk ourselves on yer rock bread, lad. We're less than a day's ride from Tordenet Castle now. Tomorrow we reach our destination."

The reminder of what lay ahead dampened everyone's spirits, or at least it seemed that way to Dani. Chatter died off and there were no funny stories of family shared this night as they quietly finished their meal and made ready for bed.

As on prior nights, Hamund prodded and nudged at one of the larger stones ringing the fire pit, using a long stick to push it over to where Dani and Elesyria had laid out their bedding.

"It's a cold one tonight," he said, not bothering to tell them the story he had on each of the prior nights about how he made sure his daughter always slept with a heated stone for her feet in the winter.

Dani snuggled down into her covers, thankful

for Hamund's kindness as her toes touched the fur-covered stone.

As tired as she was, sleep eluded her.

Tomorrow, tomorrow, tomorrow, sang through her head, lilting like a top-twenty tune on the radio.

Tomorrow they would arrive at Tordenet Castle. Tomorrow she would see Malcolm. Tomorrow they would know whether or not their plan would be successful.

If only she had some way of getting word to Malcolm.

Maybe she did have a way.

Elesyria had told her there were examples of Soul-Mates out there who had been able to communicate with one another across vast distances in their dreams. If she could experience the Dream Mating as she had, there should be no reason she couldn't pass along a message.

If she could focus her thoughts and if—and this was the big "if"—*if* she could get past the black door.

Twenty-nine

"No."

Eric leaned against the doorframe, wearing a grin that appeared beyond his ability to wipe away.

"No?"

Patrick was not happy with that response.

On the day before Danielle and Elesyria had departed for Tordenet Castle, Dermid had retired to his chamber in a fit of pique on learning that he would not be allowed to accompany them.

At first Patrick had thought to ignore him, too busy with preparations for their journey. Once he had them on their way, and Dermid still refused to come out, he'd done little more than see to it that food was taken to the lad. But it had been five days now that his brother had refused to leave his bedchamber.

Patrick had just about, by the gods, had enough of the spoiled cur's pouting.

"No," Eric repeated. "She says he'll no be bothered to come out until he's treated with the respect he deserves."

"The respect he deserves?" The insanity of that

statement brought Patrick to his feet. "I'll show that damned, spoiled—wait. *She* says? She who?"

"The strumpet what guards his door." If possible, Eric's grin widened. "It would seem yer wee brother has chosen to work through his sorrows in the eager arms of a busty willing lass."

Little wonder Malcolm continually thought of their brother as being a child. He behaved as one.

"And what does he say?"

"Nothing." Eric shrugged. "He does all his talking through the lass. In his temper, he's apparently no speaking to any of us."

"No a word himself? No one single word in these five days past?"

Eric shook his head, his brow wrinkling as he apparently considered the direction of their conversation.

While the pouting and hiding in his room might well be typical of what Patrick had come to expect of his youngest brother, the idea that he'd not spoken a single word rang false.

"Dermid has no the ability to bridle his tongue. No for five minutes and certainly no for five days." Patrick strode to the door and past his captain. "I'd see this for myself."

He should have checked for himself five days ago.

Up the stairs and through the hallways, his suspicions built until at last he reached his brother's chamber.

"Open up, Dermid," he called, pounding on the door. "Dermid!"

The door opened a thin crack, allowing a young woman wearing what appeared to be nothing more than a blanket wrapped around her body and a long, neat yellow braid, to peer out.

"What do you want?" She braced one leg behind the door, allowing no more than a few inches of open space.

"Remove yerself, lass. I'd have a word with my brother."

She was a head shorter than Patrick and he made full use of that advantage, scanning the room over the top of her head. A large lump occupied one side of the bed. His brother?

"Master Dermid has already said he dinna want to be bothered. He said yer to go away."

"No, sweetling, my brother has said nothing. No a word from the lad in five days. *You* said he dinna want to be bothered. *You* said we should go away."

He leaned his weight against the door, watching her eyes widen as she struggled to hold it in place. Through the wider opening he noted a chair that had been pulled in front of the fireplace. And next to that, a basket of needlework lay at the ready, as if its owner had just been interrupted in her work.

She shifted her weight to put more force into holding the door in place.

"He told me to tell you and yer men to leave us be. He . . . he wants an apology, and until he gets it, he's staying right here. In bed with me. You should go now."

Two red blotches bloomed on her cheeks even as she continued to stare at him.

A failing, that, the inability to hide true emotion. A disadvantage of fair-skinned peoples.

"I can see I've been settled too long at Castle Mac-Gahan, Eric."

"And why might that be, Master Patrick?" Eric responded, following Patrick's lead as he had so many times in the past.

"Because the ways of the world appear to have changed muchly since I was out and about. I was unaware that whores carried their needlework along with them."

"I'm no a—," she began to protest before clamping her mouth shut. A deep breath and she started again. "Master Dermid says yer to leave us alone. He says . . ."

Patrick had had enough of this little game.

He shoved against the door with his full weight, grabbing the girl's arms to keep her from falling to the floor as the door jerked from her hands and pushed her back. The blanket she'd held in front of her fell, exposing her sham.

She wore both her shift and her overdress. They'd merely been lowered to expose her arms so that it might appear as if she wore nothing.

Patrick handed her off to Eric and strode to the bed, where he grabbed a handful of the covers and swept them to the floor.

A roll of furs occupied the spot that should have held his brother.

"By Freya," he hissed through gritted teeth. His brother had played him the fool. "How long has he been gone?"

The girl had stuffed her arms back into her clothing. "He paid me three silvers to keep everyone away."

Patrick's patience wore thin.

"How long . . ." A pause to keep from raising his voice. ". . . has he been gone?"

She dug her fingers into her pouch, pulling out the coins to display on the flat of her palm. "Three silvers, you see? I was only doing what I was paid to do. He said—"

"How long?" Patrick yelled at her, all semblance of patience completely disappeared.

The girl scrambled backward toward the fire, covering her face and head with her arms as if she feared a beating. Only Eric's intervention saved her from stumbling into the flames.

"How long?" Patrick asked again, holding tight rein on himself this time.

"Five days." Her voice quivered and tears ran down her cheeks. "He left the night before those he had wanted to accompany."

The night before.

He should have known.

"Ready the fastest horse we have."

He gave the order without waiting to see if Eric obeyed. He had no need to see, only a need to gather his things as quickly as possible. Time was of the essence now. He might already be too late.

He should have known.

He should have seen it, should have recognized it for what it was. He'd sensed something from the first but he'd charged it off to the groomsman, Rauf.

Fool.

He should have known.

And because he hadn't, he could well have the lives of six innocents hanging over his soul for all eternity.

Thirty

THE MIST OF sparkling lights gave it away.

Dani felt as if she floated, but surely that was only because it was too dark to see where her feet touched the ground. She'd begun to think she'd wandered off from the others and lost herself in an inky black forest, but then she'd seen the mist up ahead and she'd known.

She'd entered a dream.

Not a regular dream. Not like being naked on test day or thrown into a restaurant with customers screaming for orders she couldn't find. No, this was entirely different.

She was aware that this was a dream. And more than that, she knew she'd come here with a purpose.

Up close the sparkling mist was more like a river made of millions of infinitesimally tiny creatures, writhing and splashing in unison against its banks, tossing up a multicolored living spray into the black void around her.

It beckoned her and she took several steps toward the flow until she remembered she'd come here for a purpose.

"Malcolm?"

He wouldn't be in the waters, so she turned her back to them, searching for the black door within the black world.

"Malcolm?"

A spray of the tiny creatures followed after her, winging their way around her head, around her body, and off to her left. She hesitated, unsure which way to go, and the lights buzzed down on her again. A circle around her head, a circle around her body, and then they dashed to the left, hovering there.

"Like Lassie leading me to Timmy in the well," she murmured, and followed the lights.

There were more now, coalescing around her, darting and twisting, twinkling in every color of the rainbow. They lifted her from her feet and carried her forward, invisible winds blowing her hair as they flew.

And then they were gone.

Alone, she stood in front of an enormous black door, larger than it had been before. Malcolm had been putting effort into keeping her out, it would appear.

As she reached out toward the door, a small silver circle appeared. It grew as she watched, morphing from one object to another, expanding with each change until at last it reached its final shape.

A doorknob.

It felt warm under her hand, more like skin than metal, and she turned it, slowly, half expecting it to be locked.

The door gave way, opening slowly, silently, a sliver of width, barely enough to allow her to see inside.

A mighty stench slammed into her, turning her stomach, causing her to gag. She covered her face with her arm, fitting her nose and mouth into the crook of her elbow, and pushed the door open farther. Far enough to step one foot inside a pit of unbelievable filth and death.

A figure crouched across from her, face buried in its hands.

"Malcolm?"

His head snapped up and their eyes met.

"No!" he roared, launching his body toward the door.

"Tomorrow," she cried out as the door slammed shut. "We'll be there tomorrow."

The crash of the door threw her off-balance and she stumbled backward, losing her footing to fall weightlessly into the black void.

Down and down she fell, gathering speed, until her eyes flew open.

She lay on her bed of furs, gasping for air, heart pounding, the stone at her feet gone cold.

Her stomach roiled with the disgusting odor that lingered in her nostrils, and she pushed back her covers to climb out of her warm little nest and make her way out of the circle and through the brush to a stream that ran nearby.

At its bank she dropped to her knees and leaned over it, splashing icy water onto her face. After a moment or two, she began to feel enough better that she no longer feared she'd lose her dinner.

That had been maybe the worst nightmare she'd ever had. Even now her heart still beat much faster than normal.

Another splash of water to her face and she looked up in time to see the figure of an enormous bird silhouetted against the moon. Round and round it circled overhead, in tight, silent loops, almost directly above her.

She couldn't take her eyes from the creature as it dipped and soared like it rode its own personal air current. It was enormous and absolutely mesmerizing, beautiful and scary, all at the same time.

"He hunts."

"Rauf!" Dani all but squealed the man's name, he'd scared her so badly when he spoke. "Lord, man. I had no idea anyone was even awake, let alone out here with me."

The groomsman smiled, offering a hand to help her to her feet. "Sorry for any fright, my lady. When I saw you'd left the camp, I worried for yer safety."

"I had a bad dream, but I'm fine now. I was just watching that bird up there. Look at him. It's so eerie to see him flying across the face of the moon with his wings spread out that way. He's beautiful."

"He's lethal. Hunting this night, I'd say," Rauf repeated his earlier assertion. "The great owl. From his flight, I'd guess he had targeted his prey and begun to move in for the kill, though it would appear as though the victim may have eluded him this time. It's best we return to the others now, my lady."

"You're probably right. We do intend an early start tomorrow."

Dani cast one last look up at the big bird, still circling directly overhead, and a shiver ran down her spine. He'd targeted his prey, had he? Obviously, it was the way of nature, but it didn't make her feel any better for the poor little creature here on the ground. She rustled the plants on both sides of her, making more noise than was at all necessary as she followed Rauf back to their campsite. Hopefully anything around here would be frightened into hiding.

As for her, she needed her rest. Tomorrow, just like that owl, she would be on the hunt. Except that she intended her hunt to end in success.

HE'D DOZED OFF again but a scraping noise from above him brought him wide awake.

Malcolm squinted his eyes against the light as the wooden cover slid away from the opening to the oubliette to reveal a maliciously grinning guard.

"Awake, are you? That's good." The guard picked up a basket and turned it upside down, allowing its contents to fall freely into the hole.

Malcolm had learned this lesson. He was quick this time, launching to his feet to catch what he could of the table scraps as they fell.

"Wouldn't want our good laird's guest to go hungry, now would we?" The guard's laughter disappeared only when the wooden cover slid back over the opening.

Malcolm clutched the soggy chunks of bread he'd caught, tearing into them as a starving dog might. Especially appropriate since these were the scraps normally cast out to the strays roaming the castle grounds. At least, they had been used for that purpose when his father had been laird.

Knowing Torquil, any castle strays had starved to death by now.

Much as Malcolm had expected he would.

And yet, after what felt like days in this hellhole, the cover had slid away and food had rained down on him. He hadn't been ready that first time and the bounty had scattered around him, landing in the wet slime of waste and straw that covered the floor.

He needed food to rebuild his strength. Even food such as that had been. In the dark he'd managed to find a few pieces, convincing himself as he choked it down that it was only leftovers from the table that soaked the bread.

His lesson learned, when the cover had moved this time, he'd been ready.

Resting his head against the wall, he finished the last of what he'd been able to catch.

Thanks to the scraps, and time, he had healed. His strength had returned, a fact that Torquil must have anticipated.

Which led him to only one conclusion: His brother had some reason of his own for keeping him alive. If he could only determine what that reason might be, perhaps it would give him the advantage he needed to escape when the time came.

One other possibility haunted him. A thought he'd have preferred to avoid, but with nothing to do but think, his worry would not be denied.

As he'd slept, Dani had often come to him in his dreams. At least, he thought she had.

In this hole bereft of light to mark the division between day and night, he'd begun to wonder whether his mind might not be playing tricks upon him.

Still, each time had seemed real. Real enough that he'd forced her away, blocking her entry to his world, determined not to allow her to experience the abomination of his hell.

He'd been successful at it, too. Until the last time she'd come to him.

Exhaustion had taken its toll and he'd slept soundly. So soundly that he'd not heard her approach. He'd not heard her at all until he'd looked up to meet her gaze, her eyes reflecting her revulsion from what she saw.

He'd quickly closed off that part of himself and forced her back, shielding her from the horror of his existence.

But not before he'd heard her voice. Not before she'd said the words that drove terror deep in his heart. Not before she'd claimed she was coming to him, not in the dream, but in the real world.

"Tomorrow. We'll be there tomorrow."

Surely Patrick had more sense than to allow Dani to travel to Tordenet Castle in search of him. He'd made a point of stressing to his brother the importance of keeping Dermid safe. But he'd never considered the need to order Dani's safety. It had seemed a given to him at the time. It still did.

And yet, the worries lingered, eating away at the edges of his sanity.

If Dani were to fall into Torquil's hands, if Torquil were to recognize her importance to him, it would grant his elder brother the power to access whole new levels of hell for Malcolm.

It wouldn't happen. It couldn't. Patrick would never have allowed it.

"Tomorrow. We'll be there tomorrow."

He might have been able to push the worries turned to fear aside if not for one unanswerable question.

Why had Torquil kept him alive?

Thirty-one

A<small>T LEAST SHE</small> didn't have to pretend to be a nervous and worried new wife.

The feelings were all too real as Dani waited for the massive gate of iron bars to lift and allow their party entrance to Tordenet Castle.

They rode forward, into the mouth of the long tunnel separating freedom and the castle grounds. Dani fought the desire to turn her head and watch when she heard the heavy chains clanking behind them. She had no need to confirm with her own eyes what reason told her. The iron portcullis that had allowed them entry now barred their exit.

"Like a rat in a barrel of rainwater," Elesyria muttered from her left.

Goose bumps spread over Dani's arms at the analogy. She'd plucked too many dead, swollen rats from rain barrels back on the farm not to understand its meaning.

She swallowed hard, fixing her eyes straight ahead of her.

The tunnel through the castle wall had been strategically placed, framing the entrance of the keep so that anyone arriving might be properly intimidated. The keep itself, as well as the castle walls, had been covered in whitewash. Sunlight reflected off the whole, allowing Tordenet Castle to be seen long before it was reached, a shining beacon in the distance.

Rauf rode at the head of their little procession, leading them through the long tunnel. She couldn't help but notice that Eymer drew his animal up beside hers as they passed out of the confinement of the wall's tunnel. At the same time, Guy came forward to a spot on the left and, with Hamund close at their rear, the guards had formed a protective circle around her and Elesryia.

Any comfort she might have taken in their action was lost with one look at the numbers of armed soldiers surrounding them on their way across the courtyard. No wonder Malcolm had thought he needed the might of the MacKilyn on his side.

At Rauf's signal, they drew their animals to a halt while he slid off his mount and hastened forward, dropping to one knee at the foot of a great flight of stairs that led up to the castle entrance. There he waited, head bowed, like a reverent statue.

Dani's horse pawed the ground nervously. Whether it was because the animal felt hemmed in by Eymer on one side and Elesyria on the other or something else altogether, she couldn't be sure. She only knew that she and her horse shared a similar choking apprehension.

After a few minutes' delay, a man appeared at the top of the stairs. He paused, obviously surveying those who waited below, and, as impossible as it was to determine from this distance, Dani could have sworn he stared directly at her.

Nerves.

"A fine specimen of manflesh, that one is," Elesyria murmured approvingly. "The elder brother, do you suppose?"

One and the same, Dani guessed.

He was beautiful, all right. A romance-cover version of Dermid. But where the younger brother was cherubic in his blond good looks, the elder was seriously heartbreaker handsome, with a come-hither confidence in his stride that could easily knock a cowgirl right off her horse.

If she needed more proof of who he was, the obsequious way Rauf followed after him as he passed down the stairs and headed toward their group of horses was it.

He paused not five feet from her horse, definitely staring directly at her now.

"You'll do the honors, Rauf?"

She mentally added a voice like honey-coated candy to her description of him.

Rauf stepped forward, head still bowed. "Our lord, Torquil of Katanes, laird of the MacDowylt, chosen son of Odin. My lord, may I present yer brother's wife, Mistress Danielle MacDowylt, of the MacGahan and her companion, Mistress Elesyria MacGahan."

Three of the soldiers placed their bodies between Eymer's mount and her own, pressing him back and away from her as Torquil approached.

He stopped beside her horse and held up his arms to help her down.

"Welcome to Tordenet Castle, my lady," he said as he gripped her waist and lowered her to the ground.

It seemed to Dani that he held her a bit closer and perhaps a bit longer than absolutely necessary. Long enough that she began to feel the others watching. Long enough that she tilted her head up to meet his gaze.

Her breath caught as she realized how wrong she'd been about Torquil's looks. No amount of external beauty could ever make up for the internal ugliness reflected in this man's cold eyes.

At last he released his grip and backed up a step.

"Allow me to escort you inside," he offered. "My people will see to it that your things are delivered up to yer bedchamber and then perhaps you and yer companion would agree to join me in my dining hall."

"If that's what you'd have us do," Dani answered, deciding for the moment to play it low-key.

"It is indeed," he confirmed, catching her hand in his and placing it on his forearm, his free hand covering hers, to lead her up the stairs and into the keep of MacDowylt Castle. "It's always best, I say, to leave yer business discussions until after a good meal."

His touch felt every bit as cold as his eyes had looked.

Two more sets of stairs and a long hallway led to a door where he at last stopped.

"I hope you'll find these accommodations to yer liking."

He still hadn't released her hand.

"I'm sure they'll be just fine. Elesyria will, of course, be nearby?"

There was no way in hell she wanted to be separated from the Faerie in this place. It gave her chills just thinking of the possibility.

"But of course. I've taken the liberty of having the chamber adjoining yers prepared for yer companion. This is satisfactory?"

"Yes, thank you." As if she had any choice in the matter.

"I'll leave two of my men outside yer door to . . . watch over you and see that you find way to the dining hall."

He paused, as if waiting for her to catch up with his meaning. He didn't need to. She understood quite well that she wasn't exactly free to go exploring in the castle.

"And the men who saw me safely here?" The laird's wife would surely want to know about her people. "You'll see that they're taken care of, as well?"

"Without a doubt, dear lady. They will be taken care of as well. Is there anything else I might send up for yer comfort?"

She smiled and pulled her hand from his grip, covering the obvious move by reaching out to push open her door.

"You could send up my husband. That would be nice."

His laughter echoed through the stone hallway. "I

begin to suspect it's no just yer beauty that attracted my brother to you."

With an almost imperceptible dip of his head, he turned and walked away, leaving his two stone-faced guards behind.

Nothing ventured, nothing gained, as the old saying went.

Dani slipped inside her room, pushing the door shut behind her to lean against it.

Nothing felt right about this place. God, but she hoped they hadn't made a horrible mistake in coming here.

When the door between her room and Elesyria's opened, she very nearly screamed.

"It's only me," the other woman said.

"So how weird was all of that?" Dani asked, crossing over to climb up on the bed her friend leaned against. "And what do you think of *him*?"

"It was all perfectly normal." Elesyria began to pace the length of the bed. "In fact, if anything was unusual, it was how very normal it was. We were greeted as relatives arriving for a long-expected visit. He'd even prepared our rooms. *Our* rooms," she repeated for emphasis.

"Maybe he's not easily surprised?"

Though he certainly should have been surprised at having two women show up instead of his younger brother.

"And did you notice that he never even questioned Dermid's not being with us?" Dani shared her concern. "I'll admit that after that little poop had his total hissy fit about being forced to stay behind, I was sort of worried that it might be a problem when we showed up here without him."

"Young Dermid has an overly developed sense of self-importance, I suspect." Elesyria waved a hand as if to dismiss that whole discussion. "He's not our worry at the moment."

"Then what is our—" Dani's question was interrupted by a knock at the door. "Hold that thought."

She slipped off the bed and crossed the room to answer the door. Two more of Torquil's men waited outside, bearing the things they'd brought along on their journey, including the six small bags of coin and treasures.

"Just put them there next to the hearth," she instructed, pointing out a spot by the massive fireplace that dominated one wall of the room. She waited with the door open until the men had deposited their load and made their exit past the guards standing outside.

When they were gone, she climbed back up on the bed and fixed Elesyria with a stare.

"You were just about to tell me what you thought we needed to be worried about." As if she couldn't come up with enough on her own.

Elesyria rounded the bed and sat down beside Dani. "You asked me earlier what I thought of Torquil. I'd answer that question first. The man reeks of Magic. Very ancient and very powerful Magic. The whole castle seethes with it. It's so strong, I can all but see it."

"I assume that's bad?"

It had been the major concern Elesyria had expressed as they'd worked out their plan to rescue Malcolm.

"Bad? Let's see," The Faerie pushed her hair away from her face and sighed. "It would only be bad if I needed to use my Magic. Surrounded by the Power of Asgard as I am here, I'd be lucky to strike a spark to dry kindling, let alone try to force an entire army to free Malcolm."

That definitely fell under Dani's definition of *bad*.

"I'm exhausted just holding on to my present form."

"Okay, then." Dani patted Elesyria's hand and climbed off the bed. "Don't worry about it. We can still do this. If we don't have any Faerie Magic at our disposal, I guess we'll just have to be about conjuring up some Mortal magic. You ready for dinner with the in-laws?"

At the Faerie's blank look, Dani picked up two of the little bags and tossed them to her. "Come on. Let's take our blood money and go have it out with my new brother-in-law."

Thirty-two

A CHANGE OF PLANS was most certainly in order. Torquil smiled to himself as he crossed the bailey, headed for the old tower that housed Christiana's quarters.

He had imagined so many different options for torturing his brother in the days since he'd learned Malcolm's wife would be bringing the ransom to him. But none of them had actually taken the woman herself into consideration, a serious miscalculation on his part. Not even when he'd spotted her last night had he realized what an opportunity she afforded him.

The owl's lack of color vision had done the woman a disservice.

This new sister-in-law of his was no ragged Scot. And no filthy Tinkler. Looking at that blond hair and her fair skin, he'd be willing to bet all the silver she carried with her that her ancestry stretched to his own people's shores. And her eyes! Her eyes sparkled like rare green jewels. There was something special about the woman. He could feel it.

He should have guessed as much when he'd been

told she had some mysterious connection to a stone circle.

How Malcolm had managed to ensnare such as Danielle to be his wife was a mystery, but a mystery Torquil intended to have solved before his guests left his table tonight.

Stopping at the door to the old tower, he pounded his fist against the wood.

"Christiana!" he called, impatient for once to speak with his sister.

When she opened the door, he grabbed her arm and pulled her along with him.

"Where are you taking me?"

He liked the thread of fear in her voice.

"I'd have you take yer meal at my table this day. I've someone I want you to meet. Have you any idea who it is?"

He watched her closely in an attempt to determine whether or not she'd been keeping information from him.

She closed her eyes, lifting her chin as she was wont to do, an irritating habit that reminded him of an animal sniffing the air for scent. When she opened her eyes, she shook her head, a confused furrow forming on her brow.

Interesting. She'd obviously seen nothing of this in her visions, so it was likely the Norns had woven no outcome yet. He was free to do as he pleased.

He hurried her along, knowing full well she had trouble keeping up with his longer stride. At another time he might have walked even faster, but he needed her fresh at dinner. He wanted to observe Danielle's interactions with her husband's sister. Often, in the beginning at least, he learned more by watching than by asking.

He chose to forgo his regular spot on the dais, seating Christiana at one of the smaller tables instead. He wanted a more intimate experience. He wanted to be able to hear all conversations. He wanted to watch Danielle's eyes as she experienced the evening.

A word to his captain and the hall was cleared of all people and guards set at all the entrances. There would be no distractions. The scores of hangers-on who devoured his food at every meal would have to find someplace else to feed their faces this day.

All was in readiness with only moments to spare. Danielle, followed by her traveling companion, entered the hall, their arms loaded down with three small bags each.

The homage he'd demanded?

Even with her arms filled, she moved with the grace of a special being. He waited while they stacked the bags on the nearest table and then led them to their seats.

He made sure he sat directly across from Danielle with Christiana at his side. All the better to observe.

With an uplifted hand, he signaled for the courses to begin, waiting for everyone to be served before he made introductions.

"Have you any idea who our guests are, dear sister?" He watched Christiana closely for any reaction.

"This is Danielle, Malcolm's wife, and her traveling companion."

He wasn't disappointed.

Christiana's hand paused midway to her mouth, her eyes darting up to the other woman and back to her food again. It occurred quickly, but he'd seen it because he'd been looking for it. Surprise like that was impossible to hide.

"Welcome to Tordenet Castle, ladies."

"And you must be Christiana. Malcolm has spoken of you."

Tensions ran thick at the table, inhibiting conversation. That could work to his advantage if he used it properly. He lifted his hand again and maids rushed to fill all the goblets with his favorite mead.

He timed his next round of questions to coincide with the beginning of the second course. After two cups of the mead, he expected tongues would begin to loosen.

"Tell me of yer family, Danielle. How did my brother come to wed you?"

"I arranged for Danielle and Malcolm to be together."

The companion, an older woman whose name he'd instantly forgotten, smiled cheerily at him, lifting her cup for another refill. His look must have reflected as much.

"Surely you realize that I'm Isabella's mother. No?" She took a sip, her smile even brighter than before. "Marrying my Isabella is what made Malcolm laird of the MacGahan. And with my Isa gone, I felt the lad needed a good wife to see that Castle MacGahan was well cared for. I found Danielle for him and the rest is, as they say, history."

With all her blethering, the woman must have enjoyed his mead overmuch.

"When will you release my husband?"

Dani's question seemed to spring from nowhere, catching him off guard. He waited to answer her until after the next course of food had been served.

"Begging yer pardon, my good woman, but it feels a wee bit presumptuous to be speaking of Malcolm's release when we've yet to discuss the details of either his homage or his oath of fealty, does it no?"

"In that case, let's go ahead and discuss the money. I'll be more than happy to turn it over to you just as soon as I see Malcolm. To verify he's unharmed, you understand."

He had no intention of allowing her to see Malcolm. Not yet, at least. That move did not yet suit his needs.

"I fear that's not possible."

"Will you be serving anything other than fish at this meal?" The mother-in-law frowned at her plate and then at him. "Any fruit or vegetables of any sort?"

As if he had anything to do with what came from the kitchens!

"I have no idea what—"

"That being the case"—Danielle folded her hands on the table in front of her, focusing her attention there as she spoke—"I fear I'm not at liberty to give

you any of the coin we've brought from the people of
the MacGahan."

"What?"

Somewhere along the line, his plans for this meal
had been completely dashed. These women had taken
charge.

"Since you say it's impossible for me to see my
husband, I need some proof that Malcolm lives. I
don't even know for sure that he was ever here."

"I can assure you that I do indeed hold your husband as my . . . guest."

"Oh, you assure us of that, do you?" The mother-
in-law, at last concerned with something other than
her palate.

"I'm afraid that's simply not good enough." Danielle looked up, her enormous green eyes boring into
him as if she were attempting to search his very soul.
"I'm not turning over the entire fortune of the MacGahan clan merely on your say-so. No offense intended.
I'm sure you understand this is purely business."

"The word of your own husband's brother is not
good enough for you?"

"No." The mother-in-law pushed back her chair
and rose to her feet.

"Elesyria is correct," Danielle confirmed, rising to
her feet as well. "Not when that brother claims to be
holding my husband prisoner. Or 'guest,' as you seem
to prefer to call it."

This was beyond absurd. Did these women not
realize he could merely take that which they had
brought and toss their broken bodies into the sea?

And yet, he felt compelled to continue what had become an entertaining game for him. Toying with prey so full of surprises provided a fascination to see what their next move might be.

Though once he tired of the game, the annoying one called Elesyria would be its first victim.

"Christiana. Tell them you've spoken to your brother."

"I have spoken to my brother."

Even he would have doubts based on the girl's demeanor and he knew for a fact that Malcolm languished in the oubliette below.

"Nope." Danielle pushed her chair to the table and began to gather her bags. "Not good enough. At this point, I need proof."

The next move was his, in the form of a new hurdle for his toys to overcome. He stood and walked around the table to place a restraining hand on the woman's wrist.

"If that's the treasure you think to deliver, then it would seem we already have a problem. I canna believe that holds the amount I required of you."

Danielle pulled at his grip but he refused to release his hold. Time she began to understand the power she sought to battle.

"Well, sir, it's all you're getting." Brazenly, she fixed that brilliant gaze upon him again. "And there's nothing we can do about that because it's everything we have. All the coin, all the silver, right down to the only two candlesticks I could find that were worth anything. We've even collected every piece of jewelry we could lay hands on. So, you want the wealth of the MacGahan in return for my husband's release? There it is. But you don't get one single piece of it until I have proof that he's here and that he's alive."

She tugged her hand again and he glanced down to where he held her, an idea springing to life as he noted the jewel upon her finger.

"As you say." He released his grip and stepped back. "This is business, not family, so I have a business proposal for you. In exchange for one trinket from your treasure, I will deliver to you proof that Malcolm is indeed here. A good-faith gesture on both our parts."

He could well imagine her mind ticking off the possibilities as she continued to stare at him. By the gods, but Malcolm did not deserve one such as this. Beauty, wit, and a quick mind combined in a single package.

Though hardly quick enough to successfully engage him in an intellectual battle.

"And once we've completed this good-faith act of yours, then you agree to negotiate Malcolm's release to me in return for the treasure I carry?"

"The treasure and the MacGahan's pledge of fealty, of course." The one piece he was certain he would never receive from Malcolm.

"Then we have a deal." She extended her hand to grasp his, pumping it up and down as a merchant at the fair might. Stepping back she swept her arm over the stack of bags. "Feel free to go through them. Choose whatever item you like."

"No need, my lady. I've already chosen. I'd have the trinket you wear upon your hand. You did say you were including all the jewelry you could find at Castle MacGahan as part of the payment."

Surprise registered on her lovely features even as she covered the ring with her other hand. Her reaction, however, was short-lived. She recovered quickly, all emotion wiped from her expression as she twisted the ring from her finger and handed it over to him.

"Elesyria and I shall await your proof in our chambers."

He waited as they gathered their precious little bags and made their way from the hall. At his nod, his guards fell in step behind them.

"Thank you for a most unusual meal, Brother." Christiana glided past him on her way to the door, stopping at the last moment. "She's an interesting woman, our new sister, is she no?"

Indeed she was, but he saw no need to share his thoughts with Christiana, and instead dismissed her with the wave of his hand.

He had more pressing matters on his mind.

"HE'S BEING FAR too accommodating. I don't like this." Elesyria lay back on the bed, one hand across her eyes. "I don't trust that vile creature in the least."

"I don't trust him either, but I'd hardly call him accommodating."

Dani sat on the floor in front of the massive stone fireplace in her bedchamber, rubbing her thumb over the newly empty spot on her finger. It was her own fault. She should have left her aunt's ring at Castle MacGahan if she'd wanted to keep it.

Still, if it made any difference in getting Malcolm out of this place, it was well worth the loss.

A knock at the door sent her scrambling to her feet to answer.

"Our lord Torquil sends these things with his compliments. He bids me tell you his part of the bargain is now fulfilled."

The guard handed over a pack and a roll of blankets that looked very much like the ones Malcolm had carried with him the night he'd left Castle MacGahan. Still, everyone who traveled could well have items just like these. And even if they were his, they only proved that he had been here at one point, a fact that was really not in question for her.

"You can tell your lord that I don't accept these as proof that my husband is alive."

"Our lord Torquil bids me convey to you his invitation to join him in breaking his fast on the morrow to continue the negotiations as you have agreed."

"Fine." Arguing with this Polly parrot was doing her no good at all. "You may tell him for me that we'll see him bright and early tomorrow morning."

There was no mistaking the relief she'd seen on the man's face as she shoved the heavy door shut.

Holding the things tightly to her chest, she returned to her spot by the hearth to go through the items Torquil claimed belonged to Malcolm.

She untied the binding on the bedroll and buried her nose in the blanket and any question of who it belonged to was gone. The fresh herbal scent that clung to his skin permeated the wool. It definitely belonged to Malcolm.

After draping the blanket across her legs, she opened the pack to look inside; her heart felt as if it skipped a beat. Just inside the pack was the pouch Malcolm always wore around his waist, as if someone had taken it from him and carelessly tossed it in with everything else.

She loosened the drawstrings on the leather bag and dumped its contents into her lap. There, among the bits of tiny wood shavings, two items stood out from the rest.

The first was Malcolm's knife. She'd seen it too often not to recognize it as his. He used it at every meal, and even in his spare moments, he pulled it out to occupy his hands by idly whittling some piece of wood he'd pick up.

The second item clutched at her heart.

"A fork," she said aloud, unable to keep her voice from breaking.

"What's that you say?" Elesyria climbed from the bed and crossed over to kneel at her side.

"Malcolm's carved a fork." She ran her finger the length of the smooth wood before offering it to Elesyria for her inspection. "A small fork. Just like I told him I wanted."

She felt as if her heart might break. Even as he'd traveled to meet God only knew what kind of fate, he'd been thinking of her. Only two wickedly sharp prongs, and those were all out of proportion, almost as long as the handle. But it was fork. A fork she had no doubt he'd made especially for her. She could almost see him sitting by a fire, absently carving away as he did when his hands were idle.

Her head felt stuffy and she rubbed at her eyes to prevent their betraying her with tears.

"I thought you said this whole true-love, SoulMate thing was supposed to be a gift. It doesn't feel the least bit gifty right now. In fact, it feels pretty awful."

"We do feel most deeply those things that are most important to us," Elesyria agreed as she smoothed one hand over the wood before lifting it to her nose. "It's rowan wood he's used."

Dani held out her hand for the fork and lifted it to her own nose. "Just smells like wood to me." How Elesyria could tell one from another was beyond her.

"Rowan trees are a home to powerful Magic left behind in the world by the ancient Fae. It's not just their smell that identifies them to me. It's the sense of power in the wood."

"Too bad we don't have ourselves a rowan tree here, isn't it? Maybe you could access your Magic then."

Elesyria shook her head and stood up, stretching her back as she did. "I doubt one tree could overcome what I feel weighing down upon me here, but they do have power. You likely could have used a single bit of wood like that when you set about to contact the Faeries instead of all those stones you told me about."

If only she'd known that at the time. It would have saved her the week's pay she'd spent on those pretty little stones. Not that she would have had any idea where to find rowan wood in Wyoming. Besides, none of that mattered now. It was all history.

Or would be in seven centuries.

She replaced all the items as they had been. All except the little fork. That she tucked into the pouch she wore around her own waist. After all, she was sure Malcolm had meant it to be hers.

Carrying his blanket with her, she crawled into bed and drew the woolen close to her face, breathing in his scent. She wouldn't allow herself to think about the circumstances Malcolm endured this night that prevented him from using his own things.

Instead she forced her eyes shut. She needed to sleep in order to try the dream again. She needed to see for herself that Malcolm still lived.

Thirty-three

*D*ON'T LET HIM *see your fear or it's all over. He'll come after you."*

Aunt Jean's caution played through Dani's mind as she followed Torquil's guard toward the dining hall, grating against her already frayed nerves. Maybe if she'd gotten any sleep at all last night it would have helped. Or if she'd been able to catch even a tiny glimpse of Malcolm in her dreams she might be less of a nervous wreck.

But neither was the case. Instead, she had only a head full of her aunt's favorite words of advice.

Of course, Aunt Jean had been warning her about the old goose that wandered freely around their farm and not some Magic-wielding Scotsman who held people prisoner in his castle. But still, the caution might well apply. Both were vile, hateful creatures that bore careful handling.

Outside the entry to the hall, she lifted her chin and straightened her back, only moderately reassured by the squeeze Elesyria gave her hand before dropping her hold.

As before, the huge room was devoid of people

except for the servants waiting at either end of the table where Torquil sat.

He neither stood nor looked up when they approached to take their seats. Apparently their negotiations had reached a new adversarial level.

She only hoped the bell ringing in her imagination signaled the beginning of the next round and not an all-out disaster alarm.

"I canna help but note that you've no brought along the wee bags yer to hand over to me today."

At last he chose to acknowledge their presence. Two could play that game.

Dani made a point of thanking each servant for every item that was placed on the table before she allowed herself to so much as glance Torquil's direction.

His amused expression did not inspire her to confidence.

"I saw no point in our carting the bags back and forth. You know where they are, and surely they'll be safe there, won't they?"

"Absolutely," he replied, his expression darkening as his eyes darted over her head.

"May I join you?" Christiana stood at the door, her entry blocked by the guards at either side.

"Of course," Dani replied brightly, her words drowning out Torquil's simultaneous response of "No."

His not wanting the girl there was all the reason Dani needed for including her. Anything to throw her opponent off his game.

She popped up out of her chair and hurried over

to the door to reach past the guard and draw Christiana inside the room.

"Don't be rude," she hissed at the man, feeling almost sorry for him as he looked first to his companion and then to Torquil for guidance.

At a gesture from Torquil, the guard stepped aside and Dani led Christiana back to the table to take a seat next to hers.

"There now." She forced herself to smile across at Torquil. "One big happy family."

"Though neither as big nor as happy as it should be," Elesyria murmured, digging her bread into the porridge in front of her. "Please tell me they didn't put fish in this."

Across from her, Torquil twisted the ring on his little finger. Her ring. And though he wore a smile, the muscle in his jaw stood rigid and there was nothing even close to pleasant in the eyes that glared in Elesyria's direction.

"Which reminds me . . ." Dani leaned to the side, drawing his attention back to her. "While I thank you for sending my husband's things to my room, you do realize there was nothing in those bundles that kept your side of the bargain."

"I beg yer pardon? You wanted proof Malcolm was here. That is what I gave you."

Even his speech sounded clipped, strained by the tension in his face.

Dani thought to push her luck once more.

"No, in exchange for my ring"—she tapped her bare ring finger—"you were to provide me proof that my husband was alive and well. That you did not do."

Satisfied that she'd successfully put the ball back in his court, Dani dipped her bread into the porridge and scooped a bite into her mouth, realizing too late that Elesyria had been correct about the fish.

"Yer telling me that yer no satisfied with what I've given so far?" Torquil leaned toward her, his eyes seeming to glow as he spoke. "I could have a body part brought to you if you like. A hand, perhaps? A foot? Whichever you prefer. It's of no matter to me. He's close enough that the severed appendage will still be warm when you receive it. Would that do to convince you?"

Dani dropped the bread she held between her thumb and fingers, praying she wouldn't pass out as she felt the blood drain from her face.

"That . . . that won't be necessary," she stammered, fighting to regain her self-control before either the fish or the conversation brought her breakfast up. "I have perhaps been unnecessarily stubborn on this question. I concede the point to you."

"As I thought you might," he said, the false smile still firmly in place.

She clasped her hands in her lap to hide the tremors she could not seem to stop, and breathed through the nausea assaulting her.

Jesus. The monster had just offered to start chopping Malcolm into little pieces and now he sat there, calmly shoving that fishy oatmeal crap into his grinning face.

With no more luck to push, all she wanted was

out of here with Malcolm in tow and all in one piece.

"Then we've only the exchange left to complete all our business dealings. Is he strong enough to ride? Malcolm, that is. As soon as we turn over the bags I'd appreciate having my men to assist my husband, if necessary, so that we might take our leave of your hospitality."

That came out pretty well, all things considered. She hadn't barfed on his table and she'd even managed not to yell anything about getting her man and getting the hell out of here.

"You needn't concern yourself with your husband's strength, my good woman. He will be, I can assure you, at least as strong as any of the men who ride with you."

Beneath the table, Christiana's foot tapped against hers.

"You look overly pale, my sister." Christiana placed a cool hand to Dani's forehead. "Perhaps I should escort you to the garderobe?"

"I don't see that as necessary."

Torquil barely had the words formed before Dani was on her feet, fingers pressed to her mouth as she nodded her agreement to Malcolm's sister.

"It's the porridge," Elesyria sighed. "I knew the fish so early in the day would do it."

With Christiana's arm around her shoulders, Dani hurried from the room, barely noticing when the guards stepped aside without question to allow them exit from the hall.

After a series of twists and turns, they reached the curved wall leading to the garderobe, but rather than settling her stomach, the smell only made it worse.

"You need some fresh air," Christiana said.

"No, it's really not that bad. Or it wasn't before we got here."

"You need some fresh air," Christiana repeated, more forcefully this time, taking her hand as she spoke to lead her down another series of hallways.

Their detour ended at a set of large double doors, which Dani started to open, but Christiana stopped her.

"We should be safe from being overheard here. You must leave this place soon, my sister. Another day at most and then it will be too late. Time has already passed for some of your party. I am so sorry. I didn't know before."

The young woman seemed to struggle for what she wanted to say next.

"I will do what I can to help, but not all of the visions have been clear. I have seen that what's to come for you won't be easy. Yer love for my brother will be tested and only in letting go will you hold on."

Dani's skepticism alarm tripped on full alert. This was the young woman whom Patrick had sworn saw glimpses of the future, and yet she spoke like some cheesy greeting card with her *set it free and it will come back to you* line of bull.

She didn't have time for these games.

"I appreciate that you're trying to help. I already know that I overplayed my hand back there with your brother. But he's back from whatever creepy edge he fell over and we're going to end this thing. I'll give him whatever he wants to get Malcolm and we'll get the hell out of this place."

"That's what I'm trying to tell you. Torquil has no intention of releasing you. He will place a block at every turn."

Dani had to remind herself that this was also the young woman who was, for all intents and purposes, being held hostage by her older brother. And though the girl likely had her own issues with him, Dani wasn't going to jeopardize Malcolm's release by allowing Christiana to lead her down some path of rebellion.

"Look, Christiana, I understand that there's a whole history to whatever is going on within your family and I'm sorry that things are what they are for you. But my priority is Malcolm. Torquil wants the treasure we brought and I'm going to give it to him. I do worry that, after so many days in captivity, Malcolm might not be at his best, but, like I said back there, with the help of the men who accompanied me here, we'll take Malcolm and ride out of those gates and never darken Torquil's path again. Your brother has already pretty much agreed on everything but the details."

That was her new plan. She'd originally hoped to make it out with some of the MacGahan treasures in her possession, but she no longer cared anything about the silver.

"Torquil has agreed to nothing. He plays with you.

He has no intention of allowing you or yer men to ride out of here. See for yerself."

Christiana pushed open the big doors and led the way out onto a small balcony that overlooked what appeared to be a central courtyard two stories below. Almost immediately she dropped to her knees by the railing, pulling Dani down next to her.

"There," she whispered, pointing directly below them to a swarming crowd of men.

Two massive timbers thrust up out of the ground supporting a third timber across their top like some giant child's swing set. Only it wasn't play equipment dangling from the topmost pole. It was bodies. Two of them. Hanging limp and lifeless, gently rocking back and forth as if kept in motion by an invisible hand.

It must be some war games practice with dummies. That had to be it. They were simply stuffed dummies, which would explain everything right down to the bags covering their heads.

But it didn't explain their legs. Dummies would not have those bare, lifeless legs.

Words very nearly failed Dani.

"Who are they?" She couldn't make herself do more whisper as she gripped Christiana's hand.

"Can you no tell from here?"

"No, I—"

The crowd ebbed and parted as a third man was dragged to the gallows. His hands were bound behind him and a rag tied over his mouth to muffle his screams, but in the moments before the bag was dropped over his head, his face was unmistakable.

"Eymer?"

For a moment it was as if her brain and her body were completely disconnected, the parts of her at odds over what she saw.

If that was Eymer, the other two had to be Guy and Hamund!

"We have to go get Torquil. He can stop this." Surely he didn't know what his men did.

"He'll no stop it, Danielle. He ordered it."

Then she would have to stop it. When she attempted to stand, Christiana held her down, throwing her body over Dani's and holding a hand over Dani's mouth.

"Shhh. Listen and think! There's naught that you can do. It's too late for them, but no for you. You must no let on to Torquil that you've seen this. If he realizes that you ken what he's done, you and yer friend Elesyria, and likely Malcolm as well, will be swinging alongside yer men. Do you hear what I'm saying to you?"

Dani nodded her head to acknowledge her understanding, waiting for the tears choking her throat to fall. As if some dam had formed deep inside, they would not come.

"They did nothing wrong," she managed when Christiana moved her hand. "They were good men with families who loved them. Why would he—?"

"He named them traitors because they followed Malcolm, but in truth he did it because he can," Christiana said flatly. "Because he wants to. Because he takes pleasure in the suffering of others. We must hasten to return to the dining hall. We've already been gone overly long. We will explain to Torquil that you've been ill, aye? That and nothing more. Dinna fail me on this point, my sister."

Dani allowed Christiana to help her to her feet and lead her back into the castle. She followed the young woman blindly, her mind filled with the horror of what she'd seen.

How would she ever explain to Jeanne what had happened to her husband? Or to Hamund's daughter? How would she ever wipe those memories from her mind or the guilt she felt from her soul?

As they rounded the corner closest to the garderobe, she rushed inside and dropped to her knees in front of the drafty hole to empty the contents of her stomach, heaving again and again, long after there was nothing left to come up.

The horrors of the last few minutes had assured that she wouldn't have to pretend she'd been ill.

"My lady?" A male voice, tentative and absolutely unsure.

Christiana, who had hovered at her side, lifting her hair from her shoulders, responded with a desperation in her voice that sounded absolutely credible.

"Thank Freya someone finally came to check on us. Hasten to the kitchens. Mistress Danielle has need of a cloth dipped in cool water. Hurry!"

When the young guard returned, Christiana wiped Dani's face and helped her to her feet.

"Are you ready to go before him again?"

As ready as she could ever be.

They reentered the dining hall and Dani took her seat, keeping her eyes focused on her hands, willing them not to shake. Even with her new understanding of the monster sitting across from her, she still had to try once more.

"I apologize if my absence delayed your meal." She forced a smile to her face and met the monster's gaze.

"Not at all, my lady. I trust yer feeling better now?"

That he could sit so calmly at this table after what he'd done!

Bury that for now. This was not the time to think of what had happened but instead to concentrate on what was to come. Dani lowered her hands to her lap, where she could grip them together tightly without his seeing.

"I am, thank you." A deep breath, a brighter smile. "Shall we set a time, then? Say, noon, perhaps? I'll deliver the bags to you and you can deliver Malcolm to me."

She couldn't force herself to make mention of the men who had accompanied her. That horror was too near the surface for her to be sure of her emotions.

Across from her, he twisted the ring on his finger and stared up toward the ceiling as if he considered her suggestion.

"On the morrow, my lady. I think that would be best. I'll carry yer greetings to yer husband and, if he agrees to pledge his fealty, we'll plan to convene at midmorning. In the courtyard. How does that sound?"

It sounded like a death sentence.

Still, Dani nodded as if it were completely acceptable to her.

"I am reminded, my laird, of my original purpose in coming here this morning." Christiana broke the lengthening silence as if she sat at a normal table, with normal people. "I've a boon to ask of you."

Torquil responded with only a hard stare in his sister's direction.

"My herbs run perilously low," she continued. "I'd ask yer permission to carry barrels of flour to Orabilis this day. Though we have guests to entertain, I have already delayed this errand overly long."

"Granted," Torquil pronounced after a long pause. "Go see yer witch. As our guests will be in their quarters, they'll have no need of your company. Ulfr! Set a detail to accompany Christiana on her errand."

"Thank you, my lord. And if I may now be excused?"

"Go," Torquil replied, turning his gaze back to Dani. "You and yer companion should return to yer chambers now, as well. I've much to do to prepare for tomorrow's . . . exchange."

A shiver ran down Dani's spine as she stood and turned her back on evil incarnate.

At the doorway, Christiana stopped her with a hand to her shoulder.

"I do hope yer feeling stronger now, Sister."

"I am," Dani acknowledged, in spite of the desperation clawing at her gut. Not only did it sound as if Torquil planned to kill them all tomorrow, but now the only person in the castle who might be even remotely considered an ally was preparing to leave.

Christiana pulled her close for a hug. "I will come for you," she whispered, quickly stepping back. "My errand will likely keep me overnight, but I hope I'll have the opportunity to see you both again before you leave for home."

"I feel certain you'll see more of yer new sister before she takes her leave of us."

Startled, Dani jumped when Torquil spoke from directly behind her.

With what she hoped was a courteous dip of her head, she edged away from him and hurried down the hallway to the stairs, followed by Elesyria and their guards.

Torquil's assurance to his sister still ringing in her ears only served to confirm her opinion of what he had planned for tomorrow.

But for now, she needed to clear her mind. She and her Faerie had some serious planning of their own to do.

Thirty-four

GRAB THE ROPE and tie it round you."

Eyes squinted against the light pouring in through the opening above him, Malcolm grabbed for the line that dangled over his head.

"But no around yer throat. At least no yet," one of his captors called down to the amusement of his fellow guard.

They wouldn't be amused for long. Not once he got close enough to get his hands on them. He'd see to that.

He fitted the rope around his chest, looping it into a heavy knot he could support above the edge of the opening once they hauled him up.

As soon as the knot on his chest cleared the level of the opening, he struck.

The guards, braced to lift his weight, were left off-balance when his weight was no longer pulling against them. Malcolm grabbed the leg of the man nearest him and heaved him forward, pitching him headfirst, screaming, into the hole that had been his home for days.

The second fell, landing hard on his back, his feet

kicking against the slick stone as he tried to scramble away.

Intent on the escaping guard, Malcolm hoisted himself up, transferring his weight to one knee in preparation to spring forward.

A move forestalled by the chill of cold metal pressed against the back of his neck.

"Tsk, tsk, tsk."

He had no need to turn to verify who was behind him.

"Another move and my man takes yer head," Torquil warned. "The Alfodr may have protected you from a sword to the heart, but I doubt even his mark upon yer chest will spare you from such as that."

Malcolm doubted it as well.

"Allow him to stand, Ulfr," Torquil ordered. "And walk him to the wall. You, fool, get up from the floor and put the prisoner in chains."

Once again the irons were fastened around Malcolm's wrists and his arms jerked above his head, stretching him to the limits of his height to ward off the pain.

"What now, brother?" Malcolm had grown tired of the waiting.

"An excellent question. One I've put many hours of thought into." Torquil approached, his attention on the bauble he twisted around his finger. "My first thought was simply to abandon you to the oubliette."

"And why didn't you?"

"In light of new events, it seemed somehow lacking in creativity."

Again Torquil twisted the trinket on his finger, a ring which was obviously too small for him. It barely fit past the first joint on his finger.

Malcolm stared at the jewel, a chill settling over his body even as recognition dawned.

Dani's ring.

"Where did you get that?" he asked, straining against the chains to get a better look as Torquil stepped away.

"This?" he asked innocently, holding his hand up to display the adornment. "Ah, this came courtesy of the new event which set me to reevaluating all my plans for you."

"What have you done with her?" Malcolm demanded. "If you've harmed her . . ." He would make Torquil pay. If it took until the fires of Asgard burned out, he would make Torquil pay.

"Yer wife is well. For the moment." Torquil rested one leg against a table near the wall. "As long as you behave yerself."

His wife? Did Torquil think to test him? Or was it possible that Torquil lied about Dani being here? Obviously his brother didn't know as much about her as he pretended. But he did hold her ring, and Dani had made quite clear the value she placed on the jewel. She would not have allowed it out of her possession willingly without good reason. Whatever trickery she was about, he had no intention of exposing her story.

"What would you have of me?"

"Yer pledge of fealty to me, to begin with. To me, above all others, as yer rightful lord."

Malcolm's teeth felt as if they might crack from the pressure he exerted on them. His honor or the woman who meant more to him than life itself?

"You'll have it. Though I find myself unable to take to my knee at the moment to give the pledge you seek."

"By Odin's eye," Torquil muttered, pushing off the table to pace. "So it's true. She is that important to you. All of Asgard has smiled on me this day."

The expression on his brother's face did not bode well.

"Release me and I will do as you ask. I'll pledge the House of MacGahan to yer service."

Torquil threw back his head and laughed. Laughed until he wrapped his arms around his midsection and leaned one shoulder against the wall.

"And what would be the fun in that?"

Malcolm stared, helpless to understand what he needed to offer to ensure Dani's safety.

"I see from yer face, great Warrior of Odin, you begin to recognize what I want."

His brother misread him. It wasn't understanding that radiated from him, but desperation. Pure, soul-killing desperation to save Dani.

"Tell me, Torquil. No games. Tell me what you want me to do."

"I want you to suffer!" the other man hissed, eyes flashing, spittle flying from his mouth. "I want yer misery to repay the disgrace my father brought upon our bloodline the day yer whore of a mother pushed you out to breathe yer first."

At last Malcolm understood. It was not within his power to appease this madman.

"I needed only to ascertain how important the woman was to you." Torquil resumed his pacing, his eyes alight with his schemes. "So many options to consider. Toss her into the oubliette to die with you? You would be miserable, but I wouldn't really be able to enjoy your misery firsthand. I could bring her here, to chain her to this table and slowly disembowel her while you watch."

A light-headed nausea settled over Malcolm as he felt the blood drain from his face. Torquil was no mere madman, but a full-fledged monster.

"And yet, that too, would be over so quickly. A matter of hours at best." Torquil shook his head, twisting the ring as he paced. "No, I want yer suffering to go on. Days, perhaps weeks or months before I allow you to escape yer pain by sending you to the oblivion of Niflheim."

"You may have yer revenge on me, but if you harm Danielle, the MacGahan will never be yers. Patrick will see to it for me."

It was a desperate card to play, but the only one he seemed to have left.

"I had considered that problem, but the arrival of yer lady here at Tordenet Castle has changed all that. And as for Patrick, I'll deal with him in his own time, just as I deal with you now."

Malcolm shook his head, denial the only defense left him.

"It was meeting yer dead wife's mother what gave

me the idea." Torquil chuckled, as if to himself. "In truth, I considered tossing her into the oubliette with you, but I'm no sure even you deserve to be held captive with that harpy."

Elesyria was here! Of course, it made sense. Dani wouldn't have traveled without another woman's company. But the Elf! And, more important yet, Torquil didn't recognize what creature he confronted.

Malcolm's mind raced as he desperately sought to understand the women's plan.

"When the woman spoke of your having become laird of the MacGahan through yer marriage to her daughter, I realized I had the means to accomplish both my goals sitting at my table. I will wed Danielle and through that marriage, the MacGahan will be mine."

He could foul Torquil's plan by revealing that he and Dani weren't husband and wife, but he couldn't be sure that the truth might not bring down his brother's wrath upon her even more quickly.

"Am I not a hindrance to yer plan? You claim yer desire to keep me alive so that you might take yer pleasure in my suffering, but so long as I live, Danielle is not free to wed another."

Torquil grinned, waving his hand in the air as if brushing away a summer midge.

"There's the beauty! No one needs to know you live. As far as all are concerned, yer lady will be a widow and I shall wed my poor, bereaved sister-in-law, laying claim to all that is hers. All that was yers. And you? You shall live out yer days with the knowledge that each night I take yer woman to my bed and I have her in as many ways as I can imagine."

"She'll never agree to take you as husband, let alone to share yer bed!"

The words slipped out before he could stop them.

"You mistake me if you think I need her agreement. In fact, I rather believe her resistance would be more enjoyable. Perhaps I shall even arrange to have you as audience for the consummation of our marriage."

"You bastard!" Again Malcolm strained at the chains that bound him.

"Ah, but that would be you, Malcolm, not I. Our father wed my mother legitimately, in the ways of our people. Yer mother was but a dalliance, a handfasting mistake he refused to recant." Torquil turned his back and headed for the door, stopping for one more jab before he left. "For now I'll leave you to yer thoughts. For me, I go to arrange for yer death, or, perhaps I should say, to arrange to convince yer lady of yer death."

Malcolm watched the madman's departure helplessly. There was nothing he could do. Once again, he had failed to protect the women whose safety was his responsibility. Whatever happened to Dani and Elesyria would be as blood on his hands, on his conscience, even as Isabella's death had been.

His only hope lay in the women themselves. For now he would have to trust that Dani and the Elf had a plan of their own.

Thirty-five

ALL I CAN say is, we better come up with something at least resembling a plan, and pretty damn soon, too, or we're going to end up down there, dangling and kicking at the end of a rope like . . ."

Dani's throat clogged with the gruesome memory of what she'd seen in the courtyard this morning, robbing her of her ability to speak. Never in her life had she seen anything so horrific. And the very thought of carrying the news of her friends' deaths back to their families at Castle MacGahan made her want nothing more than to curl into a tight little ball and weep.

"How could he sit there smiling at us like that when he knew something so evil was happening just outside? He's not even human," she moaned, wrapping her arms around her stomach as she sat on the floor in front of the hearth.

"Torquil is not Mortal," Elesyria agreed, kneeling down beside her. "At least not entirely."

"Are you trying to tell me that because he's descended from Odin he's some kind of demigod?"

Which would make total sense considering how

arrogantly evil he was. The monster belonged in a horror story.

"Not exactly. He's too many generations removed for that to be the case." Elesyria frowned as if she didn't really understand it herself. "Still, the power of Ancient Magic seethes through these halls. Power I can only assume he wields."

"So basically we're up shit creek and there's nothing you can do because he has you out-magicked."

"Were he to find himself in Wyddcol, he would be equally cut off from his power," the Faerie grumbled. "I'm conserving my strength. I can't say whether it will be enough to make a difference when the time comes, but I will do what I can. I want you to know that."

Elesyria sat down next to her, putting one arm around Dani's shoulders as they both leaned back against the carved stones framing the massive fireplace.

"I'm not doubting you, you know. Or accusing you." Though Dani had done her best not to admit how frightened she felt, there didn't seem to be a reason any longer to try to hide it. "It's just that I feel so—ouch!"

She recoiled from the stones behind her, holding a hand to her head.

"What's wrong?" Elesyria scowled first at her and then at the stones behind her with obvious concern.

"I have no idea."

Dani rubbed the spot on her head that felt as if someone had pulled hairs from her scalp, her movement halting when she spotted three long golden hairs hanging from the stone she'd leaned against.

"What the hell? What is this?" She reached out to the stone, rubbing her hand over its face to collect the strands of hair.

"Runic writing of some sort," Elesyria answered, mistaking Dani's question. "I'm not very good with runes. I haven't had a need to deal with them since I was a child."

"Not the carving," Dani huffed. "That thing pulled hair out of my head. Look."

She held the proof between her fingers, but Elesyria's attention was fully captured by the carving she traced with her forefinger.

"Three carvings, one on either side of the fire pit and one above." She rose to her feet and moved backward, eyes fixed on the stones. "The one on the right is *wunjo*. Joy. My mother had such a carving in our home."

"And the one that ripped my hair out?"

"Don't be silly. Likely you caught the hair upon it when you moved." Elesyria approached, leaning down to run her finger over the lines. "I remember the symbol. Let me think."

"Looks like a stick-figure man with his arms raised." Dani rubbed her fingers together, letting the hairs fall to the stones beside her. "Like he's getting ready to pull hair."

"Protection!" Elesyria beamed. "*Algiz*. I knew I'd remember it."

"And the one at the very top?" Dani rose onto her

knees, her hands bracing her weight against the rune that had pulled her hair. "Looks like a letter *F* to—whoa!"

The stone she leaned against moved and she shot backward, stumbling to her feet.

"Okay. No way that was my imagination. Did you see it move?"

The stone shifted again, sending a fine powder poofing into the air just before the entire left column of stones swung away in one piece, like a door, to reveal Christiana standing inside the opening.

"I think I have a way to get you out. We must hurry, though," she encouraged as she stepped out into the room. "You'll need to come with me."

"How did you . . ." Dani's words died off as she peered into the dark passageway.

"My father loved the idea of passageways. He had them built all over the castle. No one knows where they all are. No!" Christiana shook her head in Elesryia's direction to stop the Faerie from gathering her belongings. "You can take nothing. I'm sorry, but the guards must believe yer only to accompany me on my errand to trade with Orabilis. If they see yer belongings, they'll grow suspicious."

"I've no need for any this," Elesyria responded, dropping her bundle on the floor and heading for the opening.

Had both women lost what little good sense they had?

"How's this supposed to help us escape? I heard your brother say this morning that he was sending guards along with you. And even if we could manage to get away from the guards, I'm not leaving here without Malcolm."

Dani had come here to take him from this place and that was what she meant to do. Even if she couldn't say how, exactly, at the moment.

"We'll deal with the guards," Christiana assured. "And as for Malcolm—"

"Once we're clear of this place, I can deal with whatever guards accompany us," Elesyria interrupted, her head poked inside the tunnel.

"I told you, I'm not leaving here without—" Dani began again.

"I've every intention of seeing my brother set free. Trust me." Christiana took her hand and pulled her into the tunnel behind her. "Be as quiet as possible and follow close. There are twists and turns that would make it easy to lose yer way and we've no the time to go on a hunt for you."

The space behind the stones was just large enough for the three of them to huddle in together, funneling in to a narrow ribbon of black.

Christiana pulled on a long chain and the stone door slowly slid shut, leaving them in complete and utter darkness. With a touch to Dani's shoulder she indicated they were ready to move.

"How do you know where we're going in here?"

"Those were my mother's rooms. I've played in these tunnels from the time I was old enough to walk. Again, I must ask you trust me."

Silently, they hurried along. Dani's sense of direction was completely mangled after the first few minutes of incline leading to narrow stairs that spiraled down, followed by more incline and more stairs.

In the absence of light, blood pounded in her ears as if they did double duty trying to make up for her inability to see. By the time she bumped into the back of a paused Christiana, her legs had begun to tremble from the exertion of all the steps.

Or maybe it was simply nerves.

Ahead of her, metal scraped against stone and the wall in front of her shifted open. Not the wide, gaping doorway she'd seen in her bedchamber but a narrow space, not much bigger than her body's width. The opening led into a corridor, about twice the width of the tunnel they'd just traversed, and though the wavering light appeared to come only from torches, it seemed bright after so long in absolute black.

"Go," Christiana whispered with a gentle nudge to Dani's back. "Wait outside the door at the end of the passageway."

Dani slipped into the corridor, her eyes fixed on the prize, a small wooden door just ahead.

A large, callused hand clamped over her mouth was her only warning that she wasn't alone in the hallway.

Panic flooded her system with a burst of adrenaline and she fought the man's hold, unable to break free but doing some good damage with her nails and her feet, even as she twisted in his grasp to see her captor.

Rauf!

Dermid's groomsman held her braced against his chest, his face contorted in pain even as he tightened his hold. Nothing in sight but two large wooden buckets on the floor in front of her. She struggled to bend, stretching out her leg to catch one of the pails with her toe. If only she could get her hands on one of them, she might be able to use it as a weapon.

As if he read her mind, Rauf pinned her against the wall with a twist of his body, all the while making some half-witted shushing noise.

Always trust your gut about a man, her aunt Jean had liked to say.

Her gut certainly hadn't steered her wrong on this one.

A SPLASH OF water, cold and stinging, awoke Malcolm to the nightmare of his reality, bringing with it the ceaseless pain.

He struggled to shift his weight from his arms to his feet even as another bucket of water cascaded into his face.

"You stink like the shithole you were in, Mac-Dowylt," the man in front of him called out, lifting another bucket into his arms. "Or should I call you MacGahan now, since that's how you fancy yerself? *Laird* MacGahan. The mighty Malcolm, defender of Clan MacDowylt, turned traitor to yer people and gone soft in the turning. How mighty are you now, *Laird* Malcolm?"

Spitting out a mouthful of water, Malcolm glared at his tormentor through the dripping clumps of hair that clung to his face. "Loose these bindings and we'll see how soft I've gone, you putrid wee arse."

The man laughed, displaying a patchwork of missing teeth as he unleashed the third bucket of water.

Malcolm turned his head, but it did little good to protect him from the unavoidable onslaught slapping against his face. If only he had a weapon. If only he were free of the bindings that threatened to pull his bones from their joints.

Squinting against the water running down into his eyes, he watched as the door opened to admit another man, his arms stretched down with the weight of two large, obviously filled buckets.

Rauf!

He should have killed the man when he first stepped foot in MacGahan Castle.

"I've brought the water you asked for, Henry. The other lads are following along behind."

"Set them down here. Yer welcome to stay and watch, if you like. Mayhap I could be talked into letting you have a go at him, too."

Henry bent to lift one of the filled buckets, his laughter ceasing abruptly with a loud thunk as the empty bucket in Rauf's hand connected with the back of his head.

"Now," Rauf called from his spot crouching over Henry's body.

The door behind him swung open and Malcolm reconsidered whether he was awake or dreaming. Surely the women rushing in the door had to inhabit his dreams.

Dani's body slammed against his, forcing a whoosh of air from his chest as her arms tightened around him.

She felt too real for him to have been anything but awake.

"Oh, Malcolm! What have they done to you?" Her hands fluttered over his chest and across his face. "We're getting you out of here."

"My lady," Rauf called, tossing something through the air when Dani turned his direction.

Her hand shot out to catch the little item and she began to pull at Malcolm's arm, stretching up on her tiptoes to grab the chains that held him.

"I can't reach it!"

Rauf was at their side in an instant, working the bolt from the iron around Malcolm's wrist.

When the chains came off, it was as if his arms had forgotten how to lie properly at his sides where they belonged, the joints and muscles aching with what had been demanded of them. Malcolm was forced to bite back a groan of agony when Rauf once again lifted his arm to take the burden of Malcolm's weight on his shoulders.

"I can walk on my own," he managed. "Where do we go?"

"The tunnels," Christiana responded, rising to her feet after having tied the guard's hands and feet.

"Torquil kens the way to the water's edge. It's no safe to use that passage." As he'd learned the hard way.

"I'd no intent to use that way." Christiana's grin lit

her face. "You traveled the tunnels with Father, but I had the advantage of learning from a servant. We'll exit near the kitchens, where we'll stuff you into a barrel and cover you with flour."

Dani's fingers fluttered over his face once more before she grabbed his hand and lifted it to her lips. "For luck."

He was about to embark on an escape where he'd likely be suffocated in flour or captured and skewered on the spot.

Luck was exactly what he needed.

Thirty-six

THE BACK OF Malcolm's hand was hardly what she'd wanted to wrap her lips around, but it would have to do for the time being, in front of all these people.

Dani held tightly onto that hand as they followed behind Christiana through the endless maze of steps and slanting twists and turns until once again a sliver of light appeared ahead of her.

A sliver that grew into a chunk.

She hung back, allowing Rauf and Christiana to exit first this time. No more surprises for her. Popping out of that last tunnel to find Rauf waiting had given her more than enough fright to last a lifetime.

"Hurry!" Christiana hissed, urging her brother up into the back of a wagon where three barrels already stood.

Dani squeezed his hand once more and he bent to kiss her lips.

"Wife, is it? We'll be talking about that one," he whispered in her ear before climbing into the wagon and pretzeling himself into the barrel Rauf indicated.

One soft, sweet touch to her flesh that would have to hold her until they were free of this awful place. One cryptic question to set her mind worrying.

"Hold the mug over yer mouth and nose with the broken end to the hole as we cover you." Rauf emptied the first of the flour down over Malcolm as he spoke. "We'll have to put the plug in the hole until after the guards have inspected, but we'll take it out as soon as we can. You should have enough air to keep you going until then."

Should have being the operative words as far as Dani was concerned. The idea that they'd managed to rescue him from that horrible dungeon only to suffocate him under pounds of flour haunted the back of her mind.

Not that she needed to make up things to worry about. There were plenty of those already. Still, the plan seemed weak enough that she felt the need to voice an opinion.

"I don't like this. It's too dangerous for Malcolm to be confined in that barrel. He has no way to protect himself. Or even to breathe, for that matter, if we don't get that plug out in time."

For the first time, she saw something approaching anger in Christiana's expression.

"And what would you have us do? Dangerous? *Pah!*" The dark-haired woman smacked one fist against her other hand, her eyes flashing. "Where we just liberated him from, that was dangerous. Did you no see for yerself what they did to him in there? Or did you no recognize the stain on his shirt as his own blood? This is our only course, unless you have a better idea for getting him away from here?"

Dani felt as if she'd taken a slap to the face. She'd been so busy making sure Malcolm was unharmed that she'd barely noticed the stain on his shirt. Not that it would have made a difference. Stain or no, she understood all too well that staying where they were was tantamount to a death sentence. And, realistically, she also understood that there was no such thing as a safe way to escape.

"No, sorry. I know you're right. It's just . . . I've never dealt with anything like this at all before." And it was taking everything she had to deal with it now.

Christiana leaned in to put her arms around Dani, patting her back as she gave a little squeeze. "I doubt that any of us have. For now, let's concentrate on what we do once we're on the road."

Exactly. The plan might be scary as all get-out, but knowing what to expect was her best hope.

"How is Rauf going to be able to deal with the guards on his own?"

Though the groomsman had overpowered her when she'd come out of the tunnel, it hadn't been by much. Certainly not by enough to inspire her to think he could deal with the group of men who would be escorting them on this little jaunt.

"It's no Rauf what's going to save us from the guards. He must leave us here, as he canna be seen as helping us in any way. We travel on our own, the three of us, you, me and Elesyria. We'll have to watch for an opportunity along the way to break free of them."

The three of them? Against a company of trained guards? They were so screwed.

"You must calm yerself, Sister." Christiana patted her back once more before backing away. "Yer disquiet will put the guards on the defensive. Now get in the back of the wagon with the barrels. It's yer task to remove the plug as soon as we enter the tunnel. Elesyria and I will ride in the front."

Rauf had already disappeared by the time Dani climbed into the wagon and with him all traces of the opening in the wall had disappeared as well.

Dani shifted the blankets she sat upon, attempting to make them more comfortable, but the long lump underneath her didn't give. A peek under the woolen confirmed that she sat upon Malcolm's sword and scabbard. If they were to have any chance at all, she'd have to pass the weapon to him quickly once he was out of his hiding place. Though, in truth, all she could envision was six men using him for target practice the instant he tried to stand.

"Hang in there, love," she whispered, knowing he couldn't hear her but feeling better for having said it anyway.

"Orabilis is a fair odd little woman," Christiana began, speaking loudly as if for an audience. "Living out in her little hut all by herself. So old and wizened that many call her witch. But I ken her to be wise and kind and loving, so it matters no to me what others call her. Oh! Here is our escort now."

Dani leaned around the barrel to see the men who would accompany them, the thought of how screwed they were flooding back as the guards came into view.

There were six of them, three lining up on each side of the cart as it began to roll forward.

Six. All large and foul-tempered from the looks of them.

"Ulfr made no mention of the other ladies accompanying you on yer journey today, Mistress Christiana."

The guard riding next to the front of the cart appeared to be the man in charge.

"I dinna seek permission of Ulfr to take my new sister to meet the woman who cared for me after my own mother's death. It's our lord, Torquil, who would grant such a boon. Do you care to delay us, and bother him, to question what he might have ordered?"

"No, Mistress," the guard responded quickly, his face paling. "We'll no bother our lord with such as this. Move out!"

Dani released the breath she'd been holding, daring to hope for the first time that they might actually make it outside the walls of Tordenet Castle.

Passing through the long, narrow tunnel, the guards were forced to take positions three in front and three in back of the cart. Dani made use of the filtered light and the distance of the guards to dig her fingers into the air-blocking plug to work it from the hole in the barrel. When it gave way to her frantic efforts, she was certain the gasp for air she heard was not her imagination.

"Do you feel that," Elesyria sighed aloud, her face tilted toward the sun as the heavy iron gates clanged down behind them. "It's as if I am born again."

"Aye, my lady," the guard riding nearest her agreed. "It's a right fair day for this time of year."

The next couple of hours passed slowly, each jog and bounce of the wagon reminding Dani of how cramped and uncomfortable Malcolm must be in his hiding spot. The idle chatter passing between Elesyria and Christiana weighed heavily on her nerves. How could they babble on comparing one herb to another when there appeared to be no way to overpower the men who effectively held them captive?

Not even Malcolm could possibly take down all six. Especially not after having spent hours cramped into an uncomfortable squat. He'd be lucky to stand on his own two feet, let alone try to engage in battle.

"Pull up here, dear," Elesyria suggested brightly. "Just inside the trees. I've a need to stretch my legs."

Dani looked up from her worries to find the land had changed as they'd traveled from flat and brush-covered to hilly and, just ahead, heavily forested.

"This is no a good spot for us to —" the guard who had begun to protest stopped, his jaw dropping slack and his eyes glazing over.

"That's a good boy," Elesyria complimented, climbing over into the back of the cart. "What say we pop the lid on our floured warrior. These gents won't have anything to say about it."

All too true, Dani realized, looking around the circle of guards. Each of them wore the same expression, as if they'd gone to sleep with their eyes open.

Together she and Elesyria managed to pry the lid from the barrel. Once freed, Malcolm wasted little time in climbing from his confinement, though Dani was sure his legs must be cramping him something awful.

"Battered warrior, I should have said." Elesyria dusted her hands together, stepping back to put space between herself and the barrel. "Should have realized dry flour and wet warrior would not a good combo make."

Even covered in the dusty goo that clung to his skin and hair, Malcolm looked wonderful to Dani. Too wonderful to postpone any longer the kiss she'd wanted.

Rising on her tiptoes, she fastened her hands around his neck and pulled his head down until their lips met.

With a possessive growl, he pulled her close, delivering a kiss that didn't disappoint until he pulled away.

"We've no the time we need for that now, love."

"The six of you lads, into the cart now. Sit with your backs together like good boys." The Faerie beside them smiled brightly as she jumped from the cart to climb up into the saddle of the nearest recently vacated saddle. "We'll be needing these."

"Yer an Elf," Christiana stated admiringly from her perch at the front of the cart. "But no exactly an Elf."

"Faerie," Elesyria confirmed. "Much better than Elf, to my way of thinking. Come on with the lot of you. Who knows how long we have before someone thinks to come looking for us?"

Malcolm strapped on his sword and confirmed

Dani's suspicions of his physical state by allowing her to help him from the cart.

Once mounted, he scanned the horizon as if getting his bearings for where they were.

"How long will they be like that?" he asked, motioning toward the catatonic guards.

Elesryia shrugged. "Hours at the very least. Maybe a day or more. I've been shut off from my Magic long enough for its results to be uncertain."

Malcolm nodded, clearly already planning their next move. "We ride south, under the cover of forest as far as we can."

Dani mounted the horse next to his after assuring herself he would be all right. She'd simply have to trust in his ability to judge his own strength.

Christiana unhooked the horses that had pulled the cart, sending them off with a slap to the lead animal before climbing up onto one of the guards' mounts.

"Just in case," she said with a frown. "No point in making it easy for them to return for help."

No point, indeed.

With one last look back at the vacant stares of the guards, Dani leaned low over her horse's neck, racing to keep pace with her companions as they made their escape.

Thirty-seven

EXCITEMENT BUBBLED IN Torquil's chest, almost like in the days of his childhood when his father had returned from some journey bearing gifts for him. Except that today, he was giving the gift to himself.

He measured his steps, keeping his pace under control, refusing to give in to the giddy need to hurry as he strode the hall toward Danielle's chamber, Ulfr at his side.

He'd envisioned her reaction to the news he carried of her husband's "death" a hundred times since early morning. Now, at long last, he'd have the pleasure of living what so far had been only a fantasy in his imagination.

An accident, of course. A fall from the highest battlements in a misguided attempt to escape, the body too mangled for viewing by one with such delicate sensibilities as she.

Stepping between the guards stationed at either side of her door, Torquil filled his lungs and exhaled, striving to achieve the proper balance of emotions the grieving widow would expect before he knocked.

His knock went unanswered.

She dared ignore him?

After the second unanswered knock he stepped to one side, signaling for his men to gain him entry. With their battery, the door swung open and he stormed inside.

Empty.

He strode to the adjoining chamber, amazed to find it empty as well.

"What's the use of setting a guard if they sleep on the job?" His anger laced the words as he'd intended.

"We have not slept, my lord," one guard asserted, his voice shaking. "As you ordered, no one has come or gone from the chamber since the good ladies returned early this morning."

"I've had two sets of guards alternate," Ulfr added. "I do not doubt their word."

"And yet the chamber is empty," Torquil murmured to himself, making a slow sweep of the first chamber.

If the guards told the truth, how could he possibly explain this?

He paused in front of the fireplace, his eyes drawn upward to the rune carvings there. Centered above all, the *ansuz*, his father's symbol, Odin's rune.

A closer scan disclosed a fine, dusty powder on the hearth at his feet. As if something long closed had been opened.

Damn!

He'd forgotten these had been the chambers shared by his father and his Tinkler whore. It would only make sense his father would have built in one of the ridiculous hidden passageways the old fool had loved so much.

But the entries to the passageways were so well disguised, if a person didn't know how to gain access, it could take hours to open, even if one knew where to look. Only someone familiar with this particular room, this particular passageway, could possibly utilize it.

"Has Christiana yet left for her visit to the witch?"

"Hours past, my lord," Ulfr assured him. "My men made mention of it at the guard change."

Clever lass, his sister. Or it would appear she thought herself clever. But not clever enough by half, as she would soon learn.

"Did she travel alone?"

"I will find out for you, my lord."

If indeed Christiana thought to rescue her new sister, it seemed unlikely she would have left her beloved brother behind.

Ulfr had reached the hallway when Torquil called out.

"No. You will accompany me. Send one of yer men to verify and bring word to the dungeon. Have my brother sent as well. I've use for him."

A frisson of anger sparked through Torquil's body and he increased the speed of his steps.

They thought to outmaneuver him? He was so far beyond their level, they had no idea what penalty they would pay for their impudence.

Had she stayed in her room, Mistress Danielle would have been only a pretend widow. Now she would be one in truth.

Thirty-eight

As usual in his life, the gods were having their amusement at his expense.

Malcolm glanced over his shoulder as he rode, needing a quick check on his companions to reassure himself they still followed. He'd spent the better part of his life in the saddle, leading men from one crisis to another, but this was an entirely different experience. How did one even begin to travel with a gaggle of women in tow? Strong women, to be sure, but women nevertheless.

Yes, the gods must be laughing at their latest ploy. Choose the one man in the whole of the world who repeatedly failed the women he was given to protect and surround him with a company of women to lead. And not just any women, mind you, but the three women who meant more to him than his own life.

He reined in his horse and, behind him, the women slowed as well. Circling back to join them, he made his decision.

"We'll set up camp here for the night. We've a strong lead on any who might follow and this looks to be an easily defendable location."

He would have commented on the exhaustion he saw in their faces, but he felt sure that would have gained him only their denials. As it was, they hastened to act on his suggestion with nary a protest between them.

"We've little in the way of provisions, only what I would normally carry on a day visit to Orabilis, but it should be enough for this night." His sister pulled a small pack from her animal and joined Elesyria, who already led her mount to tether in the trees.

He dismounted and fell in step beside Dani, a peace settling over him as she reached out to clasp his hand.

"Stop worrying. They probably don't even know we're gone yet."

"I'm no worried," he automatically denied, even as she smiled up at him.

"You're doing that thing again, pinching your nose. Either you're worried or your skin is starting to crack with all that dried flour coating it."

He loved that she'd learned so very quickly to read him so well and best of all, that even when she knew she was right, she allowed him his dignity, in giving him an escape from the truth.

Pulling her close, he kissed her soundly, laughing aloud when she pushed him away.

"Okay. Officially now, the only thing worse than several days' growth of beard is having dried dough caked in the beard. You need a bath. Real bad."

"Then a bath I shall have, love, as soon as I see to the animals so that the three of you can set about building a fire."

The stream would be sheer misery with the cold, but it mattered not. He needed this crackling mess off of him. Perhaps, if his luck held, he'd even come back with a fish or small animal to add to their night's meager bounty.

"WHAT AILS THEM?"

Without dismounting, Torquil reached toward the men in the cart, ignoring the young guard who'd spoken. A sparkle of power bit at his hand, sizzling its way up his arm before he could pull back.

Irritating, to be sure, but harmless. Magic with a flavor he did not recognize.

"Interesting," he murmured, anxious to test it again.

He rounded the cart, studying the men sitting inside. They appeared to be asleep with their eyes open, frozen in motion and time.

Now that he'd felt the Magic, he judged a response and pushed his hand through the barrier once more, ignoring the sizzle to clasp the nearest man's shoulder. With a thought, his own power pulsed toward the man, sending a shower of sparks into the air surrounding him when the two Magicks met. The shower spread until it encompassed all six men in the cart and gradually they began to move.

"It's the witch," the young guard declared, backing his mount away.

"No," Torquil corrected. "The witch hasn't the power for this." At least not the witch they knew of. Orabilis was far too weak to have had any part in this.

This was different. Completely foreign to him and

yet elusively reminiscent of something he'd known in the past. Perhaps something in the collective knowledge passed through his bloodline.

Christiana? Not likely. She hadn't the intelligence to hide such a power. Magic such as this could not have eluded him for so long. No, the probability lay in its belonging to one of the others.

One he'd need to deal with quickly and permanently.

He studied the ground as his guards tended to the men in the cart. With all their stomping around, any useful signs had been lost.

What he needed was a way to track them. To scent them out and to move with speed.

"You"—he pointed a finger—"come with me."

His pathetically weak half brother visibly paled at the command. Dermid. The least of the whore's offspring. With his blond hair and pale skin, he had the look of the gods about him, but Torquil wasn't fooled. He carried the taint of the Tinkler's blood as surely as any of the others.

And yet . . . this one had chosen to follow him.

"Ulfr, when Dermid returns from the forest, send three men with him to track the fugitives. You'll follow with these men as soon as yer able to round up their horses. You may use my mount for one of them. Are you clear on that?"

"Yes, my lord!"

Blind, unquestioning obedience was Ulfr's best quality and the reason he had become Torquil's right hand.

"Follow me," Torquil ordered as he dismounted.

Dermid slid from his saddle and fell into step behind Torquil as they entered the tree line.

"You must not question what you see. Simply obey and follow. I will lead you to those we seek."

Dermid nodded, an odd, obsequious dipping and bowing of his head.

Torquil moved deeper into the forest, looking for the perfect spot. He had done this only once before and, in truth, it wasn't his preference, but he was without choice. There was no good place for him to leave his body unattended here in the woods. More important—he glanced back at the dolt following him—there was certainly no attendant he could trust.

No, he'd be forced to a physical transformation rather than a spiritual one.

This place would do.

Torquil unfastened the belt from his waist and laid it on a fallen tree trunk before pulling his shirt off over his head.

"Why are you—" Dermid began, but one look from Torquil silenced him.

His plaid and boots followed, all folded into a neat stack.

"Do not fail me, brother. I do not forgive easily," he warned. "Stand back."

He squatted to the ground, willing the transformation to begin.

The change started in his face, just as it had the one other time he'd tried this. Tearing and stretching his skin and his bones as his skull enlarged and lengthened. Only the rapid change in the shape of his mouth prevented him from screaming out in pain.

"By Odin," Dermid whimpered, falling back, scrambling away like a bug on the forest floor.

It took his arms and legs next. Long claws ripped through the flesh of his hands and feet, even as his arms and legs grew longer and thicker, with heavy fur sprouting through his skin.

His bones cracked as his rib cage expanded and his backbone doubled, then tripled in length.

This, all this, he could stand. It was the next phase that demanded all his will.

Pain, like burning hot pokers, seared though his mind as he fought the beast for control. The body would do him little good if it wasn't his to command.

With the beast confined to one small corner, Torquil shook his body, feeling the air ripple through his thick fur. The metallic tang of blood flavored his mouth. His blood, left behind when the deadly fangs erupted from his jaws.

He stretched, feeling the power in his new limbs and muscles before turning his gaze on the sniveling half human huddled against the tree. It would be so easy to snap that weak little neck between his own massive jaws. He stalked toward Dermid, slow and determined, intentionally striking fear until the idiot called out.

"Spare me, my lord! I live to serve you."

Indeed, that was the only reason he yet lived.

With a toss of his head, he started forward, waiting until Dermid gathered his clothing and followed.

Now he was ready. He could already scent the direction his prey had taken.

He would hunt them and find them, and when he did, he would make them regret their decision to deceive him.

Thirty-nine

As good as it had felt to stand after a day of running full speed on horseback, lying down was close to heaven.

Dani stretched out on her woolens, enjoying the pull of her muscles as they lengthened out. With temperatures dropping as the sun prepared to sink below the horizon, it wouldn't be long before she'd need to cocoon herself in the wrap, but for now, after the day she'd had, she was determined to simply enjoy.

Not that she planned to spend this night wrapped up alone.

She rolled on her back, feeling the silly grin stretch the corners of her mouth. Though they were far from being safe here, it was the closest she'd felt to it in days.

Elesyria dropped to sit beside her wearing her own silly grin. "I cannot begin to tell you how wonderful it is to have the Magic coursing through my veins once again. Thank you, Christiana. I shall never forget the gift of freedom you have given me."

"You would do well to save yer thanks, Faerie, for that which I have asked of you. Or at least until we ken for sure that we have freedom and no simply the illusion of freedom." Malcolm's sister leaned her back against a large tree, her face drawn in a frown. "I only wish I had brought my rune stones."

"You needn't worry," Elesryia assured. "Those guardsmen are likely still sitting in the wagon where we left them. Though my powers were weakened when we left Tordenet Castle, I put everything I had into the effort."

"Mayhap," Christiana agreed. "But it's no the guards we left behind what concern me. It's Torquil. I've no a single doubt that he kens the truth and follows us even now."

"I don't understand why your brother is so set on making all of you miserable. He's obviously a powerful and wealthy man. The meals, the servants, the possessions—everything at Tordenet Castle indicated there was no want there, so, why is he so intent on taking over the MacGahan holdings? It isn't like he needs one more group of people to rule."

It was one of the questions that had puzzled Dani from the moment she'd set foot in Tordenet Castle.

"You mistake my brother's intent. Torquil doesn't seek to rule the MacGahan alone. Torquil seeks to return the glory of the old gods. He would rule the whole of the world."

So he was crazy. Like some antihero in a B-grade movie, wanting to take over the world for fun and profit.

"Well, that's one worry we don't have." Dani smiled, relieved. "Trust me when I say I know for a fact that your brother will not succeed in taking over the world."

There were distinct advantages in having seen this world from the future.

"You base this upon yer perception of time and upon where, when, you come from."

Christiana's words hit far too close to home. How could she possibly know about Dani being from the future?

"I see the need to deny in your eyes, Sister, but I ken the truth of when you come from. I have seen yer home in my Dream Visions. So I ken the reason you would feel insulated from my brother's plans, but you must understand, yer concept of time and place has no meaning here. Torquil would wield the powers of the Alfodr. His actions could change the very fabric of the world that Skuld herself has woven. The time you remember may never come to pass."

That couldn't be.

And yet, here she sat in front of a campfire, seven hundred years from where she belonged, companions to a Faerie and a descendant of Odin. By what right could she possibly claim anything couldn't be?

"How do we stop him?"

Her life in her own time might not have been the best, but she certainly didn't want to think of the ways it could have been worse if Torquil had ruled the world she'd lived in.

"I canna say. I've no seen the outcome of his plans."

"Say what you will of his future intentions." Elesyria leaned back, stretching out her legs in front of her, "I've more of an interest in the here and now. You say you believe he already follows. Can you be sure of that?"

"Without my rune stones, the only way I have to tell is the Dream Vision, though even that will no always give me what I seek." She shrugged, a small smile playing around the corners of her mouth. "The Magic has a mind of its own."

"And then some," Elesyria agreed. "In that case, let's have at it, shall we? Is there anything we can do to help you?"

Christiana shook her head and lay back flat upon her woolen, arms crossed over her chest. Within sec onds her breathing slowed.

"I've never seen anyone go to sleep that fast."

"It's not sleep," Elesyria corrected. "You'd be more correct to think of it as being in a trance. She's connecting with the Magic on a whole different plane of existence."

Though Dani knew all of this was real, it just never got any easier to accept.

"Well, trance or sleep or whatever, Malcolm will be back soon and I'm sure he'll be ready to eat."

She pushed up to her knees to lay things out so they'd be ready when Malcolm returned. She placed her knife next to the bread and cheese before getting up to wander around the edges of their campsite, gathering sticks and kindling to toss into the fire.

She gave the spot where Christiana lay wide berth. It felt uncomfortable to go too close. Granted, the woman might be in a trance and not asleep, but she didn't want to disturb her either way.

"Did you feel that?" Elesyria sat up straight and ran a hand up and down her arm as if warding off bugs. "It has the touch of the old Magic."

"Could it be from what Christiana is doing? From the vision thing she's having?"

Dani had sensed something odd when she'd walked past the woman, like static electricity that made all the hair on her body stand on end, but she'd been convinced it was just her imagination.

Elesyria clasped both hands around her arms, her head shaking slowly as she rocked back and forth. "Maybe. I cannot say what it is for sure. But I can say for a fact that I do not like it."

Squatting down next to the fire, Dani tossed her armload of wood down and nudged some of the flatter stones close in to the fire. This would be a good night to utilize the bed-warming trick Hamund had taught her.

Her heart caught at the thought of the easygoing Hamund and what Torquil had done him and to her other friends, her last memories of them hanging from that horrible pole.

She struggled to push the image from her mind. Dusk approached rapidly, and dwelling on those memories sent a chill of apprehension racing down her spine. Hopefully Malcolm would return soon and banish all the negative thoughts eating away at her nerves.

A noised sounded in the underbrush and she was

on her feet, already headed in that direction to welcome Malcolm back when a totally unexpected figure emerged from the trees only feet from where Christiana lay.

"Dermid! What are you doing here?"

Malcolm would be furious. After all he'd done to make sure his brother had stayed behind, Dani was sure they were in for a scene when he returned.

The young man grinned as he made his way past her and into their circle. "I've found you at last! You canna believe how long I've searched for you. Where's Malcolm?"

Dani had only an instant to wonder at his asking after Malcolm but not the MacGullan guards when another rustle of brush revealed a second visitor.

This one was huge and not the least bit friendly.

A wolf. White as snow and standing easily five feet from the ground to the raised hackles on his back, he drew his muzzle back into a snarl that displayed the biggest teeth Dani could ever have imagined. A low continuous growl issued from the beast's throat even as saliva dripped from his fangs.

The beast paused, scanning the circle with what appeared to be an almost human intelligence as three men, swords drawn, stepped from the trees to take up their places, one on either side of the wolf and one behind.

The beast might be a mystery, but the men were all too easy to recognize. Torquil's guards.

And then, it was as if everything happened at once.

Dermid ran toward her, away from the beast, while Dani threw herself over Christiana's prone body, hoping to somehow protect the unconscious girl. Across the circle, Elesyria was on her feet, her arms lifted upward, her mouth moving rapidly, issuing some silent prayer even as what looked like lightning speared from the sky straight into her fingertips.

When she extended her arms straight out in front of her, the beast lunged. It leaped through the air, roaring as the lightning traced two paths of fire along its sides, sending the stench of burning fur up Dani's nostrils. The huge animal smashed its head full force into Elesyria's chest, slamming her body backward against a tree in a shower of sparkling fireworks. The Faerie slumped to the ground, unconscious, and the beast stood over her, his jaws widening as he prepared to go for her throat.

A high-pitched, continuous scream stopped the beast, forcing him to swing his massive head around to look for the source of the noise.

Only as Dani found herself staring into the beast's soulless blue eyes did she realize that the screams came from her.

Forty

MALCOLM BURST UP from the cold water, flinging his head backward to send a spray of icy droplets flying through the air.

Freedom!

He breathed it in, reveling in its invigorating grasp. This was the feeling of being alive. The only thing he'd found to rival its wonder was the feel of Dani in his arms.

The sun was sinking, sending its last rays of the day to glaze the water, making it look like a pool of liquid gold. Spearing a fish under these conditions would be impossible.

He stalked from the water to the shore, his skin rippling in cold bumps as he grabbed up his plaid and wrapped it around his body, his mind already ticking off the possibilities.

A rabbit or squirrel was equally unlikely with night approaching. They would have to settle for whatever bits and pieces Christiana had managed to bring along.

He'd just reached for his shirt when the scream pierced through the forest.

It was Dani. He knew it deep inside his soul.

He dropped the shirt in favor of his sword, already running as his hand tightened around the weapon's hilt.

This could not happen. He would not allow it to happen.

His lungs swelled in his chest as he neared the campsite, close enough to survey the field of battle from the cover of the forest.

His sister was down. Dani hovered over her like an angered boar over her piglet, with Dermid off to one side of her. Where the lad had come from, Malcolm had no time to consider, only that he appeared frozen in his fear.

Three located. Three who required his protection. With Dermid's arrival there should be a fourth. The Elf. What had happened to the Elf?

To his left, the largest wolf he had ever seen, and straight ahead, three armed men, all advancing on his women.

The Battle Rage filled his heart as he burst into the circle, and he roared his fury as he struck, spearing his sword through the first guard's back. The others turned, advancing on him as he withdrew his weapon, allowing the body to fall to the side.

A haze of red colored his vision, homing his concentration on the closest target. He sliced through the next man to reach him, opening his chest collarbone to belly. The man remained on his feet for a second, his body recognizing death before his mind caught up. The third, obviously young and inexperienced, ran directly toward him, screaming his useless threats, sword held high above his head. A swift feint and Malcolm twirled, harnessing his momentum to bring his weapon around with him, delivering a clear cut that sent the man's head rolling across the forest floor to land at the feet of the massive beast.

The wolf swung its huge head around to fix him in its sights.

Good. That was as he wanted. Whatever it took to distract the animal from his original path, which led to those he loved.

As the beast lowered its head, Malcolm had a clear view beyond. A view to the body lying at the edge of the clearing.

A woman's body, her fiery red hair soaked in a pool of blood. A woman he recognized.

"Isabella?"

His step faltered and the beast, as if sensing the break in his concentration, roared, a sound so loud it was as if the ground shook under his feet. In the same instant it leaped toward him, impacting his body with an unimaginable force. Together they flew through the air, landing with an enormous thud, the beast on top of him.

Malcolm struggled to press his sword upward and out from his chest, the only barrier between him and the monster wolf. One hand on the hilt, one on the blade, he kept the snapping jaws at bay only inches above him. The heat of the beast's breath splayed over his face even as great foaming globules of spittle bubbled from the enraged animal's muzzle, stringing down into his face to mingle with drops of his own blood from the hand holding the blade.

He must be strong. He couldn't give in to the pain.

He was all that stood between this beast and his family, but with the Battle Rage broken, he didn't know how much longer he could hold him off.

NO BOOK. NO movie, not even her wildest nightmare had ever prepared Dani for the sheer terror and violence of this moment.

Just as she'd realized that Dermid would be no help at all, Malcolm had arrived, bare-chested, the mark over his heart glowing with an unearthly light. With his speed and his sword flashing, he'd been like some death dancer sent by God.

And then, in a flash of movement and sound, the beast leapt through the air, smashing Malcolm flat to the ground.

"No!" she screamed, on her feet and running.

Not even Malcolm could hold that beast back for long.

"Help me," she yelled to Dermid as she passed him huddled on the ground. No time to wait to see if he heard or not.

She threw herself at the beast, banging her shoulder into his side, hoping to dislodge him from his spot on Malcolm's chest.

He barely budged, but swung his head in a wide arc, knocking her backward to the ground.

Pushing up to her feet, she rushed him a second

time, screaming, tangling her fingers in his fur and pulling with all her might.

His muzzle lifted in a great roar and he swung his head at her again, sending her backward into the dirt.

The landing was hard and it took a moment to catch her breath. Her hip hurt when she stood this time. Walking was tough, running would be next to impossible, but she couldn't give up. From this angle she could see tracks of blood along Malcolm's side where the wolf had scored him with its claws.

Bare hands weren't working. A weapon was what she needed. Something that could hold the animal's attention long enough to allow Malcolm to get to his feet. She dug in the pouch at her waist as she limped back toward the wolf, her hand fastening around the only object even remotely weapon-like, the small wooden fork Malcolm had carved for her.

From behind him, she jumped onto his back and, using his fur to pull herself up, straddled him like a horse. He roared in obvious anger, tossing his head from side to side, but she held on, drawing back her arm and slicing down through the air, driving the tines of the fork into the animal's neck.

A scream, more human than animal, reverberated through the forest as the animal reared onto his hind legs, knocking Dani from her tenuous perch. She tightened her grip in his fur in an attempt to hang on while the animal bucked and reared, but the force of his movements slung her from his back, his fur slicing into her skin as it slid through her fingers. The ground came up to meet her quickly, slamming the air from her lungs.

The great beast reared one last time before toppling over onto his side, his legs twitching even as the rest of his body stilled.

Not waiting to catch her breath, she rolled to her hands and knees, crawling toward the spot where Malcolm laid, his body unmoving. She had almost reached him when something hit her, knocking her back toward the tree line. Something that felt like an ocean wave buffeting her, picking up and tossing her as if she were nothing more than a piece of loose seaweed.

She managed to roll to her side in time to see the wolf's body shimmer, as if she viewed it through a pane of aged wavy glass, and then erupt in a shower of sparks that flew high into the trees before they fell back to earth.

Dani ducked, covering her head with her arms as the embers rained down, burning her skin where they landed.

When she looked up again, the wolf was gone and Torquil laid in the spot where the beast had been, naked and still, the fork protruding from the side of his neck.

It didn't matter that she didn't understand. She didn't care. There was only one thing that did matter to her right now.

"Malcolm!"

Her head pulsed with the force of whatever had hit her just as her body screamed out with the battering, but she pressed on, forcing herself up to her knees.

Across from her, Malcolm struggled to push up on one elbow and then roll to his stomach. Using his sword as a crutch, he managed to pull himself up and stagger toward Torquil's body. He paused there for a moment, staring down at his brother, a myriad of emotions flowing over his face. Then, as if he'd come to some decision, he raised his sword, both hands wrapped around the hilt, prepared for the strike.

"No!" Christiana screamed, freezing his motion.

Dani had no chance to turn toward the girl before a hand fisted in her hair, jerking her head back and up. At almost the same moment, a cold, hard blade pressed against her throat.

"What is it you think to do, little brother?" Malcolm stared her direction, his face gone blank of any emotion, though he still held his sword aloft.

Little brother? Dermid did this to her?

She tried to move and the blade stung against her tender skin, stilling her instantly.

"That's right, *my lady.*" Dermid spit the appellation as if he called her a dirty name. "Best you not move if you value keeping you lovely neck in one piece. And as for you, Brother, step away from my lord and throw down yer weapon."

"Yer lord?" Malcolm repeated, slowly backing away as he'd been instructed. "How can you do this to yer own flesh and blood?"

"Because Torquil treats me as an equal. I'll sit at his right hand when he rules all. Now toss away yer weapon or yer lady won't live to see our soldiers arrive."

"Torquil uses you and nothing more. He'll never accept you as an equal because yer as much Deandrea's son as I am." Malcolm spoke softly as he dropped his sword to the ground, his gaze on his brother unwavering.

"No," Dermid denied. "I've proven my loyalty. I've killed as I've been asked and I'll do it again. You, yer woman, Patrick, Christiana, it matters no to me. Whatever my lord asks of me, that I will do."

"Yer a madman as much as he," Malcolm said, the touch of sorrow unmistakable in his voice.

"Madman, eh? We'll see about that. Mayhap you should ask this one if she thinks me mad. What say you, Lady Danielle? Am I mad? And best you use care with yer words, my lady," he cautioned.

With his knee pressing against her back, Dermid tightened his hold on Dani's hair, stretching her neck backward so that she was looking up into his grinning face.

His eyes were wild. Malcolm was right. There was no sign of sanity left in him.

"No," she whispered, closing her eyes as the sharp edge of the blade pressed into her skin.

"Well spoken," he boomed, obviously enjoying the feel of power.

"What now?" Malcolm asked.

"Now I suspect you'll all die. Ulfr and his men should be here any minute. And when they arrive to take charge of you, I'll be sure this one goes quickly, aye? Though my dagger canna take her head, it will open her up well and good to bleed her dry. And you, my beloved brother, will have the pleasure of watching as yer lady . . ." His threat unfinished, his words dissolved in an odd gurgle.

Dani opened her eyes to see the flat blade of a sword directly above her head, blood dripping down on her face a second before the grip holding her went slack. She lunged forward, away from Dermid's grasp, twisting as she did to see what had happened.

Patrick, his face ashen, stood behind his younger brother, the blade of his sword passing through Dermid's body. The younger man, eyes still open, toppled forward as his blade fell uselessly to the ground.

She opened her mouth, though whether to scream or cry she couldn't be sure, and then Malcolm was there, his arms around her, clutching her tightly to his chest, murmuring soothing noises into her ear.

"Hold me," she managed to say.

It was all she wanted in the whole of the world, just to escape in his arms, where she'd be safe forever.

His woman lived!

Malcolm tightened his hold on Dani, almost afraid to check the line of blood at her throat. She breathed; he could feel the puffs of air against his chest. Her hands clutched at his back with a strength that would not be possible if his brother's blade had hit its mark. Logic told him she was unharmed, but it was not logic that strangled his heart. It was fear.

He grasped her shoulders and pulled away from her, examining the wound for himself, a thin red line like a wee, tiny ribbon spun from blood.

"For the love of Freya, what's happened to Elesyria?"

Patrick's strangled exclamation had her struggling to get to her feet.

"Help me up," she said, pushing against his shoulders.

"But yer hurt," he protested, even as she pushed his hand away.

"It's just a little cut." She ran her hand over her throat, her eyes darting up to meet his when she touched the spot. "Hardly more than a scratch."

He understood her drive. Her friend needed her. He stood and lifted her to her feet, holding an arm around her shoulders as she limped to the spot where Patrick cradled Elesyria in his arms, stroking her hair back from her face.

"I've seen this visage before," his brother murmured to no one in particular. "In the garden, on Samhain. I thought it a trick of the moonlight."

"What visage? What are you talking about?" Dani pushed away to drop down beside her friend. "Is she all right?"

"She lives." Patrick answered. "I dinna ken how it's possible considering the blood she's lost, but she lives."

"She wore a glamour," Christiana observed as she joined them. "To disguise her true self, an Elf but not. The Magic dissipates when she's no conscious to hold it in place. You'd best bind her wounds and get out of here before Torquil's men arrive."

"You say that as if yer no coming with us," Malcolm observed, not liking the sound of it one little bit. "Which you are."

"The Dream Vision showed me what's to come. If I go with you now, everyone dies." She shook her head even as she backed away from him. "I remain behind, as I must."

Leave her behind and risk her life again? No. He wouldn't allow that. He wouldn't be defeated by the visions of the future the Norns chose to weave. If she stayed, the danger must be eliminated.

"Then you stay without the worry of what our brother will do to you."

Malcolm strode across the open ground to reclaim his weapon. In two more steps he stood over Torquil, arms raised. No guilt. This was the same man who'd murdered his people and threatened the woman he loved.

"No!" Christiana was on her feet, running toward him. "You canna! I've seen what's to come."

He could. With a war cry, Malcolm plunged the sword down, with all the force he could muster.

The tip of the sword struck with the sound of metal on stone, inches above Torquil's body, as if a shield of solid air protected the man. It reverberated through Malcolm's body, rippling through muscle and bone with the finality of the sudden halt.

Not possible.

He lifted the sword again and thrust down as hard

as he could, meeting the same invisible barrier that surrounded his brother's body.

"By Odin," he yelled, frustration filling every fiber of his being.

Christiana grabbed his arm as he prepared for a third try. "Listen to me! You canna do this. Ending Torquil's life is no yer destiny, Colm. It falls to another. Just as freeing me of Torquil falls to another. I have seen it. I swear this to you. Now you must go. The soldiers are very near."

Would his failures never end?

"I dinna want to leave without you." He'd gambled everything to save her.

"I ken the truth of what you say, Colm. But this is no the way. Believe me when I tell you this. You must go. Torquil will need time to think on what has happened. Time you must use to build yer defenses strong. Trust in the future to deliver my savior. Now take yer women and go. Hurry!"

He could toss her over his shoulder and carry her away. There was no way she could stop him. He even considered doing exactly that as she stood on tiptoe to pull his head down and kiss his cheek.

But, ultimately, he had too much faith in the powers of the old gods to go against what Christiana told him she had seen.

One last look at Torquil's body revealed something he'd missed earlier. Dani's ring. He stooped down and pulled it from his brother's finger.

That was not the hand on which this jewel belonged.

He gathered their horses and helped Dani into her saddle, waiting only a moment to make sure Patrick had the Faerie securely in his grasp before they rode.

Christiana had been correct about the soldiers. He could feel their proximity to the camp. But the soldiers would have plenty to deal with when they arrived. And with night as their cloak, they could put many miles distance between them and Torquil's men before they'd have cause to worry.

Forty-one

IF SHE CONCENTRATED really hard, and squinted, Dani could just make out the towers of Castle MacGahan across the next rise.

Home, and yet not home, in the same way she wanted so badly to be back there and yet dreaded the arrival so very much. Nothing would be the same once they passed through the gate walls and the portcullis slammed down behind them.

Preparations would begin at once to make ready for the siege they knew was yet to come. Preparations that would include recruiting as many men as possible for the coming battle and with nothing in the way of money to entice recruits, those men would mostly be made up of the MacKilyn warriors.

And with the MacKilyn came heartbreak, in the form of the MacKilyn daughter who would be Malcolm's new wife.

Dani wanted to weep with the knowledge. Instead she took a deep breath and fixed her eyes on the towers to the east.

Her sorrow was but a tiny slice of the grief they would carry into the walls of Castle MacDowylt today. Though she faced losing all claim to the man she loved, at least she had the small comfort of knowing he lived. The families of Eymer, Guy, and Hamund wouldn't be able to say the same.

"Then we'll just have to think of something, won't we?"

Patrick's voice raised in irritation drew her attention from her own miseries.

"Because I'll no allow you to waste yer Magicks on holding that damn spell or glamour or whatever you want to call it when you need yer energy to heal yerself."

"*Allow*?" Elesyria's voice pitched up a full octave. "And since when are you in any position to tell me what you will and won't 'allow' me to do? I could blast you from the saddle where you sit with one look. Allow, indeed!"

"There'll be no blasting done here today," Malcolm intervened. "Besides, you've the look of someone who's doing well to remain upright in her own saddle let alone threatening to unseat someone else."

Men. Totally lacking in anything even remotely resembling tact. At least these two men, anyway. Dani pulled on her reins to circle her horse back around beside Elesyria's.

"Your healing is more important than the disguise you wore for them. What if we invent a new story? Something that allows you to give up constantly staying on your guard. To just be yourself. More or less."

"More or less?" Though Elesyria's face was drawn and pale, a spark of interest glimmered in her expression.

"You could be Elesyria's niece." Dani invented as she went, calling on her imagination and years of reading good books. "We could say you brought word to your aunt that she was needed at home and she sent you to stay with me as my companion."

"Or she could just go home," Malcolm suggested sourly.

"No," Elesyria countered. "All things considered, I think it best I remain here for a time. I suppose dropping the disguise might not be so bad."

"We'd need a new name for you," Dani added. That should make her happy. Faeries had a soft spot for deception, or so her study of them had told her. "Is there a name you've always liked?"

"Elesyria has always appealed to me," her friend responded.

"No, I meant . . . never mind. What about a nickname? Is there a name people call you? Other than Elesyria, that is?"

"Elf," Patrick interjected, almost allowing himself a grin as he said it.

"Absolutely not!" Elesyria glared at him before turning back to Dani's question. "My father used to call me Syrie, but that's a child's name."

"That's perfect since you're playing the part of your own niece. You could be named Elesyria after your aunt, but you go by Syrie so we allay any suspicions. How's that?"

"The Fae do not name their children after living relatives," she grumbled.

"But the part yer playing is no that of a Fae, but a plain, simple Mortal. So much the better, then." Malcolm's eyebrow lifted as he turned to face them. "Or, if that's no to yer satisfaction, you could go home."

Elesyria shook her head to reject his suggestion once again. "Not a good idea right now. For the time being, I will agree to your suggestion. Syrie it is."

Dani silently wished all their problems could be so easily solved.

The castle walls were visible now and growing larger with each step their horses took. It wouldn't be long before they reached the castle gates.

"Dispatch the first riders as soon as possible."

Patrick acknowledged Malcolm's instruction, pausing before he answered as if it was territory they'd already covered. Likely it was. Dani had witnessed their hushed conversations over the past couple of days and had no doubt that they'd been over this ground repeatedly.

"Men will be hard to come by, with our empty coffers," Patrick began, relenting with a sigh. "I'll have riders on the road before sundown."

And then they were there, the big iron portcullis creaking as its weight was drawn upward allowing their horses entrance through the wall.

They crossed the bailey, stopping near the entrance stairway. Malcolm was at her side to lift her from her perch before she'd even realized he'd dismounted. She held her breath against the aches and pains of the bruises she'd received in the battle against Torquil, resting her forehead against his chest when he set her on her feet.

"Have Eric bring the families of the men we lost to my solar. I'll break the news to them, though I'm sure they've already guessed, since we've returned alone."

His voice rumbled in his chest, physically comforting though the words he spoke to Patrick speared her heart.

"I should be there with you when you speak to them since I was there when . . ." She couldn't finish the sentence. The memory was still too raw.

"No. You'll take Ele—" He caught himself and started again. "You'll take Syrie to her aunt's old chambers and see that she's settled in. This is no a place for you to be."

"I understand that I'm not the mistress of Castle MacGahan and so it's not my official place to be there, but I was there when Torquil hanged those men. I should speak to their families." No matter how much it hurt to do so. Their men had died because they had accompanied her to Tordenet in order to protect her. She owed their families.

"No." Malcolm's refusal brooked no argument. "And no because yer no the wife of the laird but because the memories you have of their men's last moments are no memories their women need to share. Leave their families the solace that their men died in glorious battle, no strung up helpless like beasts to slaughter. Now go. See to yer friend."

Dani went to Syrie, slipping an arm around the Faerie's waist to help her up the stairs.

Malcolm was right. Of course he was right. She was being selfish in wanting to try to rid herself of the guilt she carried over the deaths of Eymer, Guy, and Hamund.

But the time for selfishness was over. The time had come when she would have to consider the needs of others over her own.

Forty-two

S HE SIMPLY COULDN'T do this.

Dani stood in the center of her bedchamber, at a loss as to what she actually could do. But whatever it was, it wasn't this.

She loved this room, from the delicate table and chairs near the fire to the intricately carved fireplace itself. It felt like she belonged here.

Only she didn't.

This was the chamber belonging to the laird's wife, connected directly to the laird's chamber. And very soon, there would be another woman who should occupy this room, a thought that made her physically ill.

She'd made the decision to move while they were still a day away from Castle MacGahan. Her challenge now was to follow through on that decision. The room next to Syrie's was open. That would be the logical choice.

But logical didn't make it feel right. The more she considered Malcolm's having a wife, the more she realized she couldn't do this.

No matter what room she lived in, Malcolm would

be with another woman and she simply couldn't handle seeing that day in, day out.

As she'd helped Syrie settle in after their journey, she'd suggested that they both might leave here and go to the Faerie's home, but her friend hadn't been the least bit receptive. In fact, after mumbling something about using Magic she shouldn't have used, she indicated she'd be staying here for the foreseeable future.

That left Dani with only one real option: to return to her own time. Granted, it hadn't worked when she'd tried before, but, honestly, how hard had she tried? And that was before Elesyria had told her about the rowan wood and its supposed Magical powers.

And yet here she stood, dithering in the middle of the room, no closer to making up her mind than she had been an hour ago.

A knock at the door separating her room from Malcolm's interrupted another round of indecision and she went to answer it.

"I thought perhaps we could take our evening meal together, in my chambers."

He was freshly shaven and his dark hair was damp where the ends lay upon his shoulders, leaving little wet spots on his untucked shirt, as if he'd just bathed and hurriedly dressed. He held out an arm, clearly inviting her to cross into his room.

One step inside the door and she knew she'd made a serious mistake.

Candles burned everywhere. They lined the mantel, sat on tables and chairs and even on the floor near the walls. A tray of food waited on the table, surrounded by more candles and, next to the table, in front of the hearth, a huge wooden tub. From here she could smell the herbal fragrance of the steam wafting off the water.

"Oh, Malcolm." She felt as if her heart would truly break. "You've done all this for me?"

He shrugged carelessly, though a wicked grin crept over his face. "Maybe not entirely for you. I'm expecting I'll take a wee bit of pleasure in the evening myself."

Taking her hand, he led her over to the tub, where he began to slowly unlace her overdress. It pooled at her feet, quickly followed by her shift.

He ran his hands down her arms and grasped her waist. His fingers trailed lower, pausing when she winced as he touched the bruise on her hip. He lifted his hands to inspect her injury, leaving her feeling unaccountably vulnerable and embarrassed by his scrutiny.

"He deserved to die at my hand for what he's done to you," he growled, looking up from his examination to meet her gaze. "I wanted to kill him for this."

"I know," she said simply. "I felt the same way when I saw him attack you. I guess I was just lucky you'd made my fork from the wood of a rowan tree."

He bent, one arm behind her knees and one at her back, and lifted her off her feet to gently immerse her in the hot water before gently kissing her lips.

"Why is that?" he asked as he rolled a bar of soap

between his hands and then began to massage her back and shoulders.

Lord, but it felt wonderful.

"Elesyria says it's likely the Magic of the wood that stopped him when a regular weapon might have had no effect. She told me the rowan wood is powerful enough that it alone might have been able to have sent me here."

Dani waited to see if he might make the connection with the wood also being able to send her home.

He didn't.

"I'll carve you another soon to replace the one you left behind."

He didn't make mention of where she'd left the little fork, sticking out of Torquil's neck.

She shivered as he leaned close, his hair brushing against her shoulders as his hands moved from her lower back upward, to her neck and over, down onto her chest.

Large and warm, they covered her breasts, massaging still until his thumb and forefinger closed around her nipple, rolling the skin gently.

She laid her head back against his shoulder and he pulled her toward him until her back fit snug up against the wooden wall of the tub. His hands molded her breasts once more before moving down to stroke across her stomach.

"Your shirt is getting wet," she protested, but he covered her lips with his.

"Yer right," he whispered as he broke the kiss. "I've no need for a tunic, have I?"

A moment later, his shirt and plaid were on the floor and he was lifting her to fit her in between his legs as he climbed into the tub behind her.

When she lay back this time, it was his wet, heated skin rather than the rough wood that cushioned her back.

His hands again covered her stomach, skimming their way down to her thighs. Over and under he rubbed until at last his fingers parted the folds between her legs and found the sensitive nub centered there.

In tiny circles, he rubbed round and round, slow at first and then speeding up as if his hand attempted to keep pace with her rate of breathing.

His erection, grown large and hard, pressed into her back and, when one of his fingers slipped inside her, she began to rock against him, stopping only when her muscles exploded in a tremor of ecstasy.

HER BODY TIGHTENED around his hand in breathless little spasms until at last her full weight lay back against him, her beautiful breasts heaving as she panted for air. Her eyes were closed, but a satisfied little smile curved her lips.

He'd done that. He'd put that look on her face. Not for the first time and not for the last. She was his and he would never give her up.

He kissed her neck, her ear, her cheek, before lifting her forward and entering her from behind. She was warm and welcoming and fully ready for him as he rocked his hips against her perfect round buttocks.

Once, twice, a third time, reveling in her moans until he realized he held her hip over the large discolored area.

"Have I hurt you?" he asked, withdrawing and pulling her close, making sure he didn't touch the spot again.

"It doesn't matter," she answered breathlessly.

"It does to me."

He stood, lifting her in his arms, and climbed from the tub, fastening his lips over hers again. She tangled her fingers in the hair at his neck, driving him wild, convincing him the bed was too far away.

Dropping to his knees on the fur next to the fire, he put her down, pulling her on top of him as he lay back. With her on top, he wouldn't have to worry over putting pressure on her bruises. They would go at her pace.

She needed no encouragement.

As they entwined their hands she lowered herself onto his erection and began to move in a sensual dance of bend and sway that forced his release much sooner than he would have chosen.

"We're good at this, are we no?" he asked when he could speak again, needing to hear her confirmation of what he'd seen in her face.

"We are," she said, her head tucked against his neck.

"I canna live without this," he confessed. "I canna live without you."

She leaned up on one elbow, tracing her finger over the mark of protection on his chest, taking her time before she spoke again, obviously choosing her words with care.

"But you will. You must in order to save your people. We both will do what we have to do, but it makes it easier knowing you love me as much as I love you."

That knowledge made nothing easier.

"I will speak to the MacKilyn. I will explain. It's as simple as that. Yer the one I want to wed. You and no other."

She leaned forward and placed a soft kiss on his cheek before she withdrew. "We'll both do what we have to do," she repeated, one lone tear tracking down her cheek.

He wiped it away with his thumb, realizing as he did so that, in spite of all they'd been through together, it was the only one he'd ever seen her shed.

"Dani," he began, feeling the need to question what was on her mind, but a pounding at his door prevented his asking.

With a curse of frustration, he rose to his feet, picking up his plaid and winding it loosely around him as he crossed the room.

Eric waited on the other side of the door.

"Yer pardon, my laird, but the MacKilyn and his party have arrived. He sends his apologies for the hour of his arrival, but insists upon speaking with you now. He awaits yer audience belowstairs in the great hall. Him and those what travel with him."

"A moment."

Malcolm closed the door, stopping to retrieve a dry

shirt from the chest by his bed before he crossed back to where Dani sat.

She'd already slipped into her shift when he reached her, her eyes as closed off from him as her body.

"You'll wait for me here, aye? I'll deal with this and we'll have it over and done with."

"You're the laird of the MacGahan, Malcolm. You don't have the luxury of dealing with it as you might like. You're responsible for an entire clan. Their welfare comes before yours. Or mine."

"I'm no going to argue the point with you now. You wait here. When I return we'll have time for all yer blether."

He leaned down and kissed her forehead before heading back to the door, tucking in his shirt as he went.

"Malcolm?"

He turned once again to see her smile.

"We both do what we must. I just want to make sure you know that I'll always love you. No matter what. No matter when."

He returned her smile, easy enough since she brought such joy to him. Closing the door behind him, he followed Eric down to the great hall.

Forty-three

NOPE. THIS DEFINITELY was not going to work.

Dani tied the last lace on her dress and moved around the room, blowing out candles as she went.

Oh, she had no doubt that Malcolm had honestly meant what he said about refusing to marry the MacKilyn girl. But once he got downstairs in front of all the clan, he wouldn't be able to go through with it. She knew him too well. He would never be able to put his own interests ahead of those who depended on him. He had too much honor.

And if he did, he wouldn't be able to live with himself.

This evening with him had convinced her of what she needed to do. There was no way she could stay. All he'd have to do would be to crook his little finger and she'd be in his bed again. She didn't have the ability to refuse him now any more than she would have that ability when he was married.

And sleeping with some other woman's husband was something she could not do and live with herself.

Besides, hadn't Christiana warned her that life

would be challenging? *Only in letting go will you hold on.* She understood the meaning now. She had to let go of Malcolm so that she could hold on to her sanity.

"So there you go," she said aloud as she stepped back into her room, closing the door to Malcolm's chamber.

Her cloak was where she'd left it, folded neatly on the bed. There was really nothing else she needed. Once she had it on, she picked up a candle and headed out into the hallway.

She chose to go the back way. There'd be too many people in the main hallway and probably even in the kitchen since guests had just arrived.

Guests. The word squeezed at her heart. Malcolm's new wife and her father.

Quietly she made her way through the narrow halls, passing only one young girl on her way outside. She kept her head turned and her cloak pulled low around her face so it was unlikely the child had any idea whom she'd passed in the hallway.

The cold bit into her exposed hands when she stepped into the night, so she blew out her candle and left it on the ground, freeing her to wrap her hands inside her cloak. The moon gave plenty of light to find her way.

Beyond the gardens, the half-finished walls of the bathhouse loomed eerily in the dark. Though it would be a wonderful addition to the grounds when Malcolm finished it, it would never compare to the bath he'd prepared for her tonight.

"No!" she whispered into the night. She couldn't

allow herself to dwell on what had been. Now was the time for what would be.

She carefully picked her way across the rocky ground to what would one day be the entrance of the building, her eyes focused on her destination.

If a small piece of rowan wood would have been powerful enough to get her here, surely an entire rowan tree should be able to get her back to her own time.

Forty-four

THE GREAT HALL was ablaze with light and activity when Malcolm entered. Both fireplaces roared with freshly built fires, and torches had been lit all around the room.

From the number of bodies seated at the tables, it appeared as though the MacKilyn traveled with fully half his household. Serving girls scurried from the filled tables out toward the kitchen and back again, carrying trays and pitchers of ale for their weary guests.

Patrick sat at the main table next to an old man who could be no one else but the MacKilyn himself. A small girl and a young woman rounded out the group.

Malcolm studied the woman's face as he approached. The daughter no doubt. Pleasant enough to look at. But she wasn't Dani.

"Angus MacKilyn?" he asked as he approached, and the old man stood, holding out his arms for an embrace.

Perhaps he always greeted his potential sons-in-law in such a manner.

"MacDowylt, my lad. 'Tis good to meet you at long last. I've heard many things about you from those who have passed through my own hall."

The young woman smiled up at him and a wave of guilt swamped his conscience. He should tell them now. There would be no marriage.

No marriage and no warriors to defend Castle MacGahan when Torquil's men came seeking retribution.

Another wave of guilt, this time accompanied by the familiar feeling of failure. This failure his largest of all. This time he would fail his entire clan, possibly leading to the deaths of every man, woman, and child in the castle.

He felt the blood rush from his head and he sat down heavily in the chair Patrick had vacated.

"Are you well, lad? You've a pale cast to yer face," Angus observed.

"We've only this very morning returned from a hard journey to the west," Patrick hurried to interject. "Malcolm's no yet had a chance to rest up."

"Ah, I see." The old man nodded his understanding. "Speaking of a strenuous journey brings me to the subject of the boon I'd have of you, lad. The boon in return for the lending of my soldiers. But first, I'd have you meet my daughter, Aeschine, and her attendant, Marie."

So this was it. The time had come for him to do what needed to be done. He glanced to Patrick, heartsick when his brother quickly averted his eyes.

Had Patrick guessed his intent?

We both will do what we have to do. Dani's words echoed though his mind as he rose to his feet to meet the woman he was to wed.

"Give our host a proper curtsy, Aeschine," Angus ordered.

The little girl crawled out of her chair and curtsied clumsily. "I'm tired, Da. Can I no have my bed now?"

"Janet!" Patrick called, and the chief maid materialized from the shadows as if by magic of her own. "Will you see to settling the ladies in their quarters?"

Malcolm watched wordlessly as the old maid bustled the MacKilyn daughter and her attendant out of the great hall.

The child was Aeschine?

Malcolm sat back down, his mind reeling. This changed everything. She was hardly more than a babe, perhaps five or six years at most. The old laird must be crazed to think to marry off a bairn such as she.

"I dinna believe I can agree to meet the terms of yer boon, Angus. I will no be a party to wed a babe such as yer wee lass."

There. He'd said it. It was out in the open and he'd deal with the consequences.

"Wed my Aeschine? You?" The old man laughed. And continued to laugh, hard enough that Malcolm was forced to pound on his back when he choked.

"No, no, lad," Angus said at last, through a raspy gasp for air. "You've heard the talk, I see, but you canna believe all you hear. There's them what likes to embroider the stories, aye? Especially when they dinna have all the facts at their disposal."

"But you did ask for a boon in return for the lending of yer men. And in the past you have insisted that yer allies marry yer unwed daughters, have you no?" Malcolm had heard those stories from many places.

"A boon I did request. It is that you house my traveling party for a few days while we rest before continuing on our journey to my elder daughter's home in Perth. She's agreed to take Aeschine to live with her since the death of Aeschine's mother. And I'd have you welcome us again on our return trip home." Again the old man laughed. "And as for trading my daughters' hands for the strength of my alliance, I had no need to require it of any, though many offered such through the years. It's a story that grew out of my having naught but female children, I suppose. And perhaps the one young buck I bullied into asking before he was ready. But only because my oldest girl wanted him."

Malcolm felt like a fool. He could only be thankful that the child had left the room before he'd opened his mouth to speak.

"My apologies, Laird MacKilyn. It seems I have misjudged you. Please consider Castle MacGahan open to you at any time you'd like to stay for as long as you'd like to stay."

"Aye, well, I ken it to be a great deal to ask. I travel with a large number of my household and I'm well aware it's a drain on yer coffers to feed us when we've all suffered the bad crops of the last season."

Malcolm sat silently as the serving girl set a small tray in front of him filled with cheese and meat before filling his tankard with ale.

Ale he really felt he needed.

Once more the old man laughed, more to himself than anything. "I'd no have you take this the wrong way, lad, but it's all well and good to be yer ally. Yer a strong and able warrior and I've a respect for that. An honorable man too, as I hear it. But I've long heard the whispers of yer clan's claim to otherworldly ancestors and though I personally have no belief in such fancy, I've no desire to taint my bloodline with such whispers. Even if my lass were old enough to take a liking to you."

Malcolm joined in the laughter this time. "No offense taken, I assure you."

He dug his hand into the bag at his waist, searching for his knife to cut a slice from the meat. Instead his fingers closed around a small, hard object. One he'd all but forgotten he had.

Dani's ring.

He'd placed it in his bag after he'd taken it from Torquil's hand and in the days that followed, he'd forgotten all about it.

But he had it now. And he had a powerful need to see her and share with her all that had happened in this room tonight.

Forty-five

MALCOLM KNEW THE bedchamber was empty the moment he opened the door. Not a single candle burned, though, for a fact, there had not been time since he'd last stood in this chamber for them to have burned down. Someone had purposefully blown them out.

"Dani?"

He could feel she was gone. He called her name anyway. A useless gesture, but one he felt compelled to perform.

As useless as checking in her chamber. It too was empty.

He hit the hallway at a run, yelling for Patrick as he reached the main level.

"What in the name of the holy saints ails you, Laird Malcolm?" Janet's head popped out of a doorway he'd just passed.

"Dani," he began, his heart pounding in his chest. "Lady Danielle. She's no in her chambers and I canna find her."

"Come to think of it . . ." The old woman shook a finger in the air as if it helped her think. "Wee Joanie mentioned having seen yer lady in the back halls. Headed outside, Joanie seemed to think."

Outside.

Malcolm grabbed the old maid, kissing her forehead while she sputtered her protests, and then he ran for the back exit.

Once he stood in the silent night, he paused, trying to guess where she might have gone. What had she said just before he'd walked out the door? She'd declared her love, and there was something else, something odd he'd attributed to the strange things she was prone to saying. Something about how she would love him always.

No matter what. No matter when.

He heard the words in his memory with a whole new sense of understanding.

In spite of his claim that he'd send the MacKilyn away, she'd had faith in him that he'd do the right thing, the thing that was best for all of his people, rather than think only of himself. She was planning to return to her own time because she understood him better than he understood himself. What a fool he was. She'd all but outlined her plan to him, right down to the . . .

"Rowan tree," he muttered aloud, already running. Pray Odin he wasn't too late.

A glow hung over the bathhouse, as if someone had lit a thousand candles behind a curtain of green silk.

"Dani!" he yelled, pushing himself to run even harder until at last he reached the wall, vaulting up and over rather than, rounding the building to where the entrance would be.

She stood by the rowan tree, one hand clutching its trunk, the other shielding her eyes. Not three feet in front of her a sphere of blinding green light pulsed and seethed, seemingly alive with a million flashing colors.

"Dani!" he called again. "Don't do it, love. You belong here with me."

She turned, surprise evident in her expression. Surprise that melted into resolve. "I can't stay here, Malcolm. Not anymore."

"Because you dinna love me enough to stay? Because yer no willing to risk what is to come?" He had to know.

"You're such an idiot," she yelled over the increasing hum of the pulsing sphere. "I can't be here and watch you with someone else because I love you too much. My being here would be bad for everyone." She took a step toward the sphere.

"If you go into that light, I'll follow you. I swear it. I'll no let you leave me." He meant it. He wouldn't lose her. He searched desperately for anything to change her mind. "I'll follow because you've promised to picnic me another date in the spring."

"I have to go. I can't stand to see you with another woman and you can't risk your people's safety by refusing to marry. Just like you can't go with me because your people need you. You know that all as well as I do."

"Here's something else I ken, love. The MacKilyn

has no interest in me as husband to his daughter. He wanted only safe lodging for himself and his traveling party while they rest before continuing on their journey to Perth."

She reached out, once again clutching the tree. "Are you telling me the truth?"

"I am." He shouted now to be heard. "What's more, he told me he'd no want anyone from the House of MacDowylt to marry into his family. Doesn't want us corrupting his bloodline."

Behind Dani, the circle shimmered, increasing in size until it burst.

Malcolm ran forward, throwing his body over hers, pinning her to the ground to protect her from the shards of light that fell like sizzling rain all around them.

When the light show at last ended, he lifted his head, capturing her eyes with his. "Looks as though yer Magic vessel has deserted you. Yer mine now, love, stranded here with me for the rest of our days."

"It didn't desert me," she assured, her fingers tracking softly over his cheek. "I sent it away. There's nothing more I want in life than to be with you. I told you that before and I meant it."

Malcolm rolled over onto his knees and helped Dani to sit up, unwilling to release her hand even as he remembered what had originally sent him to find her.

He reached into his pouch and pulled out the delicate jewel. "This belongs to you."

Before he could place it on her hand, she pulled away from him, offering her other hand instead.

"I wore it on my right hand when it was a gift from my aunt. But as a gift from you, I'll wear it on my left. A symbol of our love for one another."

He slipped the ring on her finger and helped her to stand, pulling her close for a long kiss before they headed back to the warmth of the keep. Their keep. The home they would have together with her as his wife.

He had no illusions. Their trials weren't over, and wouldn't be until Torquil was dealt with and Christiana was safe. Still, Dani had helped him discover the most important lesson of all—to believe in himself. With his SoulMate at his side, he could accomplish anything. In her love he had found his true redemption.

Turn the page for a sneak peek at

WARRIOR'S REBIRTH

by Melissa Mayhue

Coming soon from Pocket Star Books

Prologue

Nothing was as it should be here.

Not this place and certainly not him. Surrounded by this kind of natural beauty, no one should feel such an overwhelming sense of disappointment.

Chase Noble loosened the shoulder straps of his pack and dropped it to the ground before settling onto the bench overlooking Fairy Falls. He pulled a long swig from his Camelbak and stared into the cascading water.

If it weren't for his unwavering faith in his father's promise, he could easily believe he'd never find the spot he could call home. The one spot where he truly belonged. The one spot where his fate awaited him.

Foolishly, he had allowed himself to have such high hopes this time. Even the name had held promise. Every word his buddy Parker had spoken in describing this location had convinced him it would be the one he'd sought his whole life. Maybe it had been because Parker had spoken so lovingly of the place he remembered from his childhood. Maybe it had been the shimmer of heat waves wafting up from the ground, lending a surreal haze to the moment. Or maybe it had been no more than the small dark patch of mud in the Kandahari dust, all that remained after they hoisted Parker's lifeless body from the ground for their return trip to the outpost.

He'd known at that moment that he had to come here, just as surely as he'd known he wouldn't sign on for another tour of duty.

Though he had no doubt he was intended for the life of a warrior, he hadn't belonged in that faraway land any more than he belonged here.

Chase squinted up toward the sun dappling down through the canopy of trees, pausing before he took his next drink.

"You could make this easier, you know, Da. You could at least point me in the right direction. One small hint is not so much to ask after all these years."

That his father wouldn't answer didn't stop Chase from speaking. He was used to it. His father rarely answered, and then only in whispered riddles that wafted to him on a breeze.

Having a full-blood Fae for a father had never been easy.

Patience.

The word settled over him even as the leaves rustled overhead.

"I've been patient, Da. It's not like I've had any other choice. But now I feel as though . . ."

He let the thought linger on his tongue, not at all sure he could find the words to explain it even to himself. Lately it had felt as though he was running out of time, as if all his options had been used up and he stood at the edge of some vast precipice.

The vision was so strong; he could actually see himself taking that first step, soaring off into a blue sky of possibilities.

"Yeah right," he muttered, leaning over to lift his pack onto the bench beside him.

He couldn't help but picture his older sister's face at that moment. If she were here, Destiny would be sternly warning him about the importance of keeping his feet planted firmly on the ground and his eyes focused on the future. It was a lecture his bossy sister had given him often before he'd taken off to find his own way in the world.

The thought of her had him smiling as he stood. It had been much too long since he'd seen his sisters.

Even in his memories of Destiny, she was correct. No more flights of fancy. For now, he needed to set some priorities and stick to them. First on the list, find a place to crash and get himself a job. His savings wouldn't last forever. Maybe after that he'd make an effort to locate Destiny and Leah.

Soon.

The wind ruffled his hair as he hoisted his pack onto his back, the feeling so much as if it was his father's fingers that he paused in his preparations to leave.

"Oh yeah?" he asked aloud, looking up toward the dark clouds billowing overhead. "How soon?"

Four fat raindrops plopped on his face, one after another, as if to tell him the conversation with his father was over.

He turned and headed back down the trail. No point in rushing now. The skies had already opened up, pelting down on him through the breaks in the foliage. As his mom used to say, he wasn't made of sugar; he wouldn't melt.

In spite of today's failure, he felt better than he had in months. He had a plan and knew what he would do next. And best of all, though he still didn't know where he belonged, half an hour on that mountain had restored his hope. Hope that he would find his spot in the world.

Soon.

One

Just because she could never tell a lie certainly didn't mean Christiana MacDowylt could never deceive. She'd become well practiced in the art of truthful deception. She'd been forced into it. The truth, the whole truth, would likely get her killed in moments like this.

She kept her eyes fixed on the retreating forms of her brothers and the women they protected as they disappeared into the forest, leaving her behind.

"I dinna want to leave without you." Her brother's words echoed in her ears as if he had spoken them only seconds before.

It certainly wasn't that she had wanted to remain behind. Staying was the only choice she had if they were all to survive. She knew it. The gift she had inherited through the blood of her ancestor, Odin, the dream visions that displayed the future, had shown it to her.

As always, the future had presented itself as multiple paths, the inherent choices of the participants reflected in each. Two had been brighter than the others. On one pathway, she accompanied her brothers in their bid for her freedom. That pathway led to a bloody battle and the deaths of all.

On the second pathway, she remained behind.

There was no real choice to consider. Her freedom was a small price to pay for the lives of those she loved.

Besides, there was a radiant light beckoning to her down this pathway. A radiant light she'd been allowed to glimpse before. A radiant light that promised the freedom she sought and more. A face. *His* face.

If only she knew who he was or when he would come. But the Norns had not chosen to share that knowledge with her. Not yet.

Still, her brothers were on their way, headed toward the shelter of Castle MacGahan. Patrick, Malcolm along with his new wife, and the Elf upon whom so much now depended.

When no trace of her brothers' party lingered, neither a hint of them through the trees nor a glimmer of sound from their escape, Christiana released the breath she had been holding. Their safety was assured.

For now, at least.

With only moments to ready herself before the warriors arrived, she scanned the grove of trees, erecting a series of mental barriers to shield herself from the carnage where she stood. A deep breath to prepare herself sent the coppery tang of blood stinging up her nostrils.

Her half brother, her captor, Torquil of Katanes, mighty laird of the MacDowylt, and descendant of Odin, lay at her feet, lifeless.

Lifeless, but not dead.

A being as powerful as he could hardly be felled by so minor an item as the fork that protruded from his neck. Had the unlikely weapon been made from anything other than the wood of the Rowan, he would never have been felled.

Even in his current state, trapped in the middle world between life and death, the evil emanating from his soul permeated the clearing, hovering, lashing out with frenzied tendrils to find release. She felt it slither around her ankles even as it bathed in the carnage littering the clearing, snaking through the hacked and decapitated bodies of the men who had accompanied Torquil. Swarming along with the flies around the body of her youngest brother, Dermid. Sweet, cherubic, maddened Dermid, who had betrayed them all.

No! She could not allow what had happened in this grove to distract her from what was to come. When Torquil's warriors reached them and revived her tormentor, she would need to be at her most vigilant.

Indeed, it was these moments for which she had been forced to perfect the art of truthful deception.

Returning to the spot where she had lain when the battle had begun, she dropped to her knees. The tears rolling down her cheeks were no falsity. She wept for those who suffered. For those who'd lost their lives so needlessly. For the younger brother she had lost, though in truth, he had been lost to her long before the battle here. She wept for the horror of the life she would return to.

Lying back, she rested her head against the root of a tree and closed her eyes. Her only possible defense in Torquil's view would be found in her having been lost in the grip of the visions during the battle. While the matter of her escape from Tordenet Castle in the first place would certainly compound his anger, she would walk that fine line when the time came to explain.

For now, she must retreat to the only place of shelter afforded her.

After pushing all that had happened from her mind, she silently called upon Skald to show her what was to come. Even as the darkness of another vision descended, she recognized the pounding of hooves nearby, the shouts of men.

But their arrival was too late to catch her. Already her mind had escaped to the crossroads that represented the future. Already her soul floated in the eyes of the warrior who would be her savior.

THE HEAVY, MURKY dark strangled him, suffocating him as it coalesced around his naked body. Its thick, sticky tendrils tightened their thorny hold, piercing into his tender skin, wrapping around him as if he were some sort of otherworld mummy.

Torquil MacDowylt fought against their overpowering strength, marshalling his will to tear them from his body. His struggles only seemed to intensify their movement. For each piece of the squirming, stinking menace he ripped away, two more replaced it, thicker, tighter, and more deadly than before.

Though his strength faded, he would not give up. He could not give up. He fought for his life.

Desperation crowded his mind as the tendrils closed over his face. He screamed, instantly regretting the explosion of air rushing from his chest even as the long, dark fingerlings tightened around him, immobilizing him and preventing his next inhale.

A sudden explosion of sound battered his ears and the tendrils burst apart, tiny pieces of them merging and re-forming above him as his body was flung away from them. It was as if he'd been catapulted into the air by some invisible giant hand.

His body flew through the dark at impossible speeds, beyond his ability to control. Beyond his ability to understand.

A second explosion slammed his body to a stop, this one a burst of light rather than of sound. Light brighter than any fire he'd ever seen.

"My lord Torquil?"

A voice filled with hesitancy. A voice he recognized. Captain of his personal guard, Ulfr.

"I . . ." His voice cracked as he tried to answer, his throat on fire with pain.

"Our lord, Torquil of Katanes, lives!" Ulfr's triumphant shout reverberated in Torquil's ears. "Lie still, my lord. Fetch his things to me, William!"

Torquil waited a moment longer, struggling to gather his bearings. The last thing he remembered was Malcolm's face. So close to his own . . . and yet, not his.

He remembered now. He'd been the wolf! His half brother's puny neck had been so close to his muzzle he could see it snapping within his jaws. Malcolm's strength had begun to weaken. He could all but taste the pleasure of his detested brother's death.

But then . . .

His eyes flickered open and he pushed up to one elbow, his other hand covering a spot on his neck.

His brother's wife had attacked him. Though he could not imagine how she'd managed it, the bitch had done something to him that had ripped the Magic from his body and plummeted him to the mercies of the between worlds.

"Where is she?" he managed at last, surprised by the raspy sound of his voice. Where, in fact, were they all?

"She sleeps, Master. We've been unable to awaken her."

"Sleeps?" With Ulfr's arm to assist him, Torquil made his way to his feet.

The last dregs of whatever had possessed him scattered from his mind as he straightened to survey the clearing, shivering as he did.

By Odin, but he was cold! And little wonder, since

he was completely naked. Where was Dermid? His brother had carried his clothing after he'd made his physical transformation into the wolf.

"I need . . ." He struggled to form the words. Pain radiated from his neck up through his face, and his jaw shivered from the cold gripping him.

"Allow me, my lord."

With a nod of permission, Torquil raised his arms, allowing Ulfr to drop a tunic down over his head, followed by his plaid and a heavy fur draped over his shoulders.

The delay had been what he needed. He could feel his strength returning and with it, his determination.

"Take me to her," he ordered.

The Lady Danielle, wife of his brother Malcolm, would pay for her crime against him now. He would wring the life from her with his bare hands. After, of course, she disclosed to him how she'd been able to do whatever it was she'd done to him.

"This way, my lord."

As he followed Ulfr across the clearing, he took stock of his surroundings for the first time.

The men who had accompanied him were dead. Yes, he remembered that now. Another crime to lay at Malcolm's feet. To his left, the crumpled body of his youngest brother, Dermid.

A pity, that. The weak-minded lad had been easily controlled to perform Torquil's bidding. No matter, really. There were others who would substitute as well.

As he approached the woman's body propped against the large tree, his irritation spiked. His sister, Christiana, laid there, not the woman he sought.

He realized as he scanned the clearing that none of the others were here. The bodies were those of his men only.

"Malcolm? The women?" He looked askance in Ulfr's direction. "Where have they gone?"

The captain of his personal guard shook his head. "There were none here when we arrived but those you see now, my lord. Only you and Lady Christiana, and we have not been able to awaken her from her sleep."

Torquil strode to the spot where his half sister lay.

Little wonder Ulfr and his men hadn't been able to awaken her. It wasn't sleep that claimed her at the moment. Though her body was present in the clearing, her spirit was gone, flying freely on the wings of her Vision. She would not awaken until Skald released her back into this world.

The red blotches staining her cheeks, the darting of her eyes beneath the delicate sweep of her lashes, the almost imperceptible movement of her full, soft lips, all these were sure signs that Christiana inhabited a vision of the future.

Her ability to see the future was the one gift she'd inherited from the bloodline of their ancient ancestor, Odin. The one gift he wanted for himself above all others. It was the only reason he allowed her to live and the one reason he would never allow her to leave Tordenet Castle.

"Bring her," he ordered, fisting his hand as he turned his back. "We return to Tordenet."

Though he was by no means finished with Malcolm, there would be no use in following after his brother now. He would wait, preparing himself, building his strength. In time, with the proper planning, he would have his revenge. Malcolm and all the MacGahan would fall to him, as would everyone else. With his powers and Christiana's Vision to guide him, he would one day return the world to the way it should be. The way it had been when the Ancient ones walked the land. He, Torquil of Katanes, heir of Odin, would take his rightful place as ruler of all.

Fantasy.
Temptation.
Adventure.

Visit PocketAfterDark.com, an all-new website just for Urban Fantasy and Romance Readers!

- Exclusive access to the hottest urban fantasy and romance titles!

- Read and share reviews on the latest books!

- Live chats with your favorite romance authors!

- Vote in online polls!

 www.PocketAfterDark.com

26119